Coney Island Siren

Some things should never be written on paper.

Ellen, 1903
Coney Island, Brooklyn

Coney Island Siren
Theresa Varela

Pollen Press Publishing LLC
2019

Published by Pollen Press Publishing LLC
P.O. Box 1572
Radio City Station
New York, NY 10101-1572
Pollenpress.com

Printed in the USA
Editor: Cindy Hochman of "100 Proof" Copyediting
Services
Cover Photo and Art Design by Patricia Dornelles
Translations by Orlando Ferrand

ISBN-13 978-1-7327167-1-1

This book is dedicated to the women who have lost
themselves in the search for love

Transitions

There's an old saying that 'death comes in threes.' When one person dies, people usually walk around in shock. Bereft family members and friends shake their heads, mutter about the unfairness of death, and float slowly along until the tide of acceptance engulfs their grief. And then a short time later, there comes news of another death. Heads shake again but this time in a knowing fashion. The smell of destiny permeates the air. Grief inexplicably turns to expectation of the death of a third. There is sometimes a certain smugness noted in comments when the third passing occurs. The inevitable 'I told you,' or 'my mother always used to say . . .' are phrases heard, usually in whispers. The fearful may stall their own untimely demises if these words are unheard by sources more powerful than themselves. Foretelling a thing so dark brings satisfaction. There is power to the philosophy that one can't change fate, or so it is told.

There is also a belief that a prophecy foretold can be transformed. A chance stroll down a different street, a decision to climb the stairs instead of riding the elevator, or the avoidance of walking beneath a building blanketed with scaffolding can each make a critical difference in a projected outcome. Today I sit at the oceanfront and watch the waves undulate, crash, and disappear. A breeze, the ripple of a small fish, or the tiny feet of a child running to and fro on the sand may alter the destiny of the wave. My life tells me that all is an illusion. Our destinies are created by our beliefs and our actions manifest our futures.

The ocean caresses the rocks

A switch flips on in me when I walk into a flea market. It's as though I'm entering another dimension or era, and I never know where until I step inside. It becomes an adventure. The Surf Avenue Flea Market is in a cavernous garage and the double doors are held wide open. The treasure trove welcomes me like an old friend, and I love to spend as many hours there as I can. It is one of the few places where I can fully immerse myself.

The musty odor hit me and I sneezed; the dank stillness was in stark contrast to the balmy Coney Island ocean air we had left outside.

"Let's look around," I said, tugging at Frank's hand. "This'll be fun!"

"No, Maggie, we're going to the beach." Frank attempted to pull me back out of the doors. "That was our original plan. We don't have that much time. We have to get to work."

I smiled, but inside I was seething. He'd been getting under my skin all day. Frank alternated between being a loving puppy and a canine trained to keep his jaw clenched onto his prey. I never knew which Frank would appear, and today I wished I knew the secret command to make him let go.

It was dim and stuffy inside the flea market, but outside it was a spectacular September day. The warm sun beat down. My arms were brown from my glorious days at the beach. We'd make it down to the sand and the ocean and all the things that filled me with life. I fought hard for days like this.

"We'll make time," I said. "Humor me."

The flea market overflowed with antique furniture, chests filled with tattered costumes, and boxes of goodies that would take me more than one afternoon to work my way through. One carton was chock full of feather boas.

"These are crazy!" I pulled a few out, threw them around my neck, and ran over to model my new plume outfit in front of an antique mirror.

"Yeah, okay, you got me there," Frank said. "You're beautiful."

Frank stood behind me and playfully hugged me close. He towered over me and had to bend down to kiss the top of my head. Through his reflection I could see why they'd chosen him for the cover of the Police calendar. His body was muscular and lean. His curly dark brown hair was close in shade to mine, but his was short while mine went down to my waist. We were *that couple*, the one that people took a second glance at because we looked the perfect match. Despite appearances, we weren't that reflection of perfection, far from it, but there was nothing I could do to break up with him. I had tried many times.

"I love you, you know," he said.

"I love you, Frank." I smiled up at him. "But come on, there's so much to explore around here. Check out those cookie jars. I think *Mamá* had one in her kitchen."

A few of them were chipped, but they were brightly colored and reminded me of being a kid. *Winnie the Pooh. The Pillsbury Doughboy.*

"Maybe it was my mother who had one. Sometimes my brain is like Swiss cheese. How could I forget something like this?" I walked further down the aisle, pulling Frank along with me. I lingered for a moment at a tray filled with ornate perfume bottles. "Smell this one. It's nostalgic, but I can't quite remember which perfume it is."

"Like I'm going to know," he answered. "Get real."

"I know this from somewhere." I waved the bottle under his nose, but he pushed it away. "Enjoy yourself, like me," I said, kissing him lightly on the chin. "There's some great stuff here."

"I guess." He nodded and walked further into the crammed room. I was hoping that he would be bitten by the market flea as I had, when he called out to me, "Check these out."

I replaced a decanter on the tray and skirted past boxes filled with vintage children's books. Frank flipped through a box filled with LPs, 78s, and 45s.

"You're not going to believe this," he said. "They have Exposé. Lisa Lisa. Stevie B. How did they end up in this crate?"

"Babe, you're stuck in the eighties." I almost giggled, until I looked at him.

Frank's face turned a smoldering red. I knew better than to make fun of his beloved Freestyle—he was weaned on it. His mother was a Freestyle and early Hip-Hop junkie. He'd be insulted if I laughed. Then I'd have to listen to him yammer on about how I had never liked his mother and what a good woman she was. That would be disastrous. I had to start over, and quickly, before he got too upset.

"See how much you can get these for," I suggested. "Joey's at the cash register today. He'll give you a good price."

"They're probably scratched," he said. I was relieved that he seemed to forget my thoughtless statement.

"Maybe they aren't." I poked him lightly in his carved abs. "You can be so negative. Sometimes people just don't have room for stuff. Take the discs out of their sleeves and look for yourself. Joey won't mind."

"Nah, I'll wait for you outside," he said, squeezing my hand. "Don't take too long."

This was my chance to explore. I wandered past the display cases. There was something here for me. I walked deeper into the market and then instinctively stopped. I closed my eyes and tilted my head; I could *listen* better that way.

I turned about ten degrees to my right and opened my eyes. There it was. A box filled with old books. An electrical sensation tingled through me. This was the reason I'd been compelled to enter this stuffy place. I knelt and began rummaging through it.

The books were fragile and seemed about to fall apart. A few newer ones were tucked into a flannel baby blanket. Flea markets were hard to figure out. *How did people decide where things went, and with what?* I browsed through the books until I came to a financial ledger. Its amethyst-colored cover was partially water-stained.

I pulled the book out of the box and gently opened the cover. When I turned the first page, it crackled in my hands. The penmanship was old and scratchy. Whoever had written in it had obviously used a fountain pen for the entries. It wasn't a record of Accounts Payable and Accounts Received. It was a journal. The second page had a name on it. *Ellen.* There was no last name. Each of the entries was dated. The notations began in the early 1900s. I felt that twinge in my muscles again; this book

4

would be mine before I left today. A thrill fluttered in my chest. This is what I was led to just by listening to my intuition. Frank always said that I was 'full of it' when I mentioned my intuition, so today I would just keep it to myself.

I lingered over a second book. It was a large softcover filled with pictures. The photographs were mostly black and white, with only a few full-color ones, depicting the freewheeling days of the 1950s and early '60s in Coney Island. I wasn't around in those days, but my *abuela* had told me stories about how different it was back then. I wished for a moment that she could enjoy this one with me too.

I hurried to pay the flea market owner. Frank waited and I knew that he hated that. Joey coughed as he bent over while searching under the counter.

"When are you going to take care of that cough?" I asked.

"It's those cigarettes. I gotta stop, I know." He couldn't hide his wheezing. "Here, let me give you a bag for those."

"I can put them in my bag; I don't need another one." I showed him my tote. My *flashy paparazzi* bag. I felt chic when I carried it. Frank said the bag was stupid because it had a picture of a cat wearing rhinestone sunglasses on it. I told him I thought it was more campy than stupid.

"Can you get me one of those breathing pumps, Maggie?" Joey smiled sheepishly.

"I'm a nurse, not a pharmacist. Seriously, you need to get your lungs checked out. I don't know what's worse, the air in here or those." I pointed to the carton of cigarettes next to the register. "Here's the money. I can't wait to read these."

Frank was standing right outside when I finally emerged from the flea market. "What took you so long? The day is almost over."

"No, it's not," I said. "We have plenty of time."

We stopped to glance at our surroundings. Coney Island. The summer crowds had disappeared and there were only a few people walking around. Schools were open and most of the children and their parents were nowhere in sight. I could make the most of my playground. The amusement area and boardwalk were practically a ghost town. We took in the Cyclone, the famed roller coaster that people traveled from all over the world to ride. It had been created the old-fashioned way, with wood, and passengers were strapped in by a leather belt and a metal rod that was simple in its design. Close by was the Wonder Wheel, which gave its riders the best view of heaven, especially during moonlit evenings. When I sat in one of the moving cars, I'd reach out and pretend to touch the moon and the stars.

A couple of blocks away were the Parachute, a relic from days gone by; the spine-chilling Hell Hole, the Round Up, and the Himalaya, all attractions. My mother had told me about the days she rode the Himalaya, with the Supremes singing "You Can't Hurry Love" in the background. I must have inherited my love for the amusement park from her. Luna Park, with its kiddie rides, was a haven for children. When little ones passed the height requirement, they could get all the whiplash injuries they wanted. I practically lived here when I was growing up, and I made it a point to get an apartment in the area as soon as I could afford to live on my own.

I loved my first place, a tiny studio that had

everything I needed. That is, until a couple of years out of nursing college, when I met Frank. He wanted *the very best for my girl* and quickly insisted that I rent a one-bedroom in a high-rise that was right next to the boardwalk, because even though I loved the amusement park, I loved the sand and the sea even more. Each morning I woke up to the beauty of the surf. I'd gotten used to being apart from my mother and grandmother, since they'd moved to Puerto Rico when I graduated. They were proud of my profession and my new guy. They believed he'd do a fine job of protecting me. Not only was he a great policeman, but he also made sure that I stopped seeing my friends on the weekends. He said that they were a bad influence on me. I missed the dancing and the movies, but Frank was all the love I needed. Or so he said.

We held hands as we passed my favorite Coney Island ride, the Carousel. The colorful lights glowed and the brightly painted horses and carriages slowly revolved around the mirrored centerpiece. There were a few small children on this one, squealing and giggling. The older ones were probably sitting at their desks at school. As a little girl, I'd tried reaching for the brass ring. By the time I was tall enough to capture it, I'd stopped getting on the ride, because I thought I was too big. It was amazing to see how small most of the kids who rode the beautiful piece were. Adults held tightly onto their tiny waists as the horses moved up and down. The organ music blared and a pint-sized tyke marched to the sound as he waited for his turn to climb onto one of the horses.

Frank and I kept a good pace going toward the boardwalk. We climbed the splintered steps, and the gritty sand filled my rubber flip-flops. We finally made it to the railing and stood gazing out to the sea.

"I don't know how many times I've stood here looking at the ocean," I reflected, as my hair blew around my face in the warm ocean breeze. "Winter or summer, I'm here. I used to wish that I was a siren."

"A siren?"

"When I was a teenager, I imagined myself living in the sea, only coming up every once in a while. I'd spend my days singing, and the sailors on the ships would think they heard me but couldn't be absolutely sure, unless they believed. *Truly believed.* Oh, Frank, I thought it would be magical."

Frank interrupted me. "What are you doing, going psycho on me? Yeah, right. You believed in that? Well, you're a real woman, baby. Enjoy that, because I am." He pulled me toward him and kissed me on the lips.

We leaned against the railing, appreciating the surf. Summer stragglers lay on their blankets and towels. A couple of sun worshippers dragged their beach chairs and umbrellas across the sandy distance, determined to keep time at a standstill. Seagulls hopped across the white sand. The ocean caressed the rocks. September clouds formed 'owl eyes,' and through them I believed that I could see things happening in other parts of the world. I kept my *magical thinking*, as he called it, to myself. He would never get a glimpse into my inner thoughts.

"I can't believe I found this." I pulled the hardcover book out of my tote. "What do you think?"

"It's junk, Maggie. That's why you found it. If it were important, it wouldn't have been there, and you wouldn't have gotten it."

"It's not junk," I said, defending my new treasure. "This is somebody's life here in my hands."

"Dramatic, aren't you?" He took it from me and gave it the once-over. "It's just a silly journal."

I snatched it out of his hands and opened it. A sense of bells seemed to tinkle out of the pages. I turned them slowly. They were brittle and yellowed. "I think it's charmed, Frank. Look at these dates! I wonder why anybody would give it away."

"Because they're dead," he said. "What's the mystery there?"

Frank had taken on that bored look I'd gotten used to. I wondered if he saw the same sea that I did, not that I ever wanted to see through his eyes. Sometimes I wished he could at least pretend to understand what I was talking about.

"The author's relatives might want to have this," I said. "People care about their ancestors' journals, postcards, and notes; whatever they can get that will link them to their families."

"Yeah, whatever," he snapped. "We should be heading back."

"Not yet. Let's look at some of the entries."

"You look at the entries," he said.

I followed his gaze out to the beach and onto a couple of women who were climbing the steps to the boardwalk. Their swimsuits revealed gleaming, voluptuous bodies, while sunglasses hid their eyes.

A gull screeched as it landed next to him on the metal rail.

"Come on. Let's get the hell out of here. Those damn birds get closer and closer. They're not afraid of people anymore. Watch out, will you?" Frank ducked and ran his hand through his crinkly brown hair.

"Gulls? I like them. They're about grace and

9

survival." I sat down on one of the benches. I had just about had it with him. I turned away and saw a cardboard box that must have held French fries or fried shrimp. It was smeared with ketchup. A couple of the birds prodded each other, trying to get the remains.

"See? Like that," I said. "Seagulls survive on other people's messes."

"What are you getting at?" Frank sounded angrier than I was.

"I'm just saying that surviving like that is something I can relate to. It's something that I've done way too long."

"What do you mean?" he said. "Watch it."

"You know exactly what I mean," I said. "I'm always apologizing for what I say to you. Imagine that, apologizing for my own thoughts."

My eyes filled with tears. The fierce sun rays had scorched my skin and my cheeks burned as the tears rolled down my face. I'd been crying way too long.

"I told you already, stop the drama!" He groped in his pocket for his sunglasses and put them on. "Chill, Maggie."

I stood up and wiped my eyes with my open palms. "No. We've got to end this."

"What?" Frank pushed his sunglasses onto his head. "You're gonna start this again? I thought we already straightened it out."

I faced him. "No, I don't think we did. We need to separate. You know this."

"You'll come back. You'll see. Just like before," he hissed as he grabbed my arm. "You think I'm gonna let you out of my life just like that?"

An elderly man shuffled by, leaning against his

walker. The wheels turned slowly. "Miss, do you need help?" he asked. His cloudy eyes looked directly into mine and I burned with shame.

"Get out of here, *viejo*," Frank snarled. "Mind your own business."

"Leave him alone," I begged. "I'm okay, thank you." The old stranger seemed perplexed and so fragile that it hurt to see him watching me. My own *abuelo* would have been heartbroken to see me like this.

"Let's just get out of here," I said.

"Well, hurry the fuck up. I don't know why I put up with you." Frank's lips had turned thin and hard. Just moments before, he'd used them to snuggle against my cheek. I turned back once and saw the old man's look of confusion as we moved away.

"Just take me home, okay, hon?" I silently prayed that he would. "My shift starts at four."

"No, I don't think so. I told you I was spending the afternoon with you, and that's exactly what I'm going to do."

"Please, Frank, I'm tired." Sometimes he listened and sometimes he didn't. I never knew which way he'd go.

We stood on the boardwalk. The old man was far in the distance and had probably forgotten we existed. Frank pushed his hands through my hair and cradled my scalp lovingly for a minute before jerking my head back.

"I don't want to do this, but you make me."

The fear that shot through my body was almost as bad as the pain that came along with his touch.

"Please let me go! My shift starts soon. I need to shower before I leave. We've talked about this already." I hated the sound of my begging voice.

11

He pulled me along and my flip-flop fell off. I bent down to retrieve it, but he yanked me by the arm, and we made our way to his parked SUV. My foot burned on the hot sidewalk and I almost tripped. His body was feverish as he pressed close to me, making certain that we kept in step. Most of the businesses were already closed for the season. The Cyclone, the Parachute, and Luna Park were places where people left their worries behind, but for me, Coney Island was becoming unbearable. We finally reached his SUV.

The Stillwell Avenue elevated trestle hid us. There was no one there to witness him push his body into mine. "You never get it, do you?" he seethed, slamming me against the door of his shiny black Escalade. "If I decide that we're over, then we are, and not a minute before."

I put my hands up to protect my face, but he pushed my head against the car's side mirror.

"Look what you did! You scraped my car!" By pulling me back far enough, I could see the damage. There were a couple of fine scratches against the lacquered paint. They'd come from the zippers on my tote.

Frank pulled the door open and shoved me inside, slamming the door behind me. He ran over to the driver's side and climbed in next to me. He turned the music on high and the words '*I got the power!*' filled the cab. Frank's jacket was open and the gun at his waist practically jumped out at me. He laughed harshly when he saw my reaction. I turned away.

"How many times do I have to tell you to look at me?" he yelled.

The thumping music hurt my ears as he grabbed the back of my neck. I tried to push him away, but he forced me to look at him. I heard '*Or I will attack and you don't want that*' as I struggled, and suddenly I was free, but that lasted only a moment. There was an excruciating pain at the back of my head and then I passed out.

⧗

"Wake up, you little bitch," Frank barked. "You're home, just like you wanted."

I opened my eyes. We were parked in front of my apartment building on Sea Breeze Avenue. I must have lost consciousness. I tried to reorient myself.

Frank loomed over me and pulled my face close to his, his fingers digging into my jaw. "I'm letting you go to work, okay? Call me when you get there. Oh, and enjoy the rest of your day." Frank laughed in that macabre way that only he was capable of.

He practically pushed me out of the SUV and threw my tote bag out after me. I stooped to pick it up from where it landed at my feet. I had only one flip-flop on. He screeched out of the parking spot and I almost passed out again. This time in relief.

2

Short and sweet

Seaside Medical Center was a health metropolis. I ducked through the lobby to get to my unit. My face wasn't bruised, but I felt vulnerable. I was afraid that someone would notice that something wasn't right. I'd managed to get through nursing report without the staff making any comments about me. I was grateful for the cardiac monitors that kept beeping, signaling a client was turning or making some movement. It kept the attention off me.

Dulce Fortunato and I stood side by side, preparing our patients' evening medications. Working on the surgical post-operative unit meant administering intravenous fluids, antibiotics, and pills. And then there was the endless supply of pain medications for the clients who were recovering from surgery.

We'd met on the first day of orientation at Seaside, right out of nursing college, and we became best friends. Her motto of "wear life like a loose garment" manifested itself in her radiance; her smile was bright no matter what the circumstance. The one thing she hid was the fact that her mother had named her Dulcinea after the character in *Man of La Mancha*. Dulce had made me promise not to share that tidbit with anyone.

I pulled some clear sterile tubing out of its cardboard box and inserted it into the IV bag for Mr. Fletcher, the fifty-year-old man who was dealing with cancer instead of the ulcer that he had ignored for several months. The rapidly developing tumor was going to be his ticket off the planet unless he started treatment soon. I was glad to assist him, but it was hard to concentrate after the day I'd spent with Frank. While my throbbing headache was awful, the intermittent flashes of light that I was experiencing were scary. They blinked on and off like the neon lights that lined the boardwalk. I knew that I had to get my head checked out; it could be a detached retina, but I didn't want anyone to know the horrible turn my relationship with Frank had taken. I put my hand to my head.

Dulce's observation skills were like laser beams and she stopped pouring the pills. She took a good look at me and coaxed me into recounting my afternoon to her. When I was done, she gave a huge sigh of exasperation.

"I understand that you're afraid." Dulce began by trying to soothe me but ended up raising her voice. "But I'll tell you, this really disturbs me. I don't understand how you can stay with that guy."

"Shh, Dulce," I said. "Just lower your voice, and please don't be mad at me."

My cheeks were inflamed from embarrassment. I felt raw and exposed, but I needed to confide in her. I knew I could trust her, but letting my guard down, even with Dulce, was not easy.

"You don't get it. I'm not angry at you; it's that animal you call a boyfriend that's so disturbing. You have to learn how to speak up, not down." She placed the plastic bottle filled with cardiac pills back into the cart. "I've already told you that you've got to end it with him."

"And how, exactly, do you suggest I do that? Because *I* don't know how."

I stared at my reflection in the mirror next to the sink. My oval face was tanned and looked so healthy. I was surprised that my eyes were clear. My hair was pulled back into a topknot and I loosened it. No one

15

would know what I was experiencing unless I told them. They could never guess the level of my inner turmoil.

"I don't know," she admitted. "Have you tried going to the precinct to get an order of protection?"

This time I laughed, but it came out more like a whimper. "Now you're the one who needs help. You know all about that blue wall of silence. They protect each other, no matter what. Remember that. I can't go into a precinct. He'd know about it within five minutes."

"You think that, but it isn't necessarily true. You have to take a chance."

I took a deep breath. "I got worried for the old guy."

"What old guy?" she asked. "Who are you talking about?"

"There was an old man on the boardwalk and he tried to stop Frank from harassing me."

"There you go; that's what I'm talking about. Frank is dangerous. What if he had pushed the old geezer? He might be dead."

I opened the refrigerator to take out the insulin syringes. I didn't know how to answer her.

"And what if he continues to push you?" Dulce persisted. "You might be dead. Did you ever think of that?"

"That's not going to happen." Tears began streaming down my face. "How did I ever get into this type of relationship? I'm not stupid. I know that, even though he likes to remind me 24/7 how dumb I am."

"Sometimes I think there should be a law against cops dating nurses," Dulce said, pushing my hair away from my forehead. She treated me better than my own mother did, but in this case, she was wrong.

"Stop. No offense, but it's not all cops who are like

that. It's Frank."

Dulce backed away. "I'm just trying to help you out. But, hey, you know what? You're right, it is just Frank. You need to wake up and get away from him as fast as you can."

"We've been together a couple of years now."

"And what? What do you have to show for it? A few bruises. Brochures for a big white Escalade on your coffee table? Big deal."

"It's black." I felt myself shrink before her eyes. Was it about the possessions? He did give me beautiful things. Frank wasn't always so terrible. Sometimes he was good to me and I felt so loved in his arms. I constantly struggled with my feelings around this. But maybe she was right.

"I'm not going to defend him," I said.

Dulce exhaled deeply. "Good. You had me worried for a minute."

"My mother says we can work it out," I said. "She loves him."

"And Satan, too?" Dulce shook her head. "Have you ever listened to yourself? You flip- flop more than a politician."

I thought about the flip-flop I didn't have time to get, which was probably still on the boardwalk or would be swimming in the sea by high tide tonight.

"I have to start giving out six o'clock meds." Dulce took one last review of her medicine cart and pushed it into the hallway. "How about we meet for our break about eight?"

"Yeah, sure," I agreed. "I still have lots to do in here."

The room was cluttered and had an old-fashioned

set-up. Once the sixth-floor renovations were completed, our entire medical-surgical unit would move upstairs. The cart would be replenished by the pharmacy and we'd have the luxury of concentrating on our priorities—the patients. Maybe Joey was right in asking me for an inhaler this afternoon. Sometimes I was more of a pharmacist than a nurse.

Before I got back to my task, I took another long glance at my reflection in the mirror, but this time I pulled down the high-neck collar that I wore under my periwinkle-colored scrub top. No one ever asked why I wore the two shirts. What I saw had to be a trick, like the mirrors at the Fun House. I leaned forward toward the mirror. The bruises hidden by my tan were fading but real. I gently rubbed at my arms. Instead of bracelets I wore shadowed welts left by Frank's callused hands. During time off from his patrol, he liked to work in his garage making wooden cabinets and curios, and his hands revealed how much he loved to use them. My arms showed how much he used his hands too but for a different reason. There was no telling when he'd pull me close, either to make love or to dig his fingers into my skin.

I jumped when I heard the squeak of the door. I quickly fixed my shirt, making sure there were no signs of the afternoon blow-up.

"Maggie, I knew I'd find you here." Dr. Peters was one in the batch of new interns.

July was the busiest and most dangerous month of the year, as the medical school graduates came in toting their brand-new sheepskins and their brightly colored ties and blouses. They looked like kids playing at being grown-up. Part of my nursing duties was to keep hawk eyes on them as they wrote their first medication orders and changed post-operative dressings, and to remind them about protocol—like not putting sterile equipment on the floor. Some of the nurses bet that the previous year was the worst in history, when Dr. Lewis let her long, flowing locks drape onto the sterile field as she irrigated a diabetic's ankle ulcer. It was September now and most of the interns were a lighter shade of green.

"Hey, Dr. Peters, how's it going?" I asked. "I guess you finished your OR rotation."

"Yep. August flew by," he said. "I'll be working with you this month. By the way, do me a favor and call me Jeff, okay?"

"Pleased to meet you, *Jeff*," I joked, offering my hand.

"The pleasure is mine," he said, as we shook hands in the close confinement of the medication room.

Jeff's sandy-colored hair, tanned face, and easy manner indicated that he came from a world of golf, luncheons, and dry martinis. Going out with Frank usually meant going to a place where the D.J. played Freestyle. I liked it but wished that we could do something different occasionally. My saving grace was that my hospital shift didn't always match his police tour, and I was grateful for that.

Jeff interrupted my thoughts. "Actually, I came in here because I have to debride Mrs. Joseph's wound. I was hoping you'd give me a hand; you know, show me where things are kept."

"Let me give you some advice, Doctor," I said. "Never, ever plan on doing a procedure at medication time unless you've got it under control. First we give out meds and then there are the tube feedings." I smiled.

"And the families want service ASAP. Always look at the time. Get what I mean?"

"Yes, ma'am, got it." He saluted. "I'll be here all night. I'm on call. You let me know when you're available."

"I'll be ready at seven fifteen. I'll meet you at the clean utility room and show you where everything is."

"I know, teach a man to fish . . . It's a deal." Jeff winked and walked toward the elevator.

I pushed the cart down the corridor. *It's so easy to set limits with a stranger, but I can't do it with my own boyfriend.* I had to erase Frank from my mind. Work was one of the few places I was away from him, and safe. I went into my patient's room. Not only did he need to be medicated, but he needed to be suctioned right away. I hurried to clear his airway before he choked on his own secretions. I hadn't seen any of the patient techs around. I was probably the sole nurse in this part of the unit. Dulce was the only other nurse whom I had spoken with since coming on shift. The day nurses had disappeared as soon as we finished with the report. I must have been in some sort of time warp; sometimes that's how it was after a day with Frank. I had to hurry. It was going to be a busy night.

After suctioning and medicating the client, I walked into the corridor and bumped into a rock-hard body. *Frank.*

"What are you doing here?" I asked.

Frank leaned in close to me and his breath was warm on my face. His thin, wet saliva sprayed against my cheek. "Didn't I tell you to call me?"

"Yes," I whispered, looking over my shoulder. "The unit was hectic and I forgot to call."

"No such thing as forgetting." Frank put his forefingers to his temples and pressed. "Actually, what you should forget is just yourself for a moment. I've got this headache. Give me something for it."

"A headache?" I was the one battling an almost unbearable migraine all afternoon, and here he was, coming to me so that I could take care of his headache. A wave of nausea passed through me. "I don't have anything on this cart. Each client has their own medication. All of the stock medication . . ."

"Why are you telling me this? I don't want to hear this crap."

"Sorry. Just wait here. I'll be right back."

"Hurry up."

I pulled the cart back to the medication room. Frank was so erratic. Now he was at my job, taking away any sense of privacy I had. It seemed like I never had a moment of time to myself without him showing up. He had a key to my apartment and walked in whenever he wanted. A special joy seemed to emanate from him when I practically jumped out of my skin or dropped something as he suddenly walked into the room. A couple of weeks earlier, he'd told me he was going to Las Vegas for a bachelor party, and I believed him, like the idiot he said I was. He walked in on me as I soaked in the tub that night. Craving any sliver of peace that I could get, I had surrounded myself with candles. After he barged in, he sat on the toilet seat for two hours, interrogating me about who it was that I expected to join me in the tub. I ended up freezing in the water with the candles flickering out and was unable to convince him there was no one else. Frank's reality was damaged. The fact that no one did show up wasn't proof enough that I was telling the truth.

I pulled out a bottle of aspirin from the cabinet; he would complain if I gave him Tylenol. Aspirin, according to Frank, was the only thing powerful enough to take care of his aches and pains. He never wanted to hear about the potential toxic side effects. When I turned to exit the room, he was standing at the door. My belly flipped.

"Babe, maybe you can rub my head a little," he said contritely. "I'm sorry. I know you're busy, but I'm stressed."

"Stressed? About what?" I couldn't keep up with Frank's mood changes.

"Did you forget? I'm up for detective. You know that. I'm still waiting to hear from them. You really forgot?"

I could swear that he turned five years old right in front of me. But I *had* forgotten, and I really did feel bad.

"I'm so sorry," I said. "We got a little off track, but now we're back where we're supposed to be. Don't worry. You're a great officer. You'll make the grade, honey; you'll see."

We hugged briefly. The phone at the nurses' station rang and I left to answer it. The respiratory therapist was looking for Dulce. The easiest way to find her was by texting. We all kept our cell phones in our pockets, and I texted her the message and returned to Frank.

"Who were you texting?" he asked.

"What are you talking about?"

"Did you text that doctor you were so interested in?" He was right on cue with his paranoia. The headache was forgotten. "I saw you talking to him."

"It was Dulce. It wasn't the doctor; just leave him

out of this. This is my job, Frank. Okay?"

A couple of respiratory therapists walked past us down the corridor. They made life look so normal. I was relieved that I wasn't alone after all.

"I have to get to work," I said. "Why did you come here? Why didn't you get aspirin outside, at a bodega or something?"

"I'm working too. I thought I'd surprise you," he said. "I'm guarding someone down in the emergency room. Dude tried to kill his wife. I should have broken his neck, but Pablo stopped me."

"So why isn't he in jail?" I asked.

"A little knife action on her part," he said. "What can I say? Being here will keep me off the streets and closer to you."

I rolled my eyes. Nothing stepped between him and his madness—only his partner did, occasionally.

"Then why are you up here?" I asked. "Shouldn't you be with the perpetrator?"

"I already told you, Pablo is downstairs." Frank again stood close to me. His body radiated heat. "You know, I think I need some surgery. Let's go inside. Nobody's around. We'll make it short and sweet. Just like you like it." He grinned.

"Stop." I put my palm up against his chest and felt the metal badge hanging under his shirt. "I can't. *I'm working.*"

His voice became a low growl. "You got time for *sweet boy*, but not me?"

"Please, I already told you to forget about him. I'll see you tonight." I moved my body nearer against his. "I know what you want. I promise I'll give it to you exactly how you want it." I glanced around. The corridor was

23

empty. I pressed my breasts against him and placed my hand against his crotch, rubbing him slowly. I could feel him harden against my fingers. Incredibly, my nipples also hardened and tingled. I couldn't figure out how my body could still respond in this way, but it did. "I promise. I love you, Frank."

"You sure?"

"Yes."

"Give me the medicine. I'll be waiting for you." He grabbed my hand back and placed it against his bulge. "This is for you. Remember that."

I nodded, dropped the tablets into his hand, and began pushing the medication cart back down the hallway. I stopped in front of one of the rooms. When I was certain he'd left the floor, I took a deep breath and began to cry. The back of my head still felt like I'd been whacked by a sledgehammer. I took some tissues off the cart and wiped my face. I opened one of the client's pill bottles. *Percocet.* It would take care of my pain. I swallowed a couple and opened the medication book. Already behind in my work, I tried to make up for time and get my tasks done.

3
He'll be waiting

Walking into Room 512, I found myself face to face with the newest patient on the unit, Amy Landry. Because of another, more acute emergency, she'd been bumped out of the intensive care unit. Amy had tried to commit suicide by jumping out of a second-story window. My friend's brother had succeeded in killing himself by doing the exact same thing. Miss Landry's head and eyes were covered with bandages and her right leg was suspended by pins that were inserted into her knee and attached to traction and stationary pulleys. She was semiconscious, and the outgoing nurse stated that each time she started to awaken, she thrashed against the metal rails. Thick restraints on both hands protected her from pulling out the tube in her throat, which was her lifeline to the ventilator that breathed mechanically for her. Amy needed someone to watch her round-the-clock.

Sonya Harris, the other patient, was about the same age as Amy. According to Dulce, there was a rumor that Ms. Harris was the victim of a carjacking. A bank robber, whose getaway driver had left the scene early, had forced his way into her car while she was at a stoplight. Ms. Harris had attempted to throw herself out of the moving car, and the criminal shot her in the back of the head. While she would probably not survive her injuries, it was expected that Miss Landry would improve, if she didn't attempt suicide again. The media made the carjacking incident a top priority, and the hospital spokesperson promised, on camera, that the hospital would do its best to keep Ms. Harris alive.

The nurse's attendant who was stationed in front of

Miss Landry snored rhythmically. The evening was growing more torturous every second.

"Amy, I'm your nurse, Maggie Fuentes," I whispered into her ear. "You're not alone."

I believed in the concept that people in comas could hear what was being said. I would do whatever I could to help this young woman. The psychiatrist hadn't been able to talk to her, since she was wavering between levels of consciousness. Only Miss Landry knew why she had tried to take her own life.

The nurse's assistant must have been a light sleeper, because she woke to the sound of my voice and coughed. The hacking sound told me she was a heavy smoker. She sat there with her arms folded over her yellow paper gown. Miss Landry wasn't on isolation precautions, so there was no reason for the attendant to be covered in paper, with goggles and latex gloves completing her ensemble.

"She can't hear you," she said.

"Just in case she can, I want her to know that she's not alone and that we're taking care of her," I responded.

I picked up the small bag of IV antibiotics. After cleansing the rubber stopper with an alcohol swab, I pierced the tubing with the thick needle, first making sure that there were no air bubbles in the clear tube.

"She don't care if she's alone; she tried to kill herself."

"Please, Mrs. Graham, I really don't want to hear that type of talk coming from you in here." I shook my head. This woman had no heart. I threw the empty box and cellophane into the wastebasket. The aide gave a shrug and closed her eyes. With her arms against her chest, she looked as if she were settling in for the night.

26

She certainly wasn't the set of watchful eyes she was supposed to be.

Mrs. Graham had been floated from the mental health unit to guard over Miss Landry, and was probably annoyed at having to miss an evening of gossip with her peers. I'd worked with her before and she was usually less irritating on her own floor. There wasn't much I could do about her attitude. I hoped that if Amy woke up and tried to climb over the rails, she would do something about it. There wasn't much more that I could do.

The Percocet hadn't given me any relief and my head throbbed. I should have taken the evening off. If I had, I would be snuggled deep under the covers right now. I left Miss Landry and returned to the medication room. Mrs. Jordan had been discharged earlier that day and her bed hadn't been filled yet. Her medication drawer held a couple of tablets of Oxycodone. I decided that I could use the pills more than the pharmacy. I sometimes pocketed extra medication, just in case someone needed it. I swallowed the tablets and this time almost immediately felt relief.

I hurried to finish my assignment. Medications were the priority and I distributed them quickly. I could help Dr. Peters—*Jeff*—with the surgical debridement and dressing later that evening. Frank had taken up too much of my time. I was finally ready for a break, and I washed my hands and got ready to meet up with Dulce. With the headache now under control, I could manage the evening routine. I was on automatic.

The corridor was still empty; the usual after-work crowd of visitors was missing today. I made sure that Frank wasn't standing at the elevator and started down the hall toward it, but then I changed my mind and walked down the stairs. He wouldn't expect me to navigate the five flights to the cafeteria that was next to the emergency room, where he was guarding the prisoner. Hopefully, his partner, Pablo, would be with him if he decided to meet me for dinner after all. Pablo was a quiet and thoughtful type of person—the opposite of Frank, who had an impulsive streak that I had first confused for spontaneity. I'd met Frank when I worked in the emergency room, and he seemed to be the most helpful and friendly of all the officers who came in to guard prisoners or psychotic people who waited to be evaluated. Frank was handsome in a boyish sort of way and always had a joke to tell. I looked forward to the evenings when he showed up. I could never have anticipated how my feelings would change.

Neither one of them was in the cafeteria, but it was filled with staff and visitors. It was odd that my unit was so empty tonight. I spotted Dulce waving at me. She was seated near the residents' table, where the doctors wolfed down their meals.

"What happened to you?" She had already started eating without me. "Got held up on the unit?"

"Not like you think," I said. "I'll be back in a second; I have to buy something for dinner. I didn't have time to prepare anything today."

I glanced around the room for Frank and didn't see him. I was glad for the short respite. I walked into the serving area, picked up a tray, and placed a bowl of corn chowder and a green salad on it. I added a small bowl of butterscotch pudding for dessert. Its sweet taste was somehow comforting, and I made sure to get it whenever it was served. Overhead, the piped-in music played a Stevie Wonder tune. The song and the thought of the pudding calmed me down even more. I paid for my food and was soon sitting next to Dulce.

"You're not going to believe this," I said. "Frank is here. He came up to see me when you left to give out meds."

"Are you kidding me?" Dulce almost spilled her spoonful of lentil soup. "How'd he get up there? He doesn't leave you alone for a second, does he?"

I closed my eyes for a moment. "It seems like that, doesn't it? He's guarding a prisoner."

"You've got to unload him somehow."

"That man isn't going anywhere anytime soon."

We continued to eat in silence, when Jeff Peters strode over to us, placed his tray near mine, and sat down.

"Can you spare a poor intern a pudding, ma'am? Pudding for the poor . . ." Jeff immediately stopped joking when he saw our expressions. "What's going on? You two look like somebody died."

I snickered. "Well, hopefully not. The patients wouldn't like that very much, would they?"

"Guess not," he said, and pulled the plastic wrap off his cold roast beef sandwich. "So, what's going on? Wait, I get it. I'm sorry. I must have interrupted you." He moved his chair back and began to lift his tray.

"No, I'm sorry; it's us—me." I put my hand on his arm. "Stay. It's hectic on the unit. They transferred Amy Landry to our floor. You must have heard about her. It seems she was the least sick of all the SICU patients and I got her. This is all in addition to fifteen other patients. She tried killing herself yesterday. We don't really know much about her. I hear there's an aunt who's been asking for her. She's semi-comatose, and when she wakes up, who knows how she'll react."

Dulce nodded. "I know what you mean. I took care of this guy once; he had a tracheostomy and was attached to a ventilator but couldn't wait for the officer who was watching him to take his eyes off him. The guy would have run away with the machine if he thought he could get away with it. It's different but the same. People do whatever they want, no matter what you do to try to help them."

"Sounds like you two have been nurses here for quite a while," Jeff observed.

"We started working here straight out of school. It's almost three years now, huh, Dulce?" I shook my head but stopped when what had been a dull ache suddenly became a sharp pain. I swallowed, determined not to let anyone know what I was feeling. "I can't believe it," I said, forcing a smile. "We've been here that long?"

"Three years that seem like forever," Dulce said.

We all laughed, and my tension dissolved. Jeff gave Dulce a sidelong glance. I had to admit that she was gorgeous. Her luxurious dark red hair was pulled back into a bun at the nape of her neck, but some of the curly tendrils escaped.

"You nurses are always busy," Jeff remarked. "No downtime?"

"Not really. We can take time, but then we have to pay for it by having to write up our notes at the end of the shift." I looked up at the wall clock. "In fact, it's time for me to head back upstairs. I have to suction a couple of my clients and make sure that Mrs. Graham turns Amy Landry. We can't have her getting a bedsore, or pneumonia. But, I'm not telling you anything you don't already know."

"We have a gunshot victim in the unit," Jeff said. "She came in today. A young woman."

I interrupted. "We heard. That's why we got Miss Landry. Hey, I've got to be heading back." I stood up and went to put my tray on the conveyor belt.

Jeff gulped down the last of his coffee and followed me out. "Like I said, you nurses are always on the move."

I agreed. "We have no choice."

Back on the unit, I decided to read Miss Landry's chart before looking over the pre-op list for the next day's scheduled surgeries. There was a lot on my agenda, but I suddenly felt compelled to learn more about her suicide attempt.

The heat in my body rose as I read through the chart. Single. No children. My mind reeled at the thought of suicide. Why had she tried to jump to her death? Did she feel as alone as I did on some days, or as suffocated on others, when I felt like I was being strangled? Those were the days that I prayed for breathing space away from Frank. It helped to go to the beach to stare out into the ocean. In high school I had learned about sirens, and believed deep inside that I could turn into one. I identified with those *myths*, as my teacher called them. Sometimes I felt that the wails that unfurled from my chest, like those of the sea nymphs, would curl into the wind and ocean foam, and bring me the peace that could come with death. Just like Persephone, the Greek goddess, I'd have no one to pull me to shore. If I wanted life enough, I'd have to do that myself.

Shaking away my morbid thinking, I closed the chart and walked into Room 512. I had to get on with my shift.

It had been a semi-private room until Amy was

transferred to the unit. Now it only fit one client. The staff had pulled the other bed out to make room for the ventilator and other machines and monitors that had accompanied her from the surgical intensive care unit.

"Mrs. Graham?" I looked around the room and saw no one other than the patient, who was still lying in the same position I had left her. "Hello, are you in there?" I knocked on the closed bathroom door. The only sound was that of the ventilator breathing for Miss Landry. There was no reason that the aide couldn't use the bathroom—the client certainly wasn't getting out of bed, and probably wouldn't be for a very long time.

I knocked again. There was still no answer. I pushed the door open and found the bathroom empty and unused. I backed into the room again and bumped right into Mrs. Graham. We stood face to face.

I didn't even try to hide my annoyance. "Where were you? You aren't supposed to leave her, not even for a minute, without getting someone to relieve you."

"I went on my break." Mrs. Graham's expression turned sour. "You had yours, didn't you?"

"Yes, but I wasn't assigned to sit with this patient. You were," I admonished. My voice had a steel edge to it. "This woman tried to kill herself. You're responsible for making sure she doesn't succeed. Don't do this again."

"I won't," she said. "Just make sure that my relief gets here on time."

Mrs. Graham was probably counting the days until her retirement. Her faded auburn hair was tinged gray. She looked tired. As far as I was concerned, her departure couldn't come soon enough.

I needed to try a different way to coax the best out

of her. I knew it was possible. A person who did this type of work had to care; it was a given. "Next time, I want you to tell me if you're having a problem. I can help, but only if you ask."

"I went to look for you earlier. I saw you with your boyfriend," Mrs. Graham said, her dark eyes gleaming. "I didn't want to bother you."

I thought I'd made sure no one was around when I was with Frank. "I don't know what you're talking about."

"Everyone here knows that you and Dr. Peters are an item," the woman said. "I saw you in the medication room with him."

The patient in the room next door could probably hear my sharp exhalation. I hadn't even realized I was holding my breath.

"There's no truth to that and you know it. We work together. God, you're something, aren't you? Be a grown-up, okay? And stick to your assignment."

Mrs. Graham sighed and proceeded to bend down and take the washbasin out of the nightstand. "I'm going to sponge her down. She had a slight fever at six when I checked her temperature. Can't say why."

"Good idea. Let me know if the fever stays up and I'll give her something." I moved closer to inspect the bandages near the client's knee. "It could be an infection at the site of the pin insertion. It's a pretty bad fracture."

"Do you mind staying a few minutes? Help to turn her a bit while I clean her?" Mrs. Graham held a pile of fresh white linen that she had retrieved from the cart in the hallway. "Her stomach has been churning all evening."

"Sure. No problem. I don't think that the antibiotic

is doing much for her other than irritating her bowel. The chart says that she had a spike when she was in the unit."

Mrs. Graham's face was grim as she gingerly pulled the sheet off the patient's body. "Look at her. She's just a kid. They play with their lives. They think they'll die and it will all be over. They never think about the consequences." Proving that she was an expert, the aide deftly pulled the soiled pad out from under Miss Landry and quickly washed and dried her skin.

"Stand here a minute, will you?" she said. "I want to apply some lotion to her rear. Her skin is starting to get red."

I nodded. While Mrs. Graham appeared to have the personality of a piece of dry bread, her actions clearly showed that she cared about her patients. The older woman knew what she was talking about. The damage to Miss Landry's body would take many months of treatment and then rehab to heal. Unsuccessful suicide attempts were often much worse than people assumed. Amy would have to learn to love herself in much deeper ways. Her physical recovery would be difficult, but the emotional aspect was likely to be even more challenging.

"How long are the doctors going to keep her sedated?" Mrs. Graham asked.

"They aren't. We expect her to wake up after some of the brain swelling goes down. She's on her own here." I read the numbers on the machine that held the bag of dripping intravenous fluid. "She's getting fluids and antibiotics, along with cortisone." From the corner of my eye, I saw her uninjured leg make a jerky movement. "She's restless. See how she sometimes moves violently? With any luck, she'll be waking up soon."

Mrs. Graham put the dirty linen in the bag. "I don't want to be here when she wakes up. How do you tell someone that they're not dead?"

"Call one of us immediately if she wakes up." I thoroughly understood her anxiety. I had to break that type of news to a client more than once. "We'll talk to her. Just try to keep her calm if she wakes up agitated—which I'm sure she will."

"You don't have to worry about me contacting any of you," she said. "You got no problem there."

Mrs. Graham shrugged and finished providing skin care for Amy Landry. She went toward the bathroom to wash the basin out but stopped short. "By the way, I almost forgot. There was a nice man who asked for you tonight."

"Really?"

"A handsome gentleman," she answered. A big smile lit her face. "Nice hunk, if I may add. He asked me to tell you not to forget to meet him at the end of your shift. He'll be waiting for you at the parking lot near the emergency entrance."

I turned away from Mrs. Graham. I didn't want her to see me grimace. My stomach churned, just like Amy Landry's.

Birds make new nests

Dulce peeked through the medication room window. The Venetian blinds were the only barrier between the hectic emergency room and sanity.

"The stalker's waiting for you." She giggled.

"Don't call him that," Maggie said. "He's sweet."

"Sweet, I don't know. Gorgeous, yes!" Dulce rolled her eyes toward heaven. "The first time I saw him come out of that squad car, I thought I'd faint."

"Me too," Maggie admitted. "Crazy, huh? When he asked me out, I almost became tachycardic. My pulse will never be the same again."

"So, where are you off to for your first date?"

"You're not going to believe this. Nathan's." Maggie tucked a stray lock of hair behind her ear. "He wants to go right after shift. I tried to convince him that we should meet later. You know, give me time to freshen up. But he insisted. Said something about wasting the time that we could be together."

Dulce pondered her with a twinkle in her eye. "Maybe the fact that you work in the emergency room and he's a cop makes the date more urgent?"

"You're being silly," Maggie said. "I think it's nice he's that interested. I'm about to leave. See you tomorrow?"

"Wait. I've been meaning to ask you. Did you hear back from the supervisor yet? I doubt that she'll let both of us transfer to the medical unit, since we've become this ER's backbone."

"I haven't heard a thing yet. We're still pretty new,

and if we are the backbone, it's only because of the quick turnover. Both of us transferring is a strong possibility because of the merge. The only thing standing in our way would be the staff from Windsor Medical Center being more experienced. We might get lucky."

"You might get lucky tonight!" Dulce said. "Let me know what happens, okay?"

"You're impossible!" Maggie laughed as she went to meet Frank, who was waiting for her by the automatic doors.

☾

Coney Island was on high voltage. The sun had gone down and by night the electrical current charged through, lighting everything in its path. Maggie felt a thrill course through her blood as she sat at one of the round outdoor tables at Nathan's. The warm evening breeze gently tousled her long ringlets. She'd removed the elastic band that kept the dark strands away from her face at work. She drank Frank in deeply with her eyes as he stood in front of her. Not even the beauty of the summer evening could distract her from his hot energy.

"My god, you're beautiful." He simultaneously straddled the bench and placed the green and yellow boxes on the heavy stone table. One box was filled with soft drinks and the other with cardboard containers holding hot dogs and French fries.

Maggie was astonished. The feeling was mutual and this was a first. She wasn't used to being admired so blatantly. She tried not to be self-conscious as she picked up the long frankfurter in the soft bun. He had already poured ketchup and mustard on hers. Mustard wasn't a favorite, but it was thoughtful on Frank's part.

"You bought onion rings too! I love these." Maggie popped a sizzling one into her mouth.

"I thought you would." Frank dazzled with his even and steady smile. He had to be at least six foot two in height. The wide expanse of his chest demanded she reach out her hand to touch him, but instead she picked up her soft drink.

"Some energy out here, huh?" He tilted his head to the lines of people waiting to order their own Nathan's Famous hot dogs. "I know the staff here. They see me on duty often enough."

"That's why you were so quick," Maggie said. "You didn't have to stand on line, did you?" She dunked a fry into the ketchup he'd poured onto a thick paper plate. Frank thought of everything.

"Dainty, aren't you?" Frank drizzled ketchup over his whole batch of fries. "We like the same things. Just differently."

Maggie blushed. "Yeah, we both work helping people in a different way. But the outcome is saving them. Is that what you mean?"

"Something like that." He took a swig of his orange soda. "I don't really know that much about you. What sorts of things do you want me to know?"

She considered his question. "I've lived in Coney Island almost all of my life. I've always had to stand in line here." She laughed.

"Well, if you hang by me, kid, your days of waiting on long lines are over."

Frank took Maggie's hand and pressed it. The sensation surged from her hands to in between her legs and felt delicious.

"Look up, babe, fireworks!" Frank pointed to the spectacular display that burst across the sky. "Tonight's a special night."

Maggie closed her eyes and pretended that one of the white flashes was a shooting star. Her wish was that Frank would always be at her side just as he was tonight.

☾

Maggie turned over to gaze out her bedroom window, which revealed a silvery early light. Morning birds warbled loudly. A sigh escaped from deep within her soul. Things couldn't be more perfect.

Frank melded his body to hers as they spooned. "Good morning, Sunshine. I was counting the minutes until you woke up."

"What number are you up to, one hundred?" Maggie yawned.

"More like one hundred thousand ninety-two, that was me waiting for you."

"You rhyme," Maggie said. "I like that we rhyme together."

Maggie turned again and pressed her body against the length of Frank's. He swiftly entered her and they began to move rhythmically against each other like waves lapping the coastal sands. Then they parted and lay next to each other, smelling the light salty wind that came through the window.

"Being with you is like lying on ocean rocks." Maggie

lazily drew imaginary circles on his chest. "I like listening to your heart."

"What do you mean by that?" Frank asked. "My heart is hard like a rock? I don't get that."

"I didn't mean that at all. I'm sorry if it sounded like that. The words just came out. I guess I should have thought it out before I said it."

Maggie could feel his sharp intake and release of breath.

"No," he said. "It's me. I'm sorry. I don't know what got into me. Forgive me?"

"There's nothing to forgive. Let's just forget it."

"I didn't mean to pressure you, you know." Frank swiftly turned over and Maggie lay underneath him again.

"What do you mean *pressure?*" Maggie shifted a bit because his hip pinned hers against the bed. "Can you lift just a teeny bit? You are pure muscle." She laughed lightly.

"Sure. Sorry about that." Frank released her by turning on his side and faced her. "It's just that this was our first date and all. It happened naturally—or so I thought."

"I wanted to be with you," she said. "We both wanted the same thing."

Frank tickled the underside of her foot with his toes. "That's for sure. Let's go to the café and get some coffee. If you want, we can go to that Georgian bakery on Neptune."

"That sounds great, but I can make a pot right here." Maggie untangled herself from Frank and the bed sheets. "I'll bring a cup to you. I'd like to."

Maggie measured the coffee grains and readied the pot. She switched it on and went into the bathroom for a quick shower while it brewed. She came to a dead halt when she returned to the kitchen to find Frank leaning with his head far out of the window. She tied the robe sash tightly around her waist.

"What's going on? I thought you were asleep."

"Nah, I'm just checking the security around here. This fire escape isn't in the best shape. See that rust there in the corner?" Frank pointed to a small crumbly area of the fire escape.

"I hadn't seen that before," she said. "I never really look out the window." She poured a cup of black coffee for him. That he didn't take milk or sugar in his coffee was something the nurses gossiped about in the ER. They came to the conclusion that this was one way he didn't keep an ounce of fat on his tall frame.

"Thanks," he said, and took a swallow. "Perfect." He sat at the table and continued looking around her compact kitchen until Maggie felt her insides squirm.

"What? Are you giving my kitchen the third degree?" she laughed. "It's no big deal, but what's up?"

"I have a friend who manages one of those high-rises on Sea Breeze. Ever think about going up a notch?"

That was not something she expected from him and she was taken aback. "I kind of like my notch. This is my first apartment. I've been here since I moved out of my grandmother's place. It's my home."

"Well, even birds make new nests. Think about it. Just say the word and it'll happen."

Maggie didn't know how to respond but didn't have to; Frank pulled her sash open as he sat her on the kitchen table in front of him.

"For the record, Ms. Fuentes, RN, contrary to what you've heard, I do like something sweet with my coffee, and you are it."

Security, rust, and birds were forgotten as Maggie tried to stifle her moans while Frank satiated her. If she continued to make so much noise, she might have to move from her tiny place in this family building. Looking for a new apartment might not be such a bad idea after all.

A few hours later, they parted at her door. Frank's warmth lingered on Maggie's skin as she was drawn to the fake desk she never used. She pulled out a pile of old journals she had stuffed into one of the drawers the day she couldn't decide whether to burn them or keep them. *Keep them*. She had listened to her inner voice.

Maggie picked one up and rubbed the cover's shiny mermaid-like finish. She opened it and the memories poured onto her fingers. *I forgot about you. It's been so long. My poems. Rafy.* A tingle shot through her spine. *Best to keep those thoughts forgotten*. She scrambled through the desk drawer and found a pen. She turned to the first empty page in the journal and began to write. The words flowed easily through her as though she were fourteen again.

The evening is warm
I am warmed
By the man with the twinkle in his eye

And the crinkle in his hair
He laughed
Not at me or what I've done
But at my glee
My happiness runs free
On this boardwalk of lovers
I've finally met one
That is my own
Kind
Lonely long enough
I'll ignore my thoughts
And listen to my heart

Maggie closed the book and held it against her chest. Words were old friends who knew everything about you but never betrayed. Words would forever keep the secrets that had threatened to keep her hostage. Words had saved her life. She had survived those times and now life had become sweet. She had Frank.

4
Rules

The shift was finally over and Frank met me at the entrance to the hospital. I had no choice but to accompany him to the Escalade. We sat next to each other in the front seat and he nuzzled my neck; his breath was warm and tickling. He curled his fingers through my hair with one hand and raised the music volume with the other. *You're my diamond girl* blasted into my brain while Frank's ring pressed into my scalp. The Oxycodone I'd taken earlier had worn off and hadn't really helped my head that much anyway. I didn't want to ask him about his headache. I just wanted to get away from him, go home, and crawl into bed.

"You forgive me?" he asked. I couldn't see his face but could picture his familiar make-up pout.

"There's nothing to forgive, really," I said. If I didn't let him off the hook, he'd spend the night begging for my forgiveness, crying sloppily all over me, and trying to convince me that he wasn't good enough for me and never would be. It would never occur to him that after working a long shift, all I wanted was sleep.

Frank rummaged through the glove compartment and took out a joint. He moved away from me briefly to light it and inhaled deeply. I already knew that this was part two of his usual tactics. He would get oblivious on weed, and maybe some drinks—anything that would help him to relax. Frank was the first to say that getting stoned was a reward for putting up with all the negativity that he experienced at work. He handed me the joint and I also pulled deeply. It helped reduced the stress of being around Frank. But tonight I decided to play the game in a very different way.

"You know what? I don't forgive you after all." I bit his lip playfully and smiled, showing him my white, even teeth, because I knew how much my mouth turned him on. I ran my tongue across my lips. He always told me that he got hard just by looking at my mouth. "You're going to have to pay for what you did tonight."

I shuffled in my seat so that I could see his expression. The astonishment on his face was stark, even with the SUV's dark lighting.

"You're going to have to make it up to me," I said, and pushed my face right up to his, licking his lips with my tongue. "You know what you have to do."

I looked over his shoulder at the empty parking lot. His partner, Pablo, and the evening-shift nurses had said their goodnights. I opened my jacket and began pulling my scrub top up, exposing my breasts in the dim light.

"Hey, wait, you can't do that here." Frank attempted to pull my top back down. "What, are you crazy? There are video cameras around here."

"No, I just want what you want. Let's do it right here. I can't wait, babe."

"No, let's get home first."

I took his hands and pressed them against my hard nipples. "Let's make love now. Please." Frank's body trembled against mine.

"No, not here," he said. "You work here and so do I, sort of." Frank pushed me back in my seat as I tried to climb over and straddle him. "Stop it! You're nuts. I'm taking you home."

This time I didn't have to pretend to sulk. The weed was powerful and I was feeling good. The pain in my head was almost gone. "But you waited for me, didn't you? It was for a reason, wasn't it?"

"Yeah, but—"

"Yeah, but nothing. Please, Frank." I enticed him by rubbing his groin. "Come on, I need you inside of me."

"No, not here. Get some rest. We'll have time for this tomorrow, when we're off." Frank put the car in reverse and pulled out of the parking space. "Fix your clothes, will you?"

When he reached my apartment, Frank opened the door for me and told me to get out. I stood at the curb. I'd made the perfect move. Sometimes the only way to get what I wanted was to do exactly what I didn't want to do. I watched the Escalade sail through the standing red light. No rules for Frank—that was the only rule. Except, standing here right now, I wasn't so sure that I wanted him to leave me. Because then I would have to take care of myself.

⌛

I made my way inside the lobby and past the unoccupied desk. It felt eerily vacant. Mr. Hussein had worked that desk for years, until his massive heart attack. The tenants had complained, but there was no replacement yet. My mailbox was also empty. I shook off the bad feeling and pressed my hand to the back of my head. There was a small, hard lump with some swelling to my scalp surrounding it. Now that I was home, I could put some ice on it.

I climbed up the stairs to my fourth-floor apartment. I had gotten stuck in the elevator once too often, so I usually took the stairs. As I turned the key into the lock, the penetrating headache that had come along with Frank's knuckles that afternoon came back. It was probably because I was tired. Another intense day, but that was my norm.

Making it into the apartment, all I could think of was some form of relief, and I poured myself water and took some Tylenol tablets out of the bottle. I held them in my palm and stared at them. Frank's insistence that *he* had the headache when he had assaulted *me* was infuriating. The clock on the wall told me it was two in the morning. My body caving in told me I should have spent the last hour in bed and not placating him.

I decided to shower in the morning and forget about everything else tonight. I got an ice pack out of the freezer and brought it to my bedroom. I stripped off my clothes and slipped under the dark blue satin comforter on my bed. Fall nights had finally arrived. If I wanted the air conditioner out before winter, I would have to let the slow-poke superintendent know now. Coney Island winters were extreme. The ice under my head was a good reminder of that.

As I tossed and turned, I remembered the two books that I had bought earlier that day. It seemed like days ago that I was in the flea market. The books were in my bag, which was still where I had dropped it when I raced inside to change into my uniform. I crawled out of the little nest made from my robe and comforter to get them.

The journal seemed to have an electrical pull. I opened it and began leafing through the first few pages. They were blank. I wondered whether *Ellen* had really used a fountain pen as I had initially thought. Maybe she would have used a quill feather pen. The journal wasn't that old, but I had no idea when the fountain pen had been invented. Her penmanship was in a light, feathery style. There were a few blotches of ink on some of the pages.

Some of the lines looked like they were smudged, and that struck a chord with me. I recognized the tear stains that marred the lines; they resembled some of the pages in my own journal. I had begun writing in diaries when I was about eleven, and kept a stack of them behind my boots at the bottom of my closet. I hadn't liked the entries that were beginning to fill the lines, so I stopped writing altogether. I didn't know whether I should discard or keep them. I didn't want anyone to read them, and I didn't want to either, but they told the story of my life.

I began to read through some of the pages in Ellen's journal.

June 12, 1903

What a wonderful gift from Miss Isabel! She said I can pore over the pages instead of pouring her bath. Writing in this journal will keep me busy while she is on holiday. When I mentioned to her that I was fearful that someone would read what I had written, she answered me with a strange look. It took me a while to figure out what her gaze meant. I need not be concerned that someone else will know my private thoughts. There is no one in my household who knows their letters. I am the only one, thanks to her. I will miss her dearly.

June 20, 1903

Cheery me
Sitting on rocks
Leery me
Mending new socks

This evening I had the great fortune of reading articles written by Miss Victoria Woodhull. To think that she had the daring to enter the race as a presidential candidate in 1872. Imagine that we are not yet able to vote, and yet, Miss Woodhull! What a power of example! What a brave leader of the women's movement! Her speech on free love invigorates yet frightens me. I dare not wish for free love but merely to live freely. If I were free, I would not be dependent on the likes of Mr. Allerton—that miser. Mrs. Allerton is probably turning over in her grave as she watches him handle Miss Isabel's affairs. I should not complain. It is due to the sweetness of Miss Isabel who is teaching me to read the literature she has collected as a hopeful suffragette that allows me the knowledge of great women. I am indebted to her.

July 13, 1903

I refused to do it. There is not a bone in my body that says I must do something so degrading. I am a lady despite what any of those mad men think. Let other girls accept crumbs or a penny for something that goes entirely against anything I believe in. There are some things that no self- respecting lady should be expected to do. I shudder at the thought.

📖

The writer must have been a servant. Having an employer who cared so much about her that they would flout the made-up rules of society by teaching her to write was mind-blowing. I skimmed some of the pages and tried to read further, but my eyelids drooped, and I fell asleep.

5
I trusted you

The bell pealed invasively. My head was so heavy that I could barely lift it off the pillow. I had taken the Tylenol only because I was afraid that the Oxycodone was still in my system. The weed had given me a bit of relief, but my mouth felt like it was stuffed with cotton.

I glanced at the clock. It was four in the morning; I had only been in bed for two hours. I tried to think of who might be ringing my bell at this time of morning. Frank was practically my only visitor and he had his own key. I moved my legs to the side of the bed and it seemed as though hands were pushing my shoulders back down. I resisted and managed to pull myself up. My whole body had become a dense rock.

I held on to the nightstand before I stood up. The dark bedroom whirled around me, and a sensation of nausea overtook me. The knot at the back of my head was probably worse than I thought. If I went to the emergency room to get it checked out, I'd be asked how the accident happened. I wasn't about to let my old ER coworkers know that much about me. The bell rang again.

I got to my feet slowly and scaled the wall to the front door. I pressed the TALK button on the intercom system.

"Who is it?" I mumbled. "Who's there?"

"Maggie, it's me, Ann Marie. Open up. I need to talk to you."

Ann Marie? Something was wrong. She hadn't even called to say she was coming over. This was proof enough that whatever news she had was bad news. Since

51

moving to Long Island, she rarely made the trip to Coney Island anymore, especially not in the middle of the night. Ann Marie was always busy with Pablo Jr., and meetings, and whatever else it was she did since marrying Pablo. I pushed the OPEN buzzer and, through the intercom, I heard the click of the door as it shut. Now I was fully awake and on guard. I wasn't looking forward to whatever it was Ann Marie was about to say. The feeling in the pit of my stomach changed from nausea to fear—it wasn't going to be good; I was certain of it. As I waited, I wondered whether there had been an accident. Frank and I weren't married, and his mother would be the one to receive any type of official news. She would never think to contact me. Maybe Ann Marie was making the courtesy call. I had told Frank that he shouldn't smoke weed and drive. It could only be bad news.

The apartment doorbell rang. I opened the door and Ann Marie walked into the foyer. The smell of her perfume was overpowering and filled the air. It traveled up my nostrils, straight to my brain. The top part of my head had started to hurt now and the pain in the back of it was stronger than it had been earlier today. I realized that 'today' was yesterday.

"What is it?" I tied my bathrobe belt around my waist. "What's wrong?"

"I need to talk to you," she said.

"Of course. Come in." I led her into the living room. The room was decorated luxuriously with an upholstered couch and glass-top tables. Frank insisted that I have the best of everything if we entertained his friends.

Ann Marie was about my height but rounder. Her long brown hair was pulled back and tinted with subtle highlights that shone under the light of the hanging fixture. She wore a belted leather coat that was lined with fur. The makeup on her face was applied heavily, which turned Ann Marie into a caricature of the woman I knew. What had happened to her? This person in front of me wasn't Ann Marie . . . but it was. The liner around her eyes was as thick as the penciled outline around her lips. There was a fine network of lines etched around her eyes. They were bloodshot and looked as dry as a fine linen napkin.

"Let me take your coat before we sit," I suggested.

"Don't bother. I'm not going to be here that long."

We sat across from each other and Ann Marie opened her bag. "You've really hurt me, Maggie. Do you know what this is?" She pulled out a small bundle wrapped in a lacy lavender fabric.

I shook my head. "No."

"I'm surprised you'd deny it," Ann Marie said, shaking her head as if to mimic me. "I never expected anything like this from you."

I reached out to take the package. I hadn't even seen what was wrapped in the material yet. Ann Marie was acting so strange. We hadn't seen each other in a long time, but we were still friends, as far as I knew. There had been no recent interaction between us, but we respected each other. We led very different lives. Once they got married and moved to Long Island, we only saw each other when Frank and Pablo had us meet for dinner or drinks. That didn't happen too often, because the two spent hours each day sitting next to each other in the squad car.

"How could you?" Ann Marie began to weep. "I know we haven't been close lately, and you may not believe this, but I trusted you."

"What are you talking about?" I opened the small bundle and unfurled the material to reveal a white thong. The underwear seemed vaguely familiar, but I couldn't place from where. Ann Marie's perfume reeked, and my head was still cloudy. "I don't understand. Why did you bring this here?"

"He told me that you would deny it."

"Who, Ann Marie, what are you talking about?"

"Pablo admitted that you and he are together." Her voice rose. "He told me that you've been sleeping with him."

I wanted to laugh. The idea was absurd.

"Pablo? Why would he tell you something like that when it's not true?"

"Why would he tell me this? You tell me." Ann Marie took a handkerchief from her handbag and dabbed at her eyes. "Do you think I'd come all the way out here if I wasn't sure? I left the baby at home. He's asleep."

"I don't know what to say," I began.

"I found the receipts."

"Receipts?"

"Please, don't embarrass me. We both know exactly the number of times you went with him to the hotel—all those nights that I thought he was working. Is Balenciaga still your favorite perfume? And the flowers. All those bouquets of flowers."

"What the hell is this all about?" I leaned forward and put my aching head against my hands. I took some deep breaths and sat up straighter.

"You know exactly what I'm talking about." Ann Marie suddenly resembled an old schoolmarm. With her hair pulled back and the thin line of her lips, she turned into a parody of herself.

Then, suddenly, I knew that this was a dream, a nightmare. Ann Marie wasn't here in my living room. She couldn't be. I rubbed my eyes, but when I reopened them, she was still seated in front of me. The lavender material cradling the thong sat open on my lap.

"This isn't mine. I don't know why you're here or why you brought this to me," I snarled. Gathering my energy, I stood up, and the items fell to the floor. "Please leave. You can't stay here."

I led Ann Marie to the front door. The back of my head was on fire.

"I'm sorry that you believe any of this," I said. "It's a misunderstanding. I was never with your husband."

"He told me you were the one. That you and he have been getting together. He went into detail. He told me exactly what you did for him. And him to you." Ann Marie sobbed, and her chest rose and fell in rhythm.

"He lied," I whispered. I put my hand firmly on the small of Ann Marie's back, guiding her out into the hallway. I closed the door and passed out.

6
A signal across the sea

The bright sunshine penetrated my eyelids. I turned away from the late-morning light and opened my eyes. The throbbing at the back of my head was only slightly better than the night before. My blurred vision cleared a bit. Fragments of the day filtered in and out of my thoughts. *The flea market. The Escalade. Amy Landry. The journal. Frank. Ann Marie.*

I rose slowly and gagged when I saw the slick spot near me on the rug. I was grateful that I hadn't choked to death on my vomit when I passed out. I had to hurry and clean it up. If Frank saw it, he would get pissed. He'd become furious with me, like the time I had too much to drink and the same thing had happened. Frank was practically phobic when it came to the white carpet. He insisted on picking out the furniture: modern, sleek, and mostly white, and repeatedly mentioned the cost of the flooring. I begged him to let me get the original parquet floor sanded instead and to buy some colorful throw rugs. But, as usual, he got his way.

I passed the living room on my way to the broom closet, where I kept the cleaning supplies. There on the floor were the lavender-colored fabric and the white thong. I picked them up, and it finally dawned on me that she was right. They were mine.

Frank had bought the thong for me a few months after we started dating. The store clerk had placed them in a tiny classic-white shopping bag filled with red tissue paper. I loved the thong and felt hot with desire for Frank, and aroused even more so that he would think of me in such a sensual way. He thought I'd look sexier in them than in my regular white cotton bikini underwear, and told me that the "nursey thing" had to go. I had slipped them on and pretended I was walking down a runway. At the time, I felt a little silly, but I was intoxicated with Frank when we first got together. He made me feel sexier than I had ever felt before. We made ardent love and Frank told me I was perfect as he playfully slapped my butt. He was upset when I refused to wear them to work, but I felt almost naked with the fabric of my uniform rubbing against my skin. He said that feeling should make me ready for him and that he was disappointed that he couldn't imagine me wearing them while on duty.

That was a long time ago, and I realized that I hadn't seen the thong again until Ann Marie brought it to me last night. Wrapping the bundle back up, I searched for a place to hide it. I had to think before confronting Frank. Knowing how he operated, it was likely he gave them to Ann Marie just to trick me, and it wasn't worth getting into another confrontation over. There was so much to figure out, and I was in no position to do that right now with the ache about to split my head in two.

As a nurse, I knew that a head injury with severe pain, blurred vision, and vomiting all made for an emergency room visit. Telling them that I fell or was bumped in the head with a door were lame excuses. I wouldn't blame them if they didn't believe me. I touched the back of my head and my fingers connected with a bit of sticky fluid. The skin in that area of my scalp was tender and must have opened when I passed out—yet another reason to get medical attention. But I was sure that I wouldn't be admitted to the hospital; there were no empty beds for a mere bruise. All I would do by going to the hospital would be opening the door to speculation, and worse, ridicule.

I decided to leave the bundle in the top drawer of my bureau until I could find a better place for it. After flattening the material and hiding it under the velvet case that held some of the necklaces Frank bought me, I felt less uneasy.

I scoured the carpet stain until it was no longer noticeable, and I was beat. I needed to shower, but it would make better sense to stay out of the tub. It would be all too easy to slip and fall. I had to laugh at myself. It was highly unlikely that anything would happen to me, because, like a cat, I had nine lives. That theory had been proven. So I took a scalding hot shower to wash away the last twenty-four hours.

As I towel-dried my hair, I noticed that the amber light on the answering machine was blinking. I pressed the PLAY button. *Frank.* He'd be here soon. The fear crept up in me again. I could never outsmart him. *Stupid. Stupid.*

It was twelve thirty. I had the evening off and didn't have to be back at work until the next afternoon. I thought about Amy Landry. Of course I wasn't supposed to get personally involved with my patients, but I was already close, in many ways, to this woman. Mrs. Graham could be so lax. I hoped she would watch Amy carefully while she was under her care. I decided to call the unit and check up on my patient.

The day clerk answered on the first ring. "Five South. Jacobs. May I help you?"

"Hi, Laurie, it's me, Maggie Fuentes. I was just wondering how the client in Room 512 is doing. You know, Amy Landry."

"Aren't you off today?"

"Yes. I'm just checking in," I said. "I took care of her last night."

"What are you doing? I promise not to let the supervisor know that you're calling. It's been crazy here. They'll try to have you come in if they think that you're home, twiddling your thumbs."

"Why, what's going on there?"

"There was a code in the unit. You know how it is. They had to move some of the clients around again."

"What about Miss Landry; is she okay?"

"She's still here." Laurie hesitated. "Do you know her? I mean, are you friends?"

I began to feel a little self-conscious. "It's just that she's so young, you know, to try to kill herself. We didn't have that much information. Did the psychiatrist see her yet?"

"I guess I could have a look at her chart. Do you want me to check? It's busy, but I can if you want."

The bell rang in my apartment. It was the second time it had happened today, and I wasn't expecting anyone except Frank.

"Never mind," I said. "I'll be there tomorrow. Sorry to bother you." I hung up and got to the door during the second set of rings. I pressed the intercom button. "Yes?"

A male voice at the other end called out, "Delivery!"

The building did not have a doorman, and my sense of safety vanished. Ann Marie had been the first to come in, with her strange claims, and now there was someone ringing the bell with an unexpected delivery. I tried to ignore my anxiety and rang the bell back to open the door. At least I was dressed, and that made me feel a little safer.

59

This time I looked through the peephole and saw a young man dressed in a black T-shirt and jeans, holding a large arrangement of flowers. I opened the door wide enough to take them from him, and remembering the tip, told him to wait there a minute.

"No, ma'am, thank you," he said. "Everything has been taken care of already." He suddenly smiled, revealing a space between his upper front teeth. *Sweet-looking dude.* I stopped myself. I'd be signing my own death certificate if Frank found out what I was thinking. I was grateful he didn't have a psychic bone in his body.

I closed the door swiftly and tore open the paper that covered the flowers. Lilacs. The fragrance from the beauties filled the air and I inhaled deeply.

I placed the spray on the kitchen counter and searched for a card but couldn't find one. I hurried back to the door but found the hallway empty. I figured that the floral shop would be able to tell me who sent the flowers, so I scanned the wrapping paper for the name of the shop. The bright pink letters across the white paper simply read *Say it with Flowers.* No name or phone number.

Weird. The thought of an anonymous person sending me flowers was disturbing. But, if Frank had sent them, he would fly into a rage if he saw them in the trash can. He sent me flowers often enough but always had his name printed on the card with a message. The messages usually said that I was the best thing that ever happened to him, or were pleas of forgiveness for some transgression.

The persistent throbbing at the back of my head reminded me that I would have to decide about going to the emergency room. I decided I'd be better off if I lay down again for a few minutes.

I poured water into a crystal vase and arranged the delicately scented lilacs before leaving them on the kitchen counter. I'd figure out where to place them later.

I lay across my bed and picked up the journal to read another couple of entries before closing my eyes.

August 1, 1903

Miss Isabel may believe she is treated like a favored child, but I'm not too sure about that. Her father does with her what he will. She never has a choice in the matter. To the Cape. To the Harbor. Wherever he sends her, she goes. There is no will or fire in her spirit. I am grateful because she has seen me as a person more than as a servant, but really! Working in the kitchen is not my strength. Cook says, "Best you air out the feather mattress. You're better suited to that." I think not.

August 3, 1903

Miss Woodhull had been arrested and spent days in The Tombs. Is that any worse than having her image changed into that of a she-devil and splashed across the papers? If only she would pass me by on the street and stop to pour her stories out to me. I would like to stand up and charge along the streets with the other women, but instead my hands are chapped from pouring boiling water and bleach into the bucket that holds the Allerton underclothes and bed sheets. There is nothing worse than being privy to the feelings of Mr. Allerton and Miss

Isabel when I touch their clothing. It's as though they leave their feelings in their dirty clothes. I must learn to ignore and not read everything I come across. I wonder, though, can one's thoughts and feelings truly get stuck in one's clothing? I must get air. The breeze is cooling and I think I will take a walk to the beach. There I can gather my thoughts and not be bothered as I write in my journal. I will wait until dusk when the boardwalk lights are aglow.

August 5, 1903

*If this is from where I come
I would like to change my identity*

August 8, 1903

Karl is on my last nerve. He came up behind me and whispered with his breath hot against my ear. He disgusts me! I stay at home for Momma and the girls. The boys will be leaving soon. There is no reason for them to stay, with that piece of hide complaining about everything. I don't know how Momma can stand to get under the covers with him at night. At least I have the Allerton home where I can take refuge. I should not complain about working in the kitchen. I wish Mr. Penny Pincher would allow me to go with Miss Isabel when he sends her abroad. Most fathers would do that, knowing their young daughters would be much better cared for by servants who are like sisters. Miser!

I sit here at the foot of the sea. How she drives me! The crescent shape of the rocks is the same as that of the moon. I stare up at her glowing face and she takes my breath away. While the lights, the rides, and the amusements take up the attention of all the visitors who stroll through Luna Park, it is the moon that captivates me. It is dusk and she reveals merely a glimpse of her magic. I know that if I were ever to leave the Allerton Manor or Momma's rooms that I would survive on the moon's filaments of light. She always fills me. I am never in want when I'm here. But why am I so silly? Cook says my imagination and wandering thoughts will be the death of me. But I know that I will never have to leave the Allerton home. Miss Isabel loves me and I her. It is only because we were born to different mothers that she is my lady and I am her servant, otherwise, we would be sisters. I will put my pages in my satchel and pretend to be a sightseer on the boardwalk. There are many exhibitions for me to amuse myself with, even without a penny in my pocket

📖

My eyes started to close, but I was uneasy about the journal. Ellen must have been very young and careless to write her thoughts on paper. She probably never expected anyone to read her private thoughts. Maybe I should learn something from Ellen and burn my old journals. I stopped writing in them, but if something happened to me, they might end up for sale in a flea market like hers. I was exhausted. Or maybe just under the spell of the moon that Ellen wrote so lovingly about. It was the middle of the day; my thinking could be so dumb sometimes. A quick nap was all that I needed.

Lying fully clothed on my bed, my breath became rhythmical. Slow. Like the waves at the ocean that calmed me on the days I needed comfort. I was just like Ellen. I, too, needed to get away from all the madness and sit at the foot of the sea. My mind began playing images that resembled a flickering movie reel of the boardwalk. Children called out to gulls, and couples walked hand in hand, oblivious to the beauty surrounding them; they were so intent on their love. While I adored walking across the hot sand, the expansive view of the beach, water, and sky was incomparable from my perch on the boardwalk. The warm breeze blew across my face, complementing the kiss of the sun. Sleep was the reprieve that I needed. The pain in my head started to subside and my sleep deepened.

The rocks far off in the ocean seemed to beckon to me from where I sat. I looked down to see that I now stood on the white, grainy sand. There was a brown-skinned boy playing alongside a woman in a yellow and blue polka dot two-piece suit whose head was covered by a large floppy hat. The child winked at me. While he couldn't have been more than four years old, his face was that of a wizened old man. The tot pointed to a small shiny object that hung from a silvery chain around his plump little neck, and then toward my chest. I looked down and saw that I, too, wore a thin necklace of silver and a polished medallion. It flashed when I picked it up between my fingers, for it had become a beacon signaling from far across the sea. The clasp opened, and the necklace and medallion slipped into my hand. I almost dropped it but was able to catch it before it fell onto the sand.

I paused and then began my trail toward the rocks, my feet leaving a set of prints in the sand. I thought of the old tale of the person who was carried by Jesus but believed they were alone. I turned back to look at my footprints and saw that, indeed, there was only one set. I was truly alone and became more purposeful in my walk. There was a keen desire within me to reach the rocks, which seemed to grow as I neared them, but it was getting harder and harder to reach them. There, at the top, I spotted the child. Somehow he'd climbed up quickly and easily. He wore a white gauzy tunic that billowed in the breeze. He called to me.

"Hurry! You must come before it's too late!"

The boy, merely a baby, could speak, but his lips hadn't moved. His large gray eyes widened as he spotted something over my shoulder. He seemed frightened, and I turned to see what he was looking at.

"Wake up! I told you to hurry up," Frank yelled into my ear. "We're going to dinner!"

I landed back in my body with a thud and immediately felt the aching sensation in the back of my head again.

7
You belong to me

I was livid. "Why do you do that? Can't you just come in like a normal person?"

"What? I let myself in. What's the problem?" Frank peered at his reflection in the mirror as he flexed the bicep of his right arm and lifted his close-fitting shirt with his left. "Look at my abs, babe. If I didn't love you already, I'd love myself."

"Who's fighting you on that? Go ahead. Break up with me, why don't you? That would be perfect. You could start dating yourself."

"What's eating you?" Frank continued to flex in the mirror. "Woke up on the wrong side of the bed? Anyway, what are you sleeping in the middle of the day for?" He looked down at me. "Didn't we say we'd meet up?"

"I don't feel well." I touched the back of my head gingerly.

"Don't tell me. You've got a headache," he snickered, and shook his head. "That excuse went out with the caveman, sweetie."

"Maybe it did, but in my case, it's true."

It probably wasn't worth bringing up yesterday's tussle. Frank didn't care. I was the one who had to remember the reasons for our blow-ups. Whenever he did respond, it was to tell me how silly I was being, and to remind me that if I behaved right, he wouldn't have to guide me into right action.

"Want an aspirin or something? I'll get it for you." He rubbed his hand on the top of my head. "I don't want my baby hurting. Not on her day off."

"An aspirin would be excellent." I turned over on

66

my side and let my eyes close.

Frank left the bedroom and walked out into the hallway. I could hear him fiddling with music on the sound bar before stopping in the kitchen for the aspirin. I could hear Whitney belt out 'I will always love you.' Maybe she could have felt that way forever, but I couldn't. Every time I thought I was nearing the end of my rope, Frank would shift and become a sweetheart—like getting me aspirin.

"Hey, come out here, will you?" Frank's voice bellowed. "What's this?"

"My God, you're impossible." I clenched my teeth as I headed toward the kitchen.

Holding the bouquet of flowers as though he were in a beauty pageant, Frank stood there with a frozen smile plastered across his face. "You want to tell me where you got these from? Or, better yet, should I ask *whom* you got these from?"

I went to pull them out of his arms. "I don't know. They came for me late this morning. Help me look for the card. I couldn't find it."

"Really? You expect me to fall for that?" Pure disgust emanated from him. "I keep giving you more and more chances, and you know what?"

I stood silently with my arms still outstretched, but Frank held the flowers just out of reach. Their fragrance was heady and strong, and I thought I would drown in the strength of the aroma. Just like Ann Marie's perfume, it was way too much.

"You won't answer because you know better than to make up some excuse. At least you learned something from me." Frank's expression hadn't changed. "I should just mash these in your face. That way you'd really enjoy them, wouldn't you?"

"Frank, I told you—" I stopped short as he threw the bouquet in its crystal vase against the sink backsplash, shattering it. He squeezed my lips hard between his fingers before pulling me close to him.

"I came here to show you how much I love you, and I expected the same from you. You disappointed me." Frank ground his body against mine as he pushed me back into the hallway, toward the bedroom. Any outsider would say we were dancing, but my feet weren't on the floor. "I love you and you belong to me. Remember that."

Frank pushed me down onto the bed. I watched the ceiling spin above me as he pulled my clothing away from my body, and I heard tearing from somewhere close to me. I pulled my energy away from him; it was a trick I had learned a long time ago. It wasn't so much that I didn't really care for the body, but I had to keep my distance from it while it betrayed me. Instead of lying there accepting his rage, I got up and sat at my tiny dressing table. I watched from afar as he roughly penetrated the body and began to hammer it repeatedly with his own rigid one. He kissed lips that were flaccid.

I continued to watch as I smoked a cigarette, played with my colorful lipsticks, and smelled the fragrances of perfumes I spritzed from the tiny, shiny bottles onto my pretty pink skin. I watched as he rammed and rammed incessantly against the body. When he was finally done, he began kissing the body all over, crying—something I loathed—while he spoke of eternal love, his desire for it to love and forgive him. "You mean so much to me," he whispered to the body that just lay there on my bed. Tolerating the blubbering part was the least I could do for the battered shell that rested beneath him. It shouldn't have to deal with that too. I had at least that much compassion for it. I re-entered the body and we became one again.

A short time later, Frank sat up next to me. "Get up. Get dressed. We're going out for dinner."

There was no more talk of the flowers or the shards of crystal that remained on the kitchen floor. I got up and silently readied myself for the exposure of strangers who turned away when they saw the effects of what Frank had done to the body.

Sugar Wafers

The gingham curtains are pink and white. They match the bedspread with the ruffled hem. Maggie lies on her side, sucking the corner of the pillow sham. It's also made of white and pink gingham.

Mami's cries pierce the wall. "Get out of here before I call the police!"

There's a bang, and then another, bigger bang, before everything becomes quiet. Maggie's bedroom door opens and Mami slinks in, practically crawling on all fours.

"Move over," she whispers. Maggie does as she's told and Mami lies next to her on the bed. Mami's hair is a mess and tears roll down her cheeks.

Maggie touches her face. "Your eye is swollen. Your lip is bleeding."

"I'm okay, *mamita*. Don't worry. I took care of him. That piece of shit isn't coming here anymore."

Maggie nods. Just like the pink walls, she's heard that promise before.

"We might have to move, baby," Mami cajoles. "You understand, right, honey?"

The two become twins as Maggie starts crying too. "But I like this house. If we move away, how can I play with Hilda?"

"Don't worry about that. You've got me. I'll play with you."

"But what about the sugar wafers?" Maggie's wails can be heard upstairs.

"What are you talking about? What sugar wafers?"

"The ones that Hilda's mother gives me when I go to their apartment," Maggie explains. "The ones she keeps in the tin. You know, the black and red tin she hides in the cabinet."

"You don't need them. They give you cavities. Remember what the dentist said. You're only in the second grade and already you had to get fillings."

"But I want them. They're sweet."

"All right, I'll get you some when we go food shopping. Just stop bawling!"

"But the ones she gets come from Spain." Maggie is inconsolable now.

"We have to leave," Mami says angrily, but then her voice softens. "I'll see if I can get them where we move to."

"We're not moving to Spain!" Maggie's tears turn into ice, like her anger. But then she looks at her mother and they turn to salty liquid again. "Your eye is turning purple, Mami. Get a cloth. Never mind. I'll do it. I'll run it under cold water."

"No, it's not that bad."

"Yes, it is. You could go blind like Jerry."

"Jerry?"

"The kid that got the pencil stuck in his eye." Maggie cries louder.

Mami's voice turns hard again. "Shh, stop that. We can't stay here anymore. That asshole keeps trying to get back with me. *Abuela* said we can move in with her."

Maggie sits up in bed. "Where am I going to sleep?"

"You can sleep with *Abuela*. She said you could."

"You said I didn't have to share anymore. That I

could have my own room from now on."

"It's just until we find another apartment."

"But you said . . ."

"Don't be an ingrate, you brat."

Maggie lies down again and turns her back to her mother. The snot gets stuck in her throat. "I don't want to sleep with you or *Abuela*. I want my own bed. I'm too old to sleep with you."

"Look, kid, this guy's bad news, and we've got to get away."

In between sobs, Maggie talks to the wall. "You say that all the time. This time it's Albert. The last time it was Freddy. Before that it was Rocky. And that was only because you found him looking in my drawers. We keep having to move."

"You're right." Mami sounds weary. "It's not fair, but sometimes life is like that."

"I like it here," Maggie says. "I like my class."

"Well, maybe you don't have to change schools this time."

"*Abuela* lives too far. I can't take the bus to school."

"I'll figure something out. I always do, sweetie, I always do."

Mami smiles and shows a cracked front tooth, but Maggie doesn't notice because she has stopped looking at her mother. Instead, she's staring at the crack in the wall.

"What will I do with my bedspread and curtains?" she asks.

"If you want, we can give them to Hilda."

This time, it's Maggie's cries that pierce the wall.

8
Torn into fragments

"What do you mean you're not hungry?" Frank scanned the menu. "Why else would we come here? To eat, baby. These prices have gone way up. Next time you'd better check them online before making me bring you to one of your favorite restaurants."

It was evening and my sunglasses were way out of place at Gargiulo's, but I was petrified someone would recognize me. Not even celebrities wore sunglasses in dark restaurants, and I was far from being a celeb. The dark frames hid my eyes but did nothing to hide my bruised and swollen lips. I could barely move them.

"I told you, I can't eat. Not like this," I answered.

"Don't ruin the evening, okay?" Frank shook his head. "You always do this. If you wanted to stay home, you should have said something."

I nodded. First, it was hard to talk, and secondly, I didn't want to incite his spiteful anger any more tonight. I could contend with the headache, which was now a migraine, but I didn't want to sit directly in front of the cause of it for the next couple of hours.

"I have to tell you something, even though, by right, it's none of your business." Frank tapped the white tablecloth with his thick fingers.

I sat there waiting for him to go on. Flames danced atop the slender tapered candles. I had the sensation of riding waves, and struggled to stay alert.

"What, are you deaf now?" he asked. "Are you listening?"

"Yes, I can hear you," I whispered. "I'm right here."

"So say something next time I talk to you." Frank

looked over his shoulder and adjusted his collar. For once, *he* looked uncomfortable. "Ann Marie is divorcing Pablo."

I held my head up with my hand as I leaned on the table, not sure how to respond. Frank was still wound up and I waited for a cue to let me know what to say. I had to agree with whatever thoughts he might have about the split. A vision of the thong swam through the muddle in my head.

"Drink some of this," he said, and poured red wine into a crystal goblet. "You know, if it were me, I'd do anything to keep you happy. Pablo messed up. There are all kinds of women throwing themselves at us. All day long. You know what it's like being on the beat? Of course you don't, but I'll tell you that I'm not like him at all. Not in that respect. He's my partner and I'd do anything for him, but I'd never treat you the way he treats Ann Marie. Nothing is too good for my woman."

I nodded. *Just agree. Go through the motions.* I stole a glance at my watch. Ten o'clock. I just had to get through dinner and it would all be over soon. But I was curious about Pablo and Ann Marie, especially after that bizarre visit in the middle of the night.

"He's seeing other women?" I asked.

"Don't you and Ann Marie talk? I thought you two got along. You used to work in the same place."

"It's been a while since she left the hospital. What's Pablo up to?" *Play the game. Find out what Ann Marie was talking about.* I sipped from the goblet and immediately knew that I would have trouble standing up without help.

"Hey, look, I'm not about to rat him out." Frank snapped his fingers to get the waiter's attention.

A pianist played music in the background and at first I couldn't make it out. Then I realized it was the easy-listening stuff. Burt Bacharach. My grandmother listened to her old records and I would imitate Dionne Warwick by mouthing the lyrics into the mirror. I loved the way my *abuela* clapped for me, and I decided to be a singer, a star—someone famous—when I grew up. My little-girl dreams never happened. No one like Frank had ever passed through my mind, and here I was, swollen and bruised, sitting across from him at Gargiulo's.

The waiter appeared at our table and Frank whispered into his ear. I could practically touch the man's bald head as he bent close to us. The veins in his neck seemed engorged, as if they were about to blow. Sometimes being a nurse was a curse. I saw everything, and it was overwhelming.

I drew my attention away and thought about what Frank had just shared. Pablo was seeing other women and Ann Marie blamed me. Knowing this seemed to make my headache worse, and the energy in the room changed. The aura around the pianist shifted from silver to kelly green. The energy surrounding Frank was more of a grayish hue. It throbbed. I lowered my eyes and took in his whole figure. I saw that the area around his feet was thick and brownish-colored. As a kid I was alone after school a lot and spent most of my time in my head. Singing and reading filled my days. As I got older, I devoured books that explained what I saw. Energetic particles. None of it meant anything in my world today. My interest in precognition, auras, and near-death experiences was useless; none of it told me how to shake Frank. Somebody once told me to follow my intuition for guidance, but my intuitive map seemed to be torn into fragments.

"Maggie. *Maggie*," Frank called to me. "Where the hell are you? Can't you pay attention?"

Frank's face seemed a million miles away and was contorted. I was sure that if I pushed my arms out, they would go right through his energy field, which was like thick consommé.

I did my best to be present. "I'm here."

He sulked. "I'm saying something really important and you're acting like nothing I'm saying matters."

"You're right. Go ahead." I shook my head slightly, trying to get the cobwebs out. "I'm just not feeling myself."

"What I was telling you is that seeing Pablo and his wife have a hard time has really made me think."

"So, what is it you're trying to tell me?" I could barely follow my own train of thought; how could I follow his?

At that moment, the waiter came up to the table with a small, round chocolate cake, lit with a sparkly candle. My favorite flavor, except that we hadn't gotten to the main course yet.

"Congratulations." The waiter's warm, garlicky breath was offensive. I edged away from him.

I turned to Frank. "Is it a special day?" I asked. "I'm not sure . . ." I was lost. It wasn't my birthday, or Frank's either.

"Don't worry, babe," he said, moving toward me for a kiss. "This is a special day that's about to happen."

He reached into his jacket and I could see the gun at his waist. The hair on the back of my neck stood up, but I knew that Frank wasn't the type to do anything in public that would land him in jail, least of all shoot me.

It was when we were in the privacy of my apartment or the car that he would do what he did best. The restaurant was a safe place for me.

"What day? Frank, tell me! Did you plan something?" I tried to look excited.

"This is for you." Frank pulled a small black velvet box out of the inner pocket of his jacket. "Open it."

"What is this?" I held the square box in my hand and pretended to savor the moment. I wasn't ready to open the lid.

Frank beamed. "I've thought about proposing to you for a while, but sometimes you're such a pain in the neck. Sometimes you make me do things that I'm ashamed of afterwards. That's not a good place to be. I've even tried to stay clear of you, but I always end up right back next to you. I'm powerless when it comes to you. When you're around, all bets are off."

Hearing this, I wanted to cry. All along, as I was thinking of ways to get rid of him, everything I did was having the opposite effect, attracting him to me even more.

He continued. "Well, with everything going on with Pablo and Ann Marie, I decided that I wanted to do right by you. I want to marry you."

I swallowed my laughter. This wasn't the time; he was so easily offended. He'd get furious if he thought that I was laughing at him or making fun of him. It was the absurdity of the situation that made me want to snicker. If I started laughing like I wanted to, I might not be able to stop. I had to think of something quickly. He stared at me, waiting for an answer.

"Marry you?" I asked.

"Yeah. Now. I love you and you love me."

I couldn't help but interrupt. "You mean *right now?*"

"Yes. Can't you hear right? Now. Not tonight, but soon. We'll get those blood tests and—"

"Blood tests? Is that necessary these days?"

"I don't know. You should know; you're a nurse."

I gave him a blank stare—that was about all I could do. I was numb inside.

"We could pick a day and go to City Hall," he said. "Nothing fancy. You can bring a witness and I will too. I'll bring Pablo."

"Wait. This is so fast, Frank."

The pianist stopped playing and came over to our table. "Excuse me," he said. "Looks like a celebration here. Would you like me to play something? Special, you know. For you two."

"No." I held my hand up as though I could just ward him away.

"Yes," Frank said. "That would be great." Then, turning to me, he said, "Something you like, Maggie. Hurry up. He doesn't have all day, you know."

"I'm not sure." I tried to think of a song for the musician to play, but came up empty.

The pianist smiled at Frank. "Why, the little lady is speechless! How about I pick something out for you, sir. I'm just about to start the next set. Give me your names and everyone in the room will be celebrating with you." He jerked his head toward his baby grand. "The ladies love this."

My lips were dry and tender. I knew the swelling and bruises on my face were hidden under the thick makeup I had applied, but I still didn't want everyone staring at me. The pianist was gone before I had a chance to say anything.

"You haven't even looked at it yet." Frank pointed to the box that sat in front of us.

"I'm surprised and overwhelmed, that's all." I slowly lifted the lid and was just about to see the contents, when Frank snatched the box out of my hand.

"I'm begging you not to ruin this moment for me." His eyes flashed in the candlelight. "Like everything else."

"Please, Frank, give it back," I begged. "I do want to see it. I'm sorry."

"That's better," he said, dropping the box in front of me.

I opened it and gasped. I'd never seen such a beautiful ring before; the facets gleamed brilliantly in the candlelight. "Oh my goodness, Frank, this is exquisite."

"You bet your sweet little ass it is. I paid a good buck for it. It's only one carat, but look how it's surrounded by those smaller round diamonds. Baguettes and a platinum band, babe. Only the best for you."

"I can't accept this," I said. "How can you afford it?"

"Told you," he said through clenched teeth. "I told you that you ruin everything. Whether I can afford it is none of your business."

"I don't want you getting into more debt. That's all. You have the car and now this. You're a policeman and I know what your salary is."

"What are you trying to say?"

The pianist was back at his bench and hitting the first chord. Suddenly I knew what he'd play before he began. Instead of saying *yes* to 'Martini & Rossi on the rocks,' it would be *yes* to Frank and Maggie on the rocks.

Was this guy for real? He was singing an old commercial that I saw once on YouTube. Everyone had. This man's repertoire left a lot to be desired.

"Sweet Maggie, say *yes*," Frank begged. His expression changed to that of an innocent child. He had so many personalities that I could barely keep up with him.

"I'm sorry, but I'm just not feeling right," I said. "I don't want to ruin this for you—I mean *us*—but I think I'm going to pass out." The candle was melting into the frosting. The sounds from the neighboring tables were deafening. Sitting in the brocade-covered chair, I knew that I looked a sight. I'd become a cadaver set to appear as though blood still flowed through my veins. I shielded my face from the scrutiny of the people at the next table. We'd gotten their attention when the pianist dedicated his rendition of a champagne commercial to us.

"Let's get the hell out of here." Frank called to the waiter, "Check, please!"

He snapped the ring box closed and put it back into his jacket pocket. We waited for the check in silence. When the server finally brought it over, he handed it to Frank, who gave me a side-glance as he plunked his credit card down on the table and signed the receipt.

"What's wrong with you?" he asked. "You look like crap. Why can't you do better with yourself? You're like a Halloween fright with all that thick makeup you wear."

Frank grabbed me by the elbow and quickly maneuvered me out of the crowded restaurant. We stood on the sidewalk. The cool, fresh evening air filled my nostrils.

"I'm sorry. Really." I'd become a robot. "This was a very special moment and I ruined it. I know that I have to do better. I promise."

He stood with his back to me, waiting for the valet to bring the SUV.

"Frank, really." I gently touched his arm to get his attention.

Turning back, Frank practically spat at me. "I'm used to you. You can't help yourself. This isn't new. You always do this. I'm not even sure why I tried to give you the ring. My mistake. I got all caught up with Pablo and Ann Marie, and that's none of my business. He's just my partner, that's all. What he does has nothing to do with me."

The Escalade pulled up in front of us. The valet came around the front of the car to hold the door open for me. I almost stumbled climbing into it.

Once we were in the car, Frank gave me a long look. "You had to do it, huh?"

"What?" I asked. "What did I do?"

The burning sensation in the back of my head was back. Swallowing a couple of Vicodin before we left my apartment only had a short-term effect. I needed something stronger. Frank turned up the volume and the Cover Girls sang about 'making the best of things.' That just about summed up my life.

"You know what you did," he said. "You had to show him your crotch, climbing up there with your dress hiked up."

"I could barely get up in here," I tried to explain.

"You disgust me," he said, taking his fist and pressing it hard against my solar plexus. "Trust me. Sometimes I hate you."

"Stop, please." My breath came in short gasps. "Please, Frank, I love you."

"I hate what you make me do." Frank pulled his fist away and began to run his fingers through his hair. Like the millions of stars in the sky, he'd said that many times before. "I'm taking you home." He gunned the engine. "Wash that crap off your face. You look like a tramp."

"Yes." I silently prayed that he would leave me off in front of the house as he'd done the evening before. We were both quiet for the rest of the ride.

Finally coming to a standstill, Frank double-parked. "There's no parking around here. I'm going home. My mother is probably worried. I haven't called her and I have a double tomorrow. You'll be all right?"

"Yes," I assured him. "Thanks, Frank. I know you tried to plan a wonderful evening. I'm sorry I ruined it. The ring is lovely. Any woman would be proud to wear it." The words spilled out of my mouth as though through a ventriloquist.

Frank kissed me lightly on the lips. "I know, babe, I love you, remember that. I'll call you tomorrow." He bent across me to pull the door lever.

I climbed out while pulling my skirt down over my knees, even though I didn't see anyone around. I wasn't about to take another chance tonight.

I stood on the curb and watched as Frank's car screeched through the red light. Again, as always, he showed that he had no regard for anyone or anything, not even the law. I wanted to call someone to talk about the last twenty-four hours, but I didn't have that many friends anymore. Once I had been dating Frank for a while, most of the people I hung around with disappeared from my life. He was "just too intense," my friend Lilly told me right before she vanished. I was afraid to tell Dulce. At some point, she had jokingly threatened to have me arrested to keep me away from him. Behind bars, I might be safe.

I entered the lobby and noticed the new doorman sitting at the counter. He stared at me as I went toward the elevator. He didn't get up to either open the door or ask who I was.

"I'm Maggie Fuentes in 5D," I introduced myself to the man, and he finally stood up. Tall and dark, he favored Frank.

The doorman nodded but still didn't say anything to me. The name tag on his lapel read *James*. Was that his first or last name? There was something odd about him, but I wasn't sure what.

"If you receive any packages for me, just leave a message," I said. "Please don't bring them upstairs until I ask for them. Also, if I receive any visitors, call me. Don't let them go upstairs until I give you the okay."

James continued to stare at me without any expression but finally nodded. I pressed the elevator button and the door slid open. This time I went against my usual routine of walking up the stairs. I was exhausted and in pain.

I entered the apartment. The flowers were still on the kitchen floor. A small puddle had formed on the counter. The crystal vase lay shattered, and glittering shards lined the bottom of the sink. There were a few slivers on the floor. I backed out of the room.

I went into the bathroom to wash my face but kept my eyes from my reflection in the mirror. I didn't want to see how I looked. The cool water soothed my bruised skin. I didn't have to report on my shift until four the next afternoon. Ice compresses and expert makeup would do the job to near perfection. I gently patted my skin with cotton wipes and smoothed a balmy crème on it.

I winced when I saw the condition of my bedroom. The top sheet and comforter were in a heap on the floor at the foot of the bed. One pillow was on the chair and the other was on the floor next to the doorway. I picked up the tangle of bed linens and saw smears of dried blood on the sheets. Two stains. One was at the head and another where Frank had pinned my hips down.

Thanks to the mercy of physical numbness, I hadn't realized I'd bled between my legs. I pulled my clothing and underwear off. Sure enough, my pink briefs were tinged dark brown. I turned the shower faucet on, stepped in, and let the scalding water stream over me. All I could think of was to *get rid of the evidence, get rid of the evidence*. Frank had repeated those words to me often enough. They became part of my cleansing ritual, and I chanted the words that had become my mantra.

I took my robe off the door hook and put it on, tying the sash around my waist. There, on an adjacent hook, was the white thong that Ann Marie had brought me during the early morning hours. I pulled it down and again felt sick. *Who had gone through my things?*

My heart thumped as I made my way back to the bedroom. I opened the bureau drawer and pushed the velvet cloth holding my jewelry aside. The thong wasn't there, of course. It was in my hands. The lavender cloth that Ann Marie had wrapped it in was gone. I shut the drawer and went over to the bed and pushed the thong deep between the mattress and the box spring.

I ran back into the foyer to make sure the front door was tightly locked. I put the chain in place. Frank would be furious if he came back and couldn't get in, but that was unlikely. Once he brought up his mother, I knew that he wanted to stay there all night. They still shared an apartment and she waited for him. He'd slipped once and told me that she became angry when he stayed out the whole night. I was grateful for that, as crazy as it was for a man in his thirties. Those breaks gave me the solitude that I needed to get myself together.

I hauled a new set of bed sheets from the linen closet and replaced the soiled ones. I opened a pillowcase and pushed the dirty sheets into it. The memory of the last time I brought bloodied sheets and towels to the laundromat was still vivid. The couple that washed and folded didn't say a thing when they handed me the sack of freshly washed items. It wasn't until I left the laundry that I realized the wife's eyes never met mine when I'd handed her the payment.

I went to bed but tossed and turned for a long time. After the last twenty-four hours, I should have just been able to collapse into a deep slumber, but sleep kept me at a distance. I picked up an antique silver powder box that I used to hold slim joints that Frank left for me. He wanted me to have *only the finest*; no fat blunts for me. I lit one and took a few pulls. I immediately felt relief. *Nothing should work this quickly,* I thought, *unless it's pushed into a vein.* I put the joint out and picked up the old journal from the floor. It seemed to be talking to me.

August 15, 1903

Rich men pinch pennies
The poor waste them foolishly

85

Believing they will never add up
Destinies and fortunes forever squandered

August 19, 1903

I make up funny little poems but, really, what does that mean for me? Nothing. I am miserable today. I would like to leave this horrid house. If I were to save a portion of my earnings, I would be out of the house within two fortnights. Momma would die if I were to leave. Then again, she wouldn't. She has that great hog to watch over her and she has become his sow. I am saddened by her. Today she asked me to retrieve the turnips from the cellar. My legs balked on the rickety stairs that moved and shook with my weight, as if in a dance. My skirts caught against the wood jamb and collected splinters. It was late and I had to hurry, as Karl was sure to walk through the door any second. My stomach turned as I heard his heavy footsteps a moment before the front door slammed. I was sure that he would not risk the steps. I have so far avoided his fleshy arms. I have become altogether sick at the sight of him. Momma never asks why I avoid him. It is as though she takes no notice. I am praying that Miss Isabel will soon return from holiday. I would much rather be at the Allerton manor during the nights than here with this large ape.

August 28, 1903

Roses float in fragrant bath water
A flurry of activity sounds outside the door
A suitor will ask for her hand in marriage
If only I were she

86

I'm proud to have an easy turn of the quill. Miss Isabel said it's the turn of my mind that is sharp and quick, and that is what guides my pen. She has finally returned. I am again pouring her bath, but that suits me fine. The gown she has picked out for this evening's dinner has the lowest of necklines. Cook calls it coquettish. I daresay, tonight there will be a suitor at her door. There is an electrical excitement in the air and I have no words to describe what is happening, except for the jingling I feel inside my being. The sound is one of fine tinkling Christmas bells.

August 30, 1903

I am tired after today's walk, but it was worth it. I walked almost the entire length of the boardwalk—as far as my legs would go. I went directly to the Infant Incubator. Such tiny babies with a chance of hope for life. If I were in one of those incubators, I too would be cared for, but here I am wishing again. Today I stood at Ruby's door. I don't believe that is her true name, because she comes from a foreign country. She hasn't spoken to me, but I listened as she quoted her prices to the customer who stood at her door. There is a painted wooden sign that hangs over her storefront. A large eye gazes down upon everything. One can choose a palm reading or a card from her tarot deck. Pick one card or a full spread. Another sign on the door says the cost for one card is two cents and five for a full spread. Behind the sheer window curtain there are two straw chairs and a rough-hewn wooden table. On the table are a deck of cards, candles, and a round sphere of a lovely violet hue. I do so wonder if this Miss Ruby can really foretell the future, or if I'd be squandering my savings. I'd best be careful, for I'm beginning to sound like that old Mr. Allerton.

September 4, 1903

Two suitors. They would both like to have Miss Isabel's hand in marriage. Her décolletage was quite the sensation. The dress was divine. The sapphire blue silk matched her eyes perfectly. The talk is that Mr. Allerton became almost apoplectic when Mr. Daniels asked for her hand, and he said he would think about it. A few moments later, Mr. Jones knocked at the old man's study door, asking the very same thing. The timing couldn't have been better! I believe that the Miss is entirely ready to be betrothed to Mr. Daniels. There is a great fortune at stake here. Let's see whom Mr. Moneybags chooses. I can't help but laugh. It's quite tickling. I don't like to be consumed with envy but can't help but wonder how my life would be if I were Miss Isabel. My imagination soars.

September 6, 1903

Tonight I sat across from Momma, who kept her face hidden in the shadows. When I came close, I saw the dark bruises on her left cheek. I tried every antic to make her laugh. When a small smile finally made its way onto her lips, I saw that her left front tooth was missing. When I asked her what happened, she didn't answer. Instead, she snuck a glance at that hideous Karl, who sat behind the newspaper. He must have been looking at the pictures, because surely that ox can't read. Both remained quiet and acted as though I never questioned her about that tooth. There is much going on and I will have to decide what I'm to do. When I am at home, I share my bed with Mary, the littlest. She is the only one I truly worry about. It would break my heart if something were to happen to her. Edith lives out. The boys are at the factory all day and come home in time to fall asleep after evenings at the pub.

I'd read enough for the night and closed the journal. Just like Ellen, I had a lot to think about. I didn't have the nerve to write things down as plainly as she did. Someone might find the entries, and then what would happen? Here I was reading the journal over a hundred years later. Nothing had happened. I wasn't doing a thing about it and neither had anyone else. It was too late in Ellen's case, but I couldn't be sure if it was too late for me. The pain in my head had improved with the weed. I touched my lips with my fingertips. The swelling was subsiding. I placed the book on the bed next to me and rummaged in my nightstand drawer. I found a few tablets of Percocet and swallowed them. I closed my eyes and was pulled into a deep, hypnotic sleep.

"I should have murdered you when I had the chance." The hiss in my ear was familiar. I could also hear my breath; it was rhythmic, like the whoosh of a ventilator. I gasped, trying to suck air into my lungs. They were collapsing. I needed to wake up, see the light. Frank's presence engulfed me; I couldn't escape even in my sleep.

89

The night was a thick black cloak that covered me. My nightgown was soaked and stuck to my body. My eyes adjusted to the light, and I saw that I was standing in the mouth of a cave. Water swirled around my body and waves broke against me, jarring my legs. I had to hold on to keep my balance in the tumultuous waters. I reached out and felt rocky walls against my fingertips. I realized that the brackish water was lower than I had first imagined it to be, but another wave hit me higher on my thighs and I knew the area would quickly fill. I tilted my head out of the small cave and saw the full moon exposed as the clouds parted. It was ethereally bright, and the night sky was illuminated. My survival depended on me getting out before the tide came in, but my feet were stuck onto the sandy floor. My legs were heavy and I couldn't move them. My breath might save me, if only I could breathe more deeply. Between pants, I tried to speak. If I could do that, I would wake up. My voice became stronger with each attempt, but my throat burned. I was drowning. Finally, I was able to utter the words "I'm awake."

I sat up in bed. The perspiration poured out of my skin and drenched my robe. The dream was so vivid. One minute I was standing in water, barely able to breathe, and the next moment I was in my moonlit-drenched bedroom, with its bluish light pouring over me. I had to get out of bed and change my wet nightgown and robe. I sat up, panting, still unable to fill my lungs, just like in the dream. I quieted my mind and eventually was able to take a deep breath. I pulled my night things off and threw them into the bag filled with the sheets I would be taking to the laundry in the morning. I got up, went into the bathroom, and filled the tub for a warm bath. I threw a few capfuls of lavender salts into it and sank deeply into the soothing water.

Afterward, I dried my body tenderly with a thick towel and put another robe on before going into the kitchen. I had to make the apartment my home again. I poured almond milk into a bowl of sweet, crunchy cereal and returned to my bedroom, where I curled up into the overstuffed chair and began to eat.

I picked up the book that was filled with pictures from the 1950s. That was about the time my grandmother had come from Puerto Rico. She had albums filled with photos, and many of them had been taken in Coney Island. I hadn't seen them in years. She must have packed them with the rest of her things when she returned to Puerto Rico.

The pictures were mostly of sailors and glamorous girls with 'leggy gams,' as captioned beneath the photos. Some of the people photographed posed on the sand and others on the boardwalk. I must have been born with the beach in my DNA. Somehow our family always ended up at the shore. My grandma returned to Rincón when she inherited my great-grandparents' house. She was the only descendant. There were no brothers or sisters to fight for possession of house or land. My grandmother was aging, and I wanted to enjoy some time with her before it was too late; *perhaps,* I thought, *I should plan for a trip after all.*

I perused the pictures in the book until I found myself yawning, and stretched. I needed to sleep; my body craved it. After finishing my snack, I placed the empty bowl and books on the nightstand. I turned out the lights, crept into bed, and sank deep under the covers. Suddenly I thought of a dog—that might be exactly what

I needed. I fell asleep thinking about a woolly dog sharing my bed with me. When I opened my eyes again, it was three in the afternoon. I barely had enough time to prepare for my shift.

9
A different perspective

Dulce and I stood next to each other in the medication room. It seemed like I was always running and making it to work just at the start of report to then enter the cycles of medication, treatments, and the rest of my repetitive life.

"You look like hell," Dulce said. "You should have stayed home." She stared at me with professional eyes as we poured medication into tiny cups.

"Thanks. I really appreciate your assessment, but I'm not a patient, Dulce." I laughed to keep things light, but I also avoided my reflection in the mirror and the gleaming steel cabinet surfaces.

"I don't want to make you feel bad, but those are the facts," she said.

I sighed. "I didn't want to stay home. It's better for me to be at work."

"What about your clients? Do you think they want their nurse to look like she's death warmed over? I'm just saying."

"Can we not talk about this anymore? I really can't deal with it." I took a quick glance in the mirror and couldn't help but cringe. I did look awful—haggard and bruised. "The makeup doesn't really cover it, does it?"

"Maybe you can get away," Dulce suggested. "Take a vacation. You have family in Puerto Rico, don't you?"

"I was actually thinking about that."

"Do yourself a favor and check out the flights. Warm air. Mangoes. The tropics. What more could you ask for? What town are they from?"

"Rincón. It's not that simple. They're not like us;

93

they're old-fashioned."

"And? What's that supposed to mean? It's just a vacation. You wouldn't be going there to stay. You have options. Have you thought about checking in to a hotel at a beach? Really, you don't even have to visit with your family."

"No, I would like to stay with my grandmother, but I wouldn't feel right going down there unless I took some time to see my mother," I said. "I've told you before that my mother loves Frank. He's just a handsome cop to her. You know how he is when he turns on the charm."

"I don't remember the last time he was charming, do you?" Dulce took the narcotic cabinet keys out of her pocket. "I have to get Percocet for 503. Do you need anything?"

"Probably not until later, when the post-op comes from Recovery. They did an extensive hernia repair. I heard he had that hernia there for years. He was lucky that it didn't strangulate."

"Don't change the subject. You should be saying that you're lucky *you* didn't get strangulated. At the risk of repeating myself, I think you should get an order of protection. Better yet, get him arrested. You have all the evidence you need. You're wearing it."

Dulce opened the narcotic log book and signed for the tablets. My mouth watered; I should probably have asked for some for myself. I tried to focus on the conversation.

"That's not going to work," I sighed. "You know that as well as I do."

"It doesn't matter if he's a police officer. He's a danger to you." Dulce bustled around while changing the plastic waste bag on the medication cart. "There are laws and he isn't exempt. I hate to say this, but you're your own worst enemy."

"That's not fair. If I try to expose him, he'll kill me."

Dulce walked over and gave me a hug. "He's already tried to do that. He doesn't even care that he's leaving evidence all over the place. It's obvious that someone is hurting you. Most abusers take care to make sure that no bruises show. He's getting sloppy, I'm telling you."

I pulled away and covered my ears. "I can't listen to this. I have to give out medication. We'll talk later."

Once alone, I busied myself looking at my client list. I was ready to check on them, and I began by going into Amy Landry's room.

Mrs. Graham stood at the client's headboard. She dropped her hands when she saw me step into the room.

"What's going on?" I didn't trust her. "What are you doing?"

"I was just brushing her hair," she said, lifting her hands to produce the brush. "She's been waking up a bit. Not really conscious but a little agitated. The brushing calms her down."

I nodded. "Okay. Just be gentle. She's had an injury."

"I know that. How dumb do you think I am?" She placed the brush in the cabinet drawer.

My voice softened. "I'm sorry. Forget it. I know that you know what you're doing."

"This is the third evening I've been with her."

Mrs. Graham had somehow bonded with the semi-comatose woman while I was off. It was good for all of us. I had to start seeing things from a different perspective. Here I was judging this very capable nurse's aide, and I was exhausted after standing up for twenty minutes.

"Really, forgive me," I said. "I shouldn't have said what I did. Miss Landry needs someone who cares about her. She obviously didn't care too much for herself."

At that moment, Amy began moaning softly and moved her head slightly. She was, just as Mrs. Graham said, beginning to wake up. This was not going to be easy for any of us.

"Miss Landry. Amy. You're okay," I whispered in her ear. "You're in the hospital. I'm Maggie, your nurse. Mrs. Graham is also here. We're here to take care of you."

Mrs. Graham stood over her charge. "She started moving around like this last night. That's the extent of it, though."

"It might take time for her to gain full consciousness, but according to the report, the CT scan apparently didn't show much, other than swelling. Once that goes down, we'll know exactly how much damage there is. I can't believe they moved her out of the Intensive Care Unit for another patient— one with a gunshot wound."

"You didn't hear?"

"What?" I half listened as I changed the intravenous tubing to reduce the potential for infection. There were all sorts of signs and symptoms I had to watch out for, the original injury being the least of them.

The elderly aide was a live news gazette. "The gunshot victim isn't doing well. It's a woman, you know. She's the same age as this one. At first they thought there was some connection. They both live in Coney Island."

"Really?" I was unimpressed. I hated to think like

this, but these types of injuries and crimes were all too common here. I scrutinized the chart that hung at the foot of the bed. "Why would there be a connection? Investors poured money into Luna Park and to refurbish the boardwalk, but people are people. Even though there's been some change since the stadium was built, there's still plenty of street crime, not to mention guns."

"We're talking about two young women, Miss Fuentes. One of them almost died by suicide and the other in a homicide attempt, and you don't think it's a big deal? Crime isn't the reason that we're taking care of Miss Landry."

"While I'd like to stand here talking about the patients, I have to move on to 514. That client hasn't been admitted yet, and I have to complete his assessment. Let me know if she does anything else."

Mrs. Graham gave a curt nod. She knew her duties better than most of the hospital staff. I moved the cart farther down the hall and surveyed the list of my assigned clients. Mr. Vladimir Zbigniew was scheduled for a colon resection early the next morning. He was high risk. They had to make sure his fluids and electrolytes were stable before submitting him to such a drastic surgery. Bowel cleansing could take a toll on such an elderly gentleman.

I peeked into the room. An old man with a shock of white hair sat in the large upright chair. A cane lay across his lap. I was stunned that I recognized him. Mr. Zbigniew was the man who had tried to stop Frank from harassing me on the boardwalk.

"Mr. Zbigniew?" I hoped he wouldn't remember the chance meeting. "I'm Maggie Fuentes, your nurse for the evening."

He gazed at me for a moment. "Do I know you, young lady? Haven't I seen you before?"

"I'm not sure how that can be possible. You haven't been a patient here before, have you?" Not even a white lie. A mere distraction.

"No," he said, and smiled, showing a row of gold upper teeth. "Maybe you remind me of my daughter."

"Oh, that's nice." I smiled back at him.

His happy expression disappeared. "She's gone. The drugs, they killed my girl in Russia."

"I'm sorry to hear that," I said. "How awful!"

"Eh, I'm an old man." Shrugging, he leaned back in his chair and closed his eyes. "I told my son that I don't want the surgery. He insists. He said I'm not dead yet."

"He's right, you know." I patted his hand. "I—"

His eyelids flickered open. "I've been dead a long time," the old man said, his faded blue eyes peering into mine. "But you're still alive." He paused, and then said, "I know you, don't I?"

Mercifully, a sharp knock at the door interrupted us.

"Miss Fuentes, she's awake," Mrs. Graham announced. She stood with one foot in the room and the other in the corridor. "Please come quick."

"Excuse me for a moment, Mr. Zbigniew," I said. "I'll be back soon."

I followed Mrs. Graham to Room 512. Amy Landry lay still, but tears were rolling down her cheeks toward her pillow.

"Are you sure she's waking up?" I asked. "What exactly did she do?"

"Don't believe me? I know what I'm talking about." Mrs. Graham started out of the room. "You said call you, so I did."

"I'm sorry. You're right," I apologized. My frustration was mounting. "It's important for me to know what you saw. Did she wake up? Exactly what did she do?"

"She shifted a little. Moved her head a bit to the side. Like she's doing now. Look!"

Amy Landry's head was moving but was held in check by pillows, which formed a protective barrier for her against the bedrails. Sometimes patients with head injuries experienced seizures and their heads thrashed; we were prepared for that possibility. I tossed one of the pillows aside and waited. Sure enough, Amy moved her head with more force. I replaced the pillow.

Suddenly, Amy began flailing her right arm, almost hitting the metal siderail. She seemed to be reaching toward the large plastic tube that was attached to the endotracheal tube in her throat. A patient's first instinct was usually to pull it out, and it was the lifeline to their breath.

"Please stay still," I instructed her, hoping that she could hear me. "It's important that you not disconnect the tubes; they're helping you to breathe." I worked on pulling her arm back down. "Mrs. Graham, get Dr. Peters. Let him know that she's awake, and please hurry!"

As I waited for Dr. Peters and the aide to return, I crooned softly in the patient's ear, hoping that it would calm her down. Amy Landry seemed to be regaining her strength quickly, along with her consciousness. She stopped struggling, and while I waited with her, the insistent throbbing in the back of my head returned. Suddenly I felt as though I might pass out again. I stuck my leg out to pull the plastic chair closer to me. Perhaps sitting might help me until the lightheadedness passed. Time seemed to drag, and I silently prayed that they would hurry back.

"Maggie, are you all right?" Dulce's voice brought me back to my senses. "Go out to the nurses' lounge. We'll keep a handle on things until we can reach the chief resident. Dr. Peters is in the OR."

"No, I can stay," I insisted. "You have your own caseload tonight."

"Listen to me. I'm not going to tell you to go home, but I don't think you should have come in tonight at all." Her tone softened. "Go wash your face, rest, do whatever you need to do. Drink something. Just take care of yourself before you go into another patient's room tonight. Got that?"

"Why are you so upset with me? What's the supervisor going to say?" I was bewildered. "She's going to think that I abandoned my patients."

"That statement shows you're not right in the head. She'll say that you took a break. Now, just go, please."

Dulce and Mrs. Graham turned away from me and focused all their attention on Amy Landry. I left the room and walked down the corridor toward the lounge, as directed.

A flashing light in the distance got my attention. Another client needed help and I couldn't ignore him. Dulce and Mrs. Graham were already swamped, and some of that was my fault; the fact that we were eternally short-staffed didn't help.

I held on to the wall railing, intended for convalescing patients, and continued my way down the long corridor. Holding on to it helped me keep my balance, but I was still off. It was early, and I couldn't figure out why there weren't any visitors or patients in the hallway. The usual busy evening activity was on hold for some reason. I walked swiftly to the room. The red flashing light had become an urgent beacon.

10
I saw them

The light blinked steadily over the door that was slightly ajar. I heard a low moan come from inside the room. It had to be a post-operative patient who was in pain. I pushed the door open and walked into the darkish room. Other than the fluorescent lighting over the first bed, the room was shrouded in shadows.

I stood at the door. The first bed was empty. The sheets were prepared for a patient's return from the Recovery Room.

"Can I help you?" I asked, moving closer to the curtain that separated the room.

The patient didn't answer, but the moaning had now become deep, guttural. I pushed the curtain slightly aside. My mouth gaped open. Frank was leaning over the client in the bed near the window. It was a woman who was tied in four-point restraint, completely nude. I stood paralyzed at the curtain. My eyes adjusted to the dim lighting and I could see his form bending closely toward the woman. Ann Marie! The moans were coming from her. My stomach lurched when I saw what he was doing. He teased her as he traced her naked abdomen with his tongue. Ann Marie's heavy breasts writhed as she arched her body up to meet his mouth. Frank buried his face between her legs and began devouring her. She slipped her hands easily out of the thick leather restraints and they slithered over his head like eels, pulling him closer and closer to her. The sounds were coming from deep within her as she urged him to consume her. He lifted his head and I could see his glossy face as he reached toward her nipples, biting them as they grew larger and turned a dark rose color. Ann Marie pushed his head back down, and his eyes and face contorted with the effort of probing her as deeply as he could. Frank's tongue had become a snake, slithering in and out, teasing, teasing, as she finally cried out, holding him close to her sex.

I held on to the wall and scaled my way out of the room. I could barely remain upright. Once outside, I took a minute to get my bearings and then moved rapidly toward the nurses' lounge. The corridor was again full of hospital staff, patients, and visitors.

I was relieved when I reached the lounge and found it empty. I wouldn't have to face anyone. My shame was that I didn't have the nerve to confront them. I sat down on the couch and shielded my eyes from the glaring lamp in the corner.

"Wake up." Dulce shook my shoulder and I woke with a start. I had passed out.

The clock on the wall said seven thirty. "I'm so late. I have to get out of here. The medication!"

"I took care of that for you," Dulce said. "I'm worried about you. I told you that already."

"My patient . . . Miss Landry . . . what happened? Did she wake up?" I was fully reclined on the couch and had a hard time pulling myself up. I felt a pulsating sensation at the back of my head. "What's wrong with me? Why can't I just get up? Be back to normal."

"I think he really hurt you this time," Dulce said, her eyes full of compassion. "You need to see one of the docs. You should probably go to the emergency room. You don't want to have permanent damage, do you?"

"I'll be all right," I said. Suddenly, the image of Frank licking Ann Marie's glistening skin filled my head. "He's here."

"Who's here, Maggie?"

"Frank." Tears started rolling down my cheeks, but I felt numb inside.

"Frank's here?" she asked. "Where? What patient is he guarding?"

"Guarding, no." I shook my head and the pain shot through my neck up to the top of my head. "He's with Ann Marie."

"Maggie, that's impossible. Of course he's not. It's your imagination. He's on a double. You told me that already." She seemed confused. "Why on earth would he be with Ann Marie?"

"I swear, I saw them together." I lowered my voice. "They were having sex in one of the rooms."

"Maggie, stop." Dulce was becoming frantic. "Please, you've got to get checked out."

I was on the verge of hysteria. "You don't understand. No one would believe what I saw right here on the unit. Just as no one would ever believe the things that Frank has done to me. He lives in a protected bubble. Come down the corridor with me; I can show you. They might still be there, or at least there'll be proof that they were in one of the beds."

I swayed as I got to my feet and held on to the couch for a moment. I took Dulce's arm and we left the room and walked back down the corridor together. The unit was quiet but not altogether barren, as it had been earlier. There was a sprinkling of clients and visitors in the solarium.

I tried to explain to Dulce why I was so shaken. "One of the lights was blinking. I thought a patient needed help because I heard moaning, but it wasn't a client, it was Ann Marie." I tried to recall exactly which room it was. "Here, I think it was here." I pushed the door open.

The bed that had been prepared for the post-op client was now filled. An elderly woman with frizzy white hair stared at the ceiling. She was moaning too, softly, not in the same throaty way Ann Marie had cried out. The bed was surrounded with monitors and intravenous poles with several lines of fluids flowing into the woman's veins. A tiny television monitor droned, competing with an alarm that sounded on one of the machines.

Dulce flinched slightly. "This is what you brought me in to see? Nancy's in charge of this section. We'd better get you to the ER."

"Shh," I whispered. "Don't let him hear you. They're on the other side of the curtain." Clinging on to the wall, I crept, eventually pulling the curtain slowly aside.

With the curtain fully open, any certainty I had was gone. Nancy, one of the senior nurses stood there, handing a pale redhead a small cup of pills. They both turned to look at us.

"Need something?" Nancy asked.

"No, I'm sorry." For the second time that night, I backed out of the room. "I'm sure I saw them together. You have to believe me." I held tightly to Dulce's hand. "I'm telling you—"

"I'll walk you down to the ER." She held on to me as if she were giving me new life. "You might have had a concussion. You'll probably need an MRI."

We got to the emergency room and waited for the triage nurse. This was the first time that I had ever sat in one of the plastic chairs as a patient. My post had always been on the other side of the desk. Dulce kept her word and stayed in the waiting room with me. How could I tell them what was going on when Frank was always in the ER, bringing in a victim or guarding a perpetrator? It would be like sharing my family secrets on network news. It wasn't anyone's business but mine.

The double doors flew open. A technician pushed a stretcher inside that carried a young man covered in blood. His clothes were torn open and monitor wiring lay over his heaving chest. Pablo rushed in a moment later, trying to keep up with the patient. That meant Frank had to be close behind; they were almost inseparable when they were on duty. *But I had just seen him upstairs a little while ago, hadn't I?* The victim was bleeding profusely from a head wound. Everyone on staff scrambled to get into position to aid in his care. Even Dulce jumped in to keep the other gawking clients away from the chaos. The ones who came in with coughs, fevers, and dizzy spells were struck by the gore. A second stretcher burst into the room. Frank, talking on his cell phone, strode in, keeping up with a female victim. There was no blood or apparent injury on her, but her skin color was an ashy gray, and I knew from experience that she could be in more danger than the client who was covered in blood.

Angie, the triage nurse, ignored me and picked up the phone that started ringing simultaneously with the patients entering the room. The unit clerk was at dinner. A volunteer assigned to take her place stood behind the counter, wringing her hands.

"An accident on Stillwell and Mermaid," Angie said, repeating the words of whoever was on the other end of the line. She wrote several important points of information down on a legal pad. "A child? About three? Sure, we'll be ready."

"I've got to get out of here." I stood up to leave the room.

Angie put her hand out to stop me. "You're here for a headache, right? We need you for a few minutes to give us a hand. Room 3. You can pick up some Tylenol from the cabinet over the sink in there."

"No, I've got to get back upstairs," I said. "I left my whole caseload. I'm sorry; I have to leave."

Angie stared at me for a moment, then turned on her heel and went over to the first patient who had been brought in a few minutes earlier. My coming down to the ER was ridiculous. I'd let Angie believe that I'd just come down for a headache. This way I could keep my private life private. I wouldn't complain to Dulce anymore. I would just let the whole thing drop.

"Wait. There's your boyfriend," one of the nurses said, and nudged me. Fortunately, Frank's back was to the triage room and he was concentrating on his handheld.

"He's busy," I said. "I am too. I'll see him tonight."

"You sure?" she asked. "He might get stuck here tonight. A couple more buses are on the way. It was a four-car collision. A fatality, too."

"Sometimes it's like that. Nurse. Officer. We get it. That's what the work is like. See you later."

I slipped out and headed toward the stairwell. My adrenaline level had zoomed up after the pandemonium of the ER, but getting up the steps was harder than I thought it would be. Holding tightly to the banister, I climbed the steps one by one. I wasn't well. Maybe I wouldn't admit that to anyone else, but I had to admit it to myself. Maybe I should get the examination. Go on vacation. Change something. I might be dead soon.

Dulce was right.

When I reached the unit, the first room I walked into was the one I was certain that I saw Frank and Ann Marie in together. Maybe he had drugged me by slipping something into my drink. Maybe I had taken a pill earlier and didn't remember. His tongue had become a serpent snaking along Ann Marie's torso. Her body was obviously hungry for him. I couldn't un-see her gyrations, begging him to taste her. It dawned on me that they were probably the ones who were together, and her accusations were merely concocted to get me off track of the truth. It wasn't me. It was them. It had to be. But they weren't anywhere in the room. The same two patients slept quietly under dimmed lights. There was nothing in here that validated what I'd seen.

I went to the nurses' station to begin writing my notes.

"Miss Fuentes, got a minute? Please come check this order for me," Grecia Cooke, the evening clerk, said. She was young, tall, and gorgeous. Many of the interns ogled her gleaming ebony skin. "It's for 512. Miss Landry."

"Who wrote it?" I asked.

"Dr. Peters wrote it," she said, and handed me the order.

"When was he here?" I tried to focus. I was still on duty.

"He came out of the OR a little while ago. They were here on rounds and wrote a few orders." Grecia looked over as I read. "They left before I had a chance to question this one. It's for a DNR."

"Do not resuscitate." I was surprised. "Why would he write that order for Miss Landry?"

"I just wanted to be sure it said *DNR*. I always like

to get a second reading on these before I place a label on a wristband." Grecia searched in a counter drawer to find one of the cards filled with neon green labels that indicated the client was not to be resuscitated in the event they stopped breathing. "I'll do it when I get up for break."

"Whoa," I said, and tugged the card out of her hand. "Are you kidding? You can't do that. What was he thinking? She's not a DNR."

"He spoke to her."

"No, he didn't. When?"

"When they were on rounds, I told you. Just a few minutes ago. You missed them."

"It can't be. It's a mistake." I scanned the corridor for the group of doctors. "Even if he did speak to her, which I know for sure he didn't, he couldn't make that kind of decision in just a couple of minutes. She needs a psych consult. Did they call for one yet?"

"He probably forgot. You know how they are when they're on rounds; always in a rush." Grecia combed through the chart. "There isn't anything here about a psych consult."

"I'll call him back to the unit. He has to explain why he wrote this order. It's impossible. She can't be a DNR. She's just starting to wake up. She tried to kill herself; there's no way she's capable of making a decision like this."

Grecia looked uncertain as she held the card in her hand.

"Forget it," I said. "Put that away. She's not that injured anyway."

"There was damage. We saw it on the CT scan."

I whirled around to see Jeff Peters. The attending

neurologist stood next to him.

"How did you get here?" I asked. "I just looked down the hall and didn't see you. Where were you?"

"Are you all right?" Jeff stared at me in the same way that Dulce had earlier that evening. "Dulce—"

"Dulce, what? Please stop. I don't know what's going on with her, but I'm all right," I fumed. "This isn't about me. This is about Amy Landry. Why would you write a DNR order for her?"

"What? I don't understand." Jeff picked up the chart. "Wait a minute; this is a mistake. This was for Mrs. Cagney in 516. This should never have been on this patient's chart." He rubbed his eyes. "I must be more tired than I thought."

"I guess we're all working under a lot of strain." The tension in the air was palpable.

"Good thing I had you check it, Fuentes," Grecia said. "Oh, wait a minute; I need that for Mrs. Cagney after all, don't I? Next time, I'm really going to check it closely."

If she hadn't already checked it out so carefully, there could have been dire consequences. I sat down on one of the desk chairs.

"Thank goodness you did," I said. "The fact that you were clearheaded enough to get a second person to look made all the difference tonight. I hate to say it, but I'm glad it wasn't me this time. I seem to be a bit out of whack lately."

Grecia looked concerned. "Really? That's not the Maggie Fuentes that I know."

"Dulce told me that you've been under the weather," Jeff said. "Are you sure you're okay? You look—"

I turned away and pretended to check another set of

orders that had been left at the desk. I didn't want him to take a good look at me. The thick makeup I wore didn't entirely hide my bruises and the overhead fluorescent lighting seemed to enhance the pale green and lavender discolorations. Maybe he'd just think I had overdone it with the foundation.

Grecia had returned to picking up orders and Jeff pulled a chair closer to sit next to me.

"Say, how'd you like to have dinner with me tomorrow night?"

No way, I thought. *For sure there'd be a murder.* "Jeff, you're sweet, and I'm flattered, but I'm seeing someone."

"Really? I didn't realize that, but of course you would be." A slight flush rose to his cheeks. "Guess I'm a little late here."

"Actually, you're a lot late," I said. "I've been dating the same person for a few years now."

"That's real dating, isn't it?"

This time my cheeks burned. "I guess you can say that."

"No wedding bells?" Jeff whirled once in his chair.

"No, no wedding bells. At least, not yet." I thought about the stunning engagement ring Frank tried to give me at the restaurant. "Maybe soon, though. We're talking about getting engaged."

"Hey, congrats. Who—wait, I'm sorry. This is none of my business. Sometimes I get carried away."

"It's all right. That was a fair question." I considered sharing more, and decided it was okay. "He's a police officer. Frank Ramirez. He works in this precinct and he comes in a lot with the ambulance. That's how we met. You might have seen him here."

"I might have. In any case, he's a lucky guy."

Jeff's name was announced over the loudspeaker. He was being paged to the Intensive Care Unit.

"Right now, I'd better get downstairs," he said. "After that, I'm off. See you tomorrow, okay?"

"Wait a minute." I held on to his forearm. "You didn't tell me about Amy Landry. Is she awake? Can we order the consult for her?"

"I gave her a little sedation. She was reacting violently when I got there. We want to keep her under."

"Oh, I see." I couldn't help but feel disappointed, and I wasn't sure why.

"Actually, there has been some improvement. The swelling in her brain seems to be going down, but she's got a long way to go. It's too early for the consult."

I sighed deeply.

Jeff took another look at me. "Maybe it's none of my business, but how invested are you in this patient?"

"Sort of. I can't understand why she'd want to take her life. Jumping is intense. Most women make attempts by pills or cutting."

"That's if you go by statistics, but this one seemed intent on going through with it."

"Yeah, you're right," I said. "That's why I told Mrs. Graham to keep a close eye on her. If she's serious, when she wakes up she might try to kill herself again."

"Yeah, you have a point there," Jeff agreed. "I've got to get out of here; they paged me again." As he left the nurses' station, he stopped and turned back. "You should get some rest. You look tired. I can say that because I'm sure I look pretty much the same. I've been on for thirty-six hours straight."

"Sure thing," I said.

When he left the station, I began looking through the thick chart in my hands. Mrs. Cagney had been there for two weeks, practically unheard of these days when the aim was to return people to their homes as soon as possible. I suddenly remembered Mr. Zbigniew. What was wrong with me? There was so much for me to do before my shift ended tonight. It was almost nine o'clock. I needed to prepare the ten o'clock treatments and medications for my caseload. If only my head would stop hurting. The ache had become background noise to me.

The rest of the evening passed quickly. I took more of the Oxycodone that I'd stashed at the bottom of my bag. No one had to know. I could work by rote when I had to. I could practically do it all with my eyes closed.

At the end of the shift, I waited by the elevator. I pushed all thoughts of Frank and Ann Marie to the back of my head, with the ache that seemed to have taken up residence there. I didn't have to do anything about them, especially tonight.

⧖

The evening seemed like it would never end, but when I got a cab home and finally lay in my bed, sleep wouldn't come. This wasn't unusual after an evening shift. There was barely any time to sit and I was still running on high. I needed to lower the volume and lull myself to sleep. The journal was across the room and seemed to be alive and reaching out for me. I went to pick it up and my hands started to tremble when I felt the energy emanating from the book. I turned on the lamp and began to read.

September 9, 1903

I finally got up the nerve and asked Ruby to read the cards for me. She said she wouldn't charge but a penny. Ruby said that no amount of money that I had to give her would make her a rich woman, but it was important to honor the reading. I found it curious that she used the word 'honor.' It's not a word that I often hear. Ruby read the cards for me, spreading them in front of her on that great round wooden table. She spoke in riddles and gave me a headache. It was intriguing for me to sit close to her. She is of flesh and blood, but her deep-set eyes become mirrors and look far off when she is reading. Ruby's hair is thick and dark, with threads of silver all the way through. It's hard to tell how old she is; she could be as old as Momma. I didn't tell her about Karl, but I'm sure she knows all about him from the cards. I will not speak of him because he disgusts me so when he pushes against me as I bend over to do the housework. I will not stand for his vile ways as Momma does. Ruby said that I am old enough to be on my own. That I must decide before I let someone else decide what my fate is, and by then it will be too late. She said that is something that I struggle with and will always struggle with, for I brought it down with me from the stars. She said that everyone comes from a star with things to weigh and to fulfill or toss. My quest is to speak up and take action for myself. It sounds courageous. Ruby said she could see the glint of a sword in my eye. If she could see that, then I am certain she saw Karl. Finally, she said, there are not many choices for me, but I must be sure to make the most of the choices I do make.

📖

Ellen had her troubles too. I wondered if she had any hope that things would get better. I also wondered if I had any hope that things would change for me. It would be wonderful if I could sit next to her and exchange thoughts and experiences, but then again, maybe it wouldn't. Maybe things hadn't turned out so well for Ellen after all. How strange to feel so drawn to this woman who lived so many years before me. I laughed quietly to myself. There was no way to speak with someone who was dead. Psychics and mediums said they could. I might be intuitive, but in my heart, I didn't really believe them.

I thought I might fall asleep when I read the journal as I had for the last few nights, but tonight was different. I couldn't be sure if I was rattled by the contents of the journal or whether it was something else, but I couldn't sleep. I tossed and turned, until I finally threw the comforter aside and got up.

I walked through the rooms of my apartment like a ghost. I took one of the joints that Frank had left for me. I lit it, taking deep pulls. My lungs felt as if they'd explode, but almost instantly I found myself relaxing. I sat on the couch in the dark. This was exactly what I needed. Frank knew what he was doing when he'd left it there, and I was glad that he did. I had to check my little box to make sure that I had more left. I returned to my bed and welcomed the empty space that enveloped me.

The morning lighting was mystical. The room shimmered in white, appearing almost sterile, like a hospital room. A steady humming pulsated, like the white-noise machines that we used to calm our patients down when they were in a lot of pain or upset. But I wasn't in the hospital, I was at home, and the insistent throbbing in my head was starting up again.

I rubbed my eyes and looked around. The brain is a tricky organ. I pulled myself up and looked over at my clock. Ten in the morning. It seemed like only a few minutes ago that I was at the hospital, getting ready to pour meds. I worked hard to retrieve bits and pieces of information about the previous evening. I finally remembered standing at the corner, hailing a cab. I read the journal and finally fell asleep.

I've got to get up and do something about this. If I don't get checked out, I might never feel like myself again. I picked up the phone and called the doctor.

"Hi. This is Maggie Fuentes. I was hoping I could see Dr. Markowitz. I'm not sure the last time I was there. It's been a while." I held my breath while I waited for a response.

The receptionist came back on the phone. "It's been a little over two years, Ms. Fuentes."

"Two years? Wow. That long? Are you sure?" I didn't want to think about the last time I was there before Frank and I were a couple. It was too painful. My boyfriend-picker needed an adjustment. "I need to see the doctor. I've had this headache. I hit my head and the pain isn't going away. I fell." Again, I waited for the receptionist as she looked for an available time.

The appointment offered was a lot earlier than I anticipated. "Okay, tomorrow at ten. Thank you."

Before hanging up, I listened to her advice about going to the hospital emergency room if I thought my injury was 'urgent.' I'd said the same thing to quite a few people before, but I had waited this long; another day wouldn't matter. In the meantime, I had to tell Frank.

Dialing his number, any inner peace I held slowly drained away, but when he picked up on the first ring and I heard his voice, I was sure that I was doing the right thing. He had to care about me. I had to be mistaken about him.

"Frank—" I began.

"Hey, look, I can't talk. I'm at the station. I've got to write up a few things here. I'll see you tonight."

"I'm working tonight," I said. He knew my schedule. I gave him my monthly work schedule as soon as I received it. If I hadn't given it to him, he would have already demanded it. That was the routine. I knew the drill.

"I told you, I gotta go," he said.

"Frank, listen to me. I had to make an appointment for tomorrow to check my head. It still hurts."

"The doctor? You made an appointment? What for?"

"I told you. My head hurts. I should have gone to get it checked right away. If you want, you can come with me." I spat those words out.

"Damn straight I'll be coming with you," he spat back. "Text me the time. I'm not sure I can come to your place after work tonight."

"That's all right. Do what you have to do. I'll just go

to sleep as soon as I get back home anyway. I could use the rest."

"You complain so much," he said. "Is this how it's going to be with you for the rest of my life?"

I held my breath for a minute. "I know you're busy and I shouldn't take what you're saying so personally, but it makes me feel bad when you talk to me like this."

"To make you happy, I'll see you at work tonight. I'll pick you up for dinner. I love you, even though sometimes you can be a pain in the ass."

"I love you too," I said. "I know it's a big deal taking time to go with me tomorrow and I appreciate it."

I hung up, relishing the fact that I had the rest of the day without Frank. I would deal with him tonight, and not a minute before.

Stretched out on my bed, I began feeling sleepy again. My eyelids were heavy, and closed quickly against the light that filtered through the blinds. I thought about work and took a minute to turn on the alarm. My supervisor had spoken to me a couple of times about being late and I didn't want any more unpleasant run-ins with her. I began thinking about Jeff, and how nicely he treated me and respected the things I had to say. He was cute too, with his sandy-colored hair and blue eyes. He reminded me of the beach. The waves, the sand, the heat. I imagined him lying with me, listening to the sounds of the ocean pounding against the surf. I began imagining him rocking against my body on the sand.

I couldn't help but touch myself while thinking of him. I moved my hands slowly and rhythmically between my thighs. My breath quickened as my body began to respond to my own touch. Very quickly, almost too quickly, I came. The tears rolled out of my eyes. Here

I was, thinking about Jeff while practically engaged to a man who beat the crap out of me. I never had orgasms with Frank unless I popped a pill or smoked a joint. It was all perfectly timed pretenses. *Fake it 'til you make it.* But I could never figure out exactly what it was that I wanted to *make*.

I rolled over on my side, and the image of Ann Marie and that stupid thong popped into my brain, but quickly turned into a visual of Frank devouring her.

⧗

The next morning, we headed over to the radiologist for an MRI. Frank was upset, but I was relieved that the previous evening had gone well. He hadn't bothered me after all, and I got to sleep easily.

"How would I know that he'd send me for an MRI?" I sat crouched in the Escalade, clutching onto the arm rest. Frank was zooming, and the buildings seemed like a movie set, sweeping by fast. "Please slow down—my head."

He turned the volume down on the radio and Exposé sang in the background as he went into one of his tirades. "If you're so sick, why'd you go to work? You begged me to take you to dinner the other night. If your head aches so badly, how come you didn't say anything? I'm telling you, Maggie, this is why, exactly why, I get sick of you. I end up in the ER when I'm working with those psychos out there, and now I have to babysit you too?"

"I'm sorry," I said. "I told you that my head was hurting. I don't want to get an MRI either, but Dr. Markowitz insisted. What are they going to say at this point? Wait it out; the pain will go away?"

"Could you just shut up?"

"Something could be wrong, you know. There is a possibility I really do have an injury. These headaches are going on way too long."

Frank pulled the car into the parking lot. "We're here. Remember what I told you. That's all I'm going to say." He squeezed my face for a second and then jerked his hand away.

Although the lot was almost full, we were able to find a parking space. I was glad that I didn't have to hear Frank's mouth go on and on had we not found one.

I dreaded going inside. This wasn't the first time that I had to have an MRI. I'd been hurt before. I already knew that the nurse would try to corner me with questions. I tried to think of what I was going to say this time. If it was busy, maybe they'd have less time to focus on me. Sometimes I felt like I was in for questioning, as though I were a criminal.

Frank came around the SUV and opened the door for me. I bit my tongue. Anyone looking at us would swear I had landed fine gold. Frank was good-looking; there was no denying that. Tall. Muscular. He dressed well. His jewelry was understated and elegant. I was forever catching women looking at him. I wondered how he responded when I wasn't around. Too bad that whatever he did do wasn't enough for them to steal him away from me.

"Remember," he whispered in my ear.

I nodded. I knew exactly what to say and what to hold back. I had to save myself. There wouldn't be anyone at home protecting me if I said the wrong thing. Frank might think I was stupid, but I wasn't that stupid.

He held open the door to the radiology offices. We went inside and the woman at the front desk had me sign in. She gave me a clipboard that required some information. I couldn't chance going to the same place I had gone to the last time I'd had 'a fall.' They kept records of me and my injuries.

Frank craned his neck over my shoulder and watched as I filled out the form. *Name, address, insurance carrier.* None of that meant anything. *Reason for MRI.* I looked at him and wrote down *Fall.* That was it. I fell.

Being at the radiologist reminded me of going to see the school nurse when I was nine years old. Our uniforms were skirts and matching socks. Usually, I wore leotards, but this time I couldn't find any clean ones in my drawer. My mother probably hadn't had time to do the laundry. I hoped that my teachers wouldn't notice my legs. Hilda, my best friend, did, and told my homeroom teacher. She took one look at me and sent me to the school nurse. Some of the bruises on my arms and legs were old and some were new. I told her that I'd fallen. I picked myself up and kept going again. Now, however, I was immobilized. It wasn't as easy as it had been when I was a kid. I was stuck.

The female technician interrupted my thoughts. "Miss Fuentes, you can come in now."

Frank dug his fingers into my wrist as he smiled at me. "Don't make me regret bringing you here. Got it?" An elderly woman sat there smiling at us. Obviously, she hadn't heard a word he'd said.

"I know. Let me go." I pulled my wrist away and turned to the technician. "Can my boyfriend come in with me?"

"You two lovebirds, you're so cute. I'm sorry, not inside, but he can wait right here for you. It shouldn't be too long."

"Thanks anyway." I batted my eyelashes at Frank. It would keep him satisfied for the moment at least.

⏳

As the technician promised, it was over practically before it began. I was putting my clothing back on, when she poked her head back into the room.

"Don't leave yet, Miss Fuentes," she said. "The doctor would like to talk to you. His office is the second to the right." She held the door open and waited for me to head there. I didn't have time to get Frank, who sat in the other direction. I knew he'd be pissed.

I stood at the doctor's open door. His back was to me as he sat looking at a computer displaying images of a brain.

"Hi. I'm Maggie Fuentes. You wanted to see me?"

"Yes, Miss Fuentes. Dr. Morales. Come in and have a seat." He stood up and pulled one of the leather chairs away from his oak desk and pointed to it. After walking around the desk, he sat back down into his own high-backed chair. The doctor looked as solid as the wood desk he sat behind. He could have been a military man with his salt-and-pepper buzz cut. He took his glasses off, put them on the desk, and began rubbing his eyes.

"I only have a few minutes," I said. "I have to work this afternoon." I needed to get out of there. Fast.

"I won't keep you too long," he said. "Would you like some water?" There was a pitcher filled with ice water on his desk. Alongside it were several disposable plastic cups. "Feel free. We have plenty more where that came from."

"Thanks. I'm okay." I sat back in my seat. I didn't

want to show him how anxious I felt.

"I guess you're wondering why I called you in." The doctor's eyes pierced any façade that I wore. "I won't waste your time. That's yours," he said, pointing to the computer images.

I nodded. "I'm a nurse."

"You're a nurse? Really? Okay, that's good to know."

"I fell and thought I should get my head checked out."

"When did you fall?"

"A couple of days ago. I had to work, so I couldn't get to my doctor right away."

"You mean you're working as a nurse in a hospital?"

"Yes."

"And you couldn't get to a doctor? Let me show you something." He pushed the computer buttons and pointed to changing imaging sequences. The brain, my brain, glowed. "There is no fracture, but you had a pretty bad fall, didn't you? Dizzy a lot? Look at these areas." He pointed to a few white spots on the screen. "This shows damage to the brain tissue. It's clear that this isn't your first fall. I'd say you've fallen—a lot."

I sat there on mute.

The doctor was like a dog with a bone. "Have you had any other work-ups done? Has your regular doctor discussed your problem of *imbalance* with you?"

I poured water; anything to stall a response. Luckily, he kept talking, because I had no idea what to say. I wasn't in the mood to be interrogated. I needed to tell him something so I could get out. Frank would be wondering what was taking me so long, and I didn't need that grief.

"Want to tell me what's going on?" he said, pointing at the computer again. "There's something to that."

I wished he would just be quiet. I would be the one paying for his bid to be a private detective. His going into the wrong profession was not my problem. The desire to smoke creeped up around my jaw.

"I'll try one more time," he said.

I had to come up with something. "Look, really, there's nothing going on. If there were, you could be sure I'd talk to my doctor."

"And I'm not your doctor. Gotcha. I'll send him the report. You be careful, little lady. A lot of people, women especially, have been killed by falls."

"Will do, Doctor. Thanks for your concern, but I'm really okay."

I stood up and hurried out to Frank, who stood there looking at his watch. As I got closer to him, his eyes searched mine.

"Let's get out of here," I said. "They didn't find anything. You were right. I don't know why I didn't listen to you in the first place. You're always right, babe."

He hugged me. "I love you and would never steer you wrong. Now let's get the hell out of here."

We made a beeline for the SUV and he swung me home.

⧗

We sat on the couch close together. Frank took my face in his hands and rubbed my cheeks softly with his thumbs.

"Look at me, Maggie. I love you and wouldn't do anything to hurt you. Got that?"

"Yes, I know that. I just got a little nervous because the headache wouldn't go away."

Actually, my head still hurt, but I wasn't about to say that. I also had another flash of the image of him greedily gorging on Ann Marie at the hospital. That was a sight I couldn't seem to shake.

"We have plenty of time before work. Let's chill a little, okay?" I squeezed his thigh with my hand. "Please."

"Are you asking what I think you're asking? What took you so long?" Frank laughed and dug into the leather bag he carried wherever he went. Safe in his possession. "My little girl, chasing the dragon."

I watched as he placed the black tar, the cigarette, foil, and lighter in front of me on the coffee table. His practiced hands told me that he did it more often than when he was with me. He brought it to my mouth and I inhaled deeply. This was all I needed for now. Everything would be all right.

⧗

"Get up. You have to get up." Frank lay next to me. "Work, remember?"

I snuggled closer to him. Everything was good. "Why can't we just stay here tonight? Loving each other."

"Because, sweetness, we have responsibilities. You owe it to those sickos and me to the losers. But first, let me get a little more of that quality snatch you got there."

We made love again—sweet, lazy love. I had one eye on the clock but didn't care so much, not like I had earlier that morning. Frank's body was perfectly matched with mine. My head didn't ache anymore.

Frank's love had eased it away.

After showering together, I made sandwiches. Roast beef and Swiss cheese. I was glad that I had thought to pick something up during the craziness of the last few days. I knew he liked when I made hearty sandwiches for him, and I was happy to please him. He had pleased me. Frank wasn't as bad as I made him out to be. Sometimes I could be frustrating. I knew that. The sound of El DeBarge came through the speakers he had installed in my kitchen. Love songs captured my feelings, or at least what I thought my feelings were.

"I need you to do me a favor," he said, as he chased a bite of the sandwich down with milk.

"A favor? Of course," I said.

"I need you to visit my grandmother. She's in a nursing home up in East Harlem."

"Since when?" This was news to me. He'd never spoken about a grandmother.

"A while. She has Alice Heimer's disease. Doesn't know any of us anymore."

"You mean Alzheimer's? Wow, I had no idea." I wondered what other important things he was leaving out of the conversation. "What about you? How come you can't go, or your mother?"

"You know how it is. It's hard for Mom to go see her. She's old and crotchety. My grandmother doesn't even recognize us and my mother ends up feeling bad whenever she goes there."

"And you don't think I'll feel bad too? She's never even met me, so there's zero chance that she'll recognize me."

"Please, just do me the favor," he said. "I'll make it worth your while."

"Worth my while?" I shook my head. "So, basically, on my day off I'm going to a nursing home to visit with your grandmother, who doesn't know me. Is that right?"

"Yes, please. I won't ask for anything else. I promise. Just this time."

"I don't know why I'm saying yes, but okay." I did know why. I'd never hear the end of it from him if I didn't agree to visit her.

Frank swept me into his arms and kissed me, grinding his body against mine. "You won't be sorry. I promise. You're the best."

"Yes, that's me, the best." I couldn't help the bit of sarcasm.

"Did you give any more thought to what I asked you the other night?"

I couldn't seem to get it together like Frank did. He jumped from one thing to another and I had a hard time keeping up with him. Part of me found it annoying, but he was in a sweet mood after our afternoon of lovemaking. I crept as close to him as I could to smell his aftershave.

"What?" I started to giggle. "I'm sorry, what are you talking about?"

"What are you, loony? The ring, *pendeja*, will you accept the ring? You know what I'm talking about. I want you to be my bride." Frank's eyes took on a feverish glow. He pulled me tighter, until I couldn't take a deep breath.

"The ring!" What was wrong with me? "Of course. I can't think of anything that I'd like to do more than marry you."

"That's the girl I love." We continued to embrace. "We'll have the whole force out. Man, it's gonna be great."

I loved to see him happy like this. It reminded me of how much we had together, that we were meant for each other.

"I've been carrying it with me wherever I go, but it really belongs only one place—your finger." With a flourish, he fished the small velvet box out of his pocket. Kneeling down on his right knee, he opened it. "Baby, will you marry me?"

The ring glittered and winked at me. "I would be happy and proud to be your wife. I love you."

Frank placed the ring on my finger and looked up at me. The tears in his eyes were real. I held my hand up to the light to admire the brilliance of the diamond.

"We may have had some bumps in the road, Frank, but I know that we love each other. I know in my heart that we can work through anything. I'll do my best to make you happy and to be the wife you deserve."

"I know you'll do your best. I'm giving you a chance to prove how much you love me." He stood up and hugged me tight.

We would be good together. I'd do anything to make that happen. Life wasn't easy and we'd have our struggles. The main thing was that we'd struggle together.

Violets and Hennessy

"C'mon, Frankie, don't be like that. Give Mommy a kiss."

Frankie's eyes connected with his mother's in the magic makeup mirror. It was the kind of mirror that stars had in their dressing rooms and was surrounded by bright yellow light bulbs. She bragged that her lip pencil never squiggled when she used that special mirror and her foundation always looked *au naturel*. Mommy promised Frankie that he could visit the Times Square theater where she danced when he turned thirteen, but that wasn't going to happen for years. For now, she whispered stories in his ears about the dancers who wore glittery costumes, when he climbed under the covers at bedtime. Mommy's eyes were just as shiny when she spoke about how excited the audience became when she danced and about the handsome men who asked her out on dates after the last show of the night.

Frankie watched as she painted the little black dot on her cheekbone. He didn't want to kiss her goodbye as she got ready for work. Instead, he jumped off her bed, went into the living room, and hid in the space between the sofa and the stereo.

He made himself invisible and pretended to be Horus in the Brooklyn Museum. Mrs. Powers, his first-grade teacher, taught them to SHHH. BE QUIET. His breath became shallower as he sat with his knees scrunched into his chest, arms hidden under his sweatshirt. The ceiling swelled downward, pressing onto him, and the music from the boombox swallowed him whole. Earth, Wind & Fire promised he would grow to be a pearl. The sound was so loud that he could scream and no one would ever hear him.

"Where'd you go, Frankie Boy?" Mommy sang. "I'm gonna count to ten and you're gonna come out before I reach nine, so I can give you a big, fat, squishy kiss before I go out. Now, Frank-i-eee!"

The end of his name was strung out long until it sounded like a low shriek. He shifted. It was hard sitting still like a mummy, even though he'd practiced every time he watched *Saved by the Bell*.

"Don't do this to me!" she yelled. "Mommy's gonna be mad."

The front door slammed shut. It was that freak, Hernan Pabón. Frankie caught his breath. But Mommy was here. That wrinkled old skeleton wouldn't dare do anything with Mommy right here. No. He would ignore him. They were quiet and probably kissing in the bedroom. Then he heard her again.

"Now, Frankie!" When she screeched like that, he couldn't hear the record playing. Frankie slowly straightened up and pulled his arms back out through the sleeves. Frankie became Bruce Lee and did a tai-chi move. If he wanted, he could be lightning. Either fast or slow, he wasn't afraid of anybody. Frankie went back into the bedroom.

"That's Mommy's baby." His mother bent over and her breasts teased his cheeks as she hugged him. "Give me a kiss, sweetie." Her red mouth was moist against his dry lips; her breath a mix of Violet Mints and

Hennessy.

"Now give Hernan a kiss. He's almost your old man."

Frankie held his breath. SHUT UP! HE'S NOT MY OLD MAN! Hernan Pabón smelled like a fart.

Wrinkled and creepy, Hernan walked up behind his mother and grabbed her around her waist, grinding his body against her as she pushed her butt up against him. They both closed their eyes and seemed to forget that Frankie was standing there. Mommy bit her lips and moaned. It didn't look like she hurt. Not like Frankie did when Hernan came up behind him and did the same thing to him. Frankie moaned but in a different way. It hurt. Real bad.

The monster opened his eyes but kept them on Frankie as he now squeezed his mother's breasts. "God, your titties are fine. You want some?" He directed his question at the little boy. "Well, you can't. These are mine."

Frankie's mother giggled from deep in her throat—not her usual laugh. "Babe, are you crazy? Not now. Not with you-know-who in the room."

"Yeah, you're right."

In relief, Frankie took a deep breath, but Hernan's sour odor drifted from across the room. He tried to just breathe into his mouth, where he couldn't smell anything. He'd learned that by practice too.

"Frankie, sweetie, remember what I told you. I'm going to work. Pay attention to Hernan. He's nice enough to help out and watch you until I come back. Remember, he's almost your father. Respect him and act like a big boy, okay?" A sigh blew out from between her ruby-red

131

lips. "I want to be proud of you."

The pair released each other, and Hernan gave Frankie a broad wink. "We'll have fun, right, Frankie Boy?"

Frankie watched as his mother left the apartment and closed the door behind her. Hot pee streamed down his leg.

"Guess we gotta change your pants, huh, kid?"

Frankie stared at the smile on Hernan's face. *I'm gonna kill you when I'm big. You'll see.*

12
An angel

We'd turned the clocks back for Daylight Saving Time and early dusk always got to me. I could never figure out why I got emotional about that. I checked the medication order for the third time. It was hard to concentrate. Maybe I shouldn't have smoked dope on a day that I was working. I didn't do it that often, and handled it whenever I did. It was that radiologist who upset me. He really pushed. Most of my doctors liked to use a light touch with me and did their best not to scare me away. Most of them respected the fact that my business was my business, and being a nurse made it easier for me.

Dulce walked into the medication room. It would be better for me to head her off at the pass. She never knew when to quit. I loved her, but she was always on my case.

"I went to the doctor to check my head," I said.

"Really?" She put the key in the narcotics cabinet. Getting pain medication was like a top-secret operation. "Great."

"Great? A couple of days ago, you couldn't wait for me to go. That's all you talked about. Now all you can say is *great*?"

I realized that I had picked up the wrong medication. I needed meds for 510, not 501. I put the packet of antibiotics back in the drawer. Thankfully, no harm done.

"I promised myself that I was going to ease up on you. If you want to stay in that mess of a relationship, more power to you, as my mom would say."

"Okay, where are we going with this?" I dug down

for the stock bottle of ibuprofen. There had never been an evening when someone didn't ask for a painkiller. "I know you better than this. What do you have up your sleeve?"

"Please, Maggie, I need to finish up with these meds. I'm not going to talk to you about your relationship with Frank. It goes nowhere."

"I'm just sort of surprised," I said. "That's all."

"A person can't win with you. One minute you're annoyed, telling me that you're okay, and the next, I don't even know."

"Dulce, please."

"See what I mean? I'm already back to doing what I promised myself I wouldn't. Like I said, I need to focus on my meds."

I blurted out my news. "We got engaged today."

"What?" Dulce's face paled.

"Never mind." I felt a chill go through me, as though someone were walking over my grave—but I wasn't dead. I was very much alive.

"I feel sad about that, Maggie. I think you're making a mistake."

"Look. My ring." I thrust my left hand in her face. "It's beautiful, don't you see?"

"I do see, but you don't." Tears skated down her cheeks. "The ring is beautiful, you're right. Excuse me." Dulce took the narcotics out, shut the door, and locked it. "I've got to get these to the post-op."

"I want us to be honest with each other. You know that. Tell me the truth about what you think."

"Sorry, I can't talk any longer right now." She signed for the pills she'd taken and placed them in the patient's drawer. "I'm ready to give meds. See you later."

"Dinner? Aren't we meeting for dinner?"

"I'm sorry. I'm going out on my break tonight," Dulce apologized as she exited the room. "I need to get a little air."

I'd shared my news with her and ended up feeling sucker-punched. But everyone went out on their own every now and then. I had to get it together. Somehow I was always behind. I looked at my medication list and a name stuck out at me. *Amy Landry!* How could I have forgotten her?

At that moment I vowed never to smoke that stuff before work again. Everything was slow and unreal. Maybe Dulce knew. She could probably see it on me and her excuse of 'getting air' was really an excuse to get away from me. I knew better than to believe what she said. I hurried to finish preparing the evening medications. I had to check on Amy Landry.

As I walked toward Miss Landry's room, I had the sudden image of Frank shattering the crystal vase in the kitchen. Sometimes it took longer than I wanted to be free of the awful visuals that would sweep in when I least expected them. Some of the 'flashbacks,' as Dulce called them, never went away, and I hoped this wasn't one of them.

Mrs. Graham blocked the doorway. "Good evening, Miss Fuentes," she said.

"Excuse me." I tried to get past her.

"She's not there." The aide didn't step aside as I expected. "She's gone …"

I interrupted her. "Of course she's there; why would you say that? Where would she be?" I ducked around her compact body.

Miss Landry lay in bed just as I had left her. The ventilator whirred in regular intervals.

"Why did you say she wasn't in here?" I took the patient's limp hand in mine.

"I never said that." Mrs. Graham crossed her arms.

"You did," I countered. "Just now."

"Are you calling me a liar, Miss Fuentes?"

"I just heard you. You said that she wasn't in here. I heard you."

"You're mistaken. I never said that. You just want to make trouble for me."

I backpedaled. "Forget it. I'm sorry. You're right, it's probably me. Maybe I misunderstood you." I decided to stop before we had an argument. I couldn't afford to have her report me to a supervisor. If things got out of hand, I could lose my job. It wasn't worth going back and forth with her.

Everything was a blur and I didn't know anything about my patient's progress at this point. I didn't know about my progress either. When the radiologist questioned me, I turned him off so quickly that I didn't find out the severity of the injuries to my brain. *Damage*. My thinking was spiraling out of control. I was panicking. My breath was short and my hands began to tremble. I had to concentrate on my work, and right now that meant Amy Landry. I looked up to see Mrs. Graham staring at me.

"Didn't she wake up at all?" I asked. "Did the respiratory therapist try to get her off the ventilator yet?"

"You know what happened. Why are you asking me? You're the nurse, aren't you?"

I racked my brain trying to figure out why Mrs. Graham was being so antagonistic. She had seemed to be

136

softening up, and now this.

I attached the small bag of medication to Miss Landry's intravenous line. Although it was only an antibiotic, the expression on her face seemed to change. She appeared calmer. Her skin took on a translucent quality and the blue veins at her temples became more prominent. The chapped lips looked softer, rosier, and fuller. Even her hair seemed to glow and curl around her face. Amy was transforming right before me. It was as though an angel now inhabited her body. I was transfixed by her altering appearance.

"Miss Fuentes, move!" Mrs. Graham pushed at me. "Call a code! Get the cart!"

I looked at Amy Landry again. This time I saw that the blood was draining from her complexion. Her skin was gray, not pink as I thought it had become. I was horrified. What had I been seeing? A moment ago, she seemed full of life, but her heart had stopped beating.

"Quick. Start compressions! I'll activate the emergency system!" I flew out of the room and had the clerk call the emergency code, while I grabbed the crash cart and pulled it back toward the patient.

The code team appeared and surrounded her. I automatically pulled the essential medications out of the cart and lined them up, ready for use. *Epinephrine. Vasopressin. Amiodarone. Atropine. Normal saline bag.* I could set these up in my sleep.

The respiratory therapist manually pressed and released the Ambu bag that had been attached to the endotracheal tube snaking out of Amy's throat. He worked in unison with Dr. Peters, who took over the chest compressions from Mrs. Graham, who stood biting her nails in the corner of the room. Everyone listened for orders from the team leader, Dr. Mantle. An intern scribbled on the clipboard, keeping track of everything.

The external defibrillator device was readied to shock her heart back into beating again. We all stood away from the bed as he pressed the button immediately, after warning us all to keep clear. The two listened for the machine's robotic instructions before resuming chest compressions and rescue breathing. I felt as though my own heart had stopped. This had happened without warning. As far as we knew, Miss Landry didn't have cardiac disease, and her ability to tolerate her medications and treatments had been assumed, at least by me. There was no response, and Dr. Mantle pressed the defibrillator button again.

After the second shock, Amy's heart responded in normal sinus rhythm. The entire team inhaled and exhaled simultaneously. It was over just as quickly as it had begun.

"Should I set up a transfer for her to go to the unit?" I asked Dr. Mantle.

"Forget that option; there aren't any beds available. We're going to have to watch her up here," he said. "The gunshot victim is at a crossroads. We must keep her there. She's a young woman."

"So is Miss Landry." The words popped out before I had a chance to censor myself.

"I'm with you on that," Dr. Mantle said, pushing his black frames up high on the bridge of his nose. "Confidentially speaking, the issue is that the Harris family has not left the hospital since she was brought in to the ER. The woman was a victim. She was shot at by a crackhead, I'd bet. She was found lying stone-cold out at an intersection. Her car was gone. Someone must have shot her and left her there for dead. Luckily for her, it was in the middle of the day and a lady who was going to the beach found her. There aren't that many people around there at this time of year. Miss Landry, on the other hand, put herself into this predicament. Take it for what it is."

"I get it. Believe me, I do. It's just that we're always short-staffed. There isn't enough of me to go around. It's fortunate she has Mrs. Graham doing one-to-one, but it isn't the same as being on the unit."

"Not to get personal, Maggie, but I haven't seen you in a while. Are you okay?" Dr. Mantle looked me straight in the eye.

"Yes. Of course."

"It's just that you seem different. You're not the same girl I worked with in the ER. Maybe you need some time off. Like you just said, there isn't enough of you to go around."

"I'm okay," I said. "Please excuse me. I have to finish up here."

I discarded the empty boxes and threw the used needles in the thick plastic Sharps container. Everyone was getting on my nerves. Even Dulce, with her well-meaning sickly sweetness. Mrs. Graham was making crazy statements that she wouldn't back up. And now I had Dr. Mantle telling me I looked like I needed time off. I was fine and, even if I wasn't, I was entitled to my privacy. I pushed the cart back to its spot near the clean utility room to replenish it with new supplies.

"Hey, that was intense!" Jeff Peters was standing next to me. "You're a pro at this, aren't you? I still haven't quite gotten quite used to it. My adrenaline goes way over the top during these codes."

"Well, yeah, you do kind of get used to it," I admitted. "I've done them so many times, it's as though a switch is turned on in the back of my head."

Jeff reached out and touched the back of my head, pretending to turn on the switch.

"Ouch!" I cringed, and immediately regretted the movement.

"Maggie, I'm sorry. I didn't mean to hurt you. I was just playing with you."

"Forget it." I continued restocking the cart.

"Seriously, I'm sorry. I know better than to touch you like that. It was just instinctive. I could kick myself."

"It's nothing, really. Forget it," I said. "I have to finish up here."

"Wait. What's wrong with your head? Did you hurt it?"

Jeff was bewildered, and I couldn't blame him. There was no way that I was going to tell him about any of my problems or the source of the pain. I wasn't planning to bring that episode back up, no matter what anyone asked me.

"I'm super sorry, but I'm busy right now. I've got to load this cart up, and I'm not even halfway through meds. I've got Amy Landry on my caseload and sixteen other people who are waiting for medications. This isn't a brush-off. Get what I mean?"

"Yeah, sure, sorry. Got it."

I softened. "Really, thanks. I appreciate your concern."

"Still dating that officer?" he asked. "Is there any way we could go out for dinner, coffee?"

"Consider this a bona fide brush-off now," I said. Jeff would probably be shocked if he found out I touched myself thinking about him. Orgasms were easy with him, but the reality was that he wasn't in the room with me while I was having them. He seemed sweet and earnest, but Frank and I were engaged now.

"I'm engaged," I said, and showed him my diamond ring.

"I see. Congratulations. I mean . . . I wish you the best. Congratulations go to the groom for being engaged to a very nice lady."

"A very nice lady? Okay. I don't think anyone has ever described me like that before. That will be my epitaph. Hmm . . . *a very nice lady*."

"With a macabre sense of humor. Your epitaph, huh?" Jeff seemed perplexed about the whole conversation. "Excuse me, I'm going to write orders for the post-op in 507."

As I restocked the drawers of the crash cart, I thought about that. My obituary. Maggie Fuentes, *A very nice lady with a macabre sense of humor*. Survived by no one because she didn't survive Frank Ramirez.

A sharp, scratchy sensation began to gnaw at the back of my head. I imagined a crow's talon scraping against my scalp, his black beak cawing a warning at me. Of what? I shook myself to get back to the task at hand. Then I had a change of heart.

Impulsively, I followed Jeff to the nurses' station. "There's nothing wrong with coffee," I said.

"Are you sure?" Jeff seemed taken aback.

"Yes." I made sure no one else was within earshot. "Let's go right after my shift is over."

⏳

Using the new electronic record wasn't easy. Dulce

pointed at the screen detailing some of the instructions I had received earlier in the month. She worked per diem at another hospital, so she was a lot more fluent in the program language than me.

"I stink at this!" I laughed. "They say that it's supposed to be intuitive. I don't think so!"

After the fast pace of the earlier part of the evening, we had a few minutes to breathe and practice the new computer program. I felt more like my old self.

Dulce started to laugh but stopped abruptly. I looked up from the monitor to see Frank approaching us from the elevator.

"I'm going to check on 505," she said, and wasted no time leaving the nurses' station. "I think he needs to be suctioned."

I had shared too much about our relationship with her and now I regretted it.

"Hey, there!" I wanted to be happy, but I was also a little ashamed. There was no getting around the fact that I'd been flirting with Jeff. I was like a train with no brakes when I smoked, and didn't know how to stop myself.

"Thought I'd come up and say hi to my fiancée." Frank came around the counter.

Grecia, the clerk, dug her nose into her work as she separated copies of advance directives and living wills. These would go into the client charts.

"Frank, let's go outside," I said. "Only staff is allowed back here. HIPAA, you know."

"HIPAA, whatever. Bullshit. I'm here to see my sweet girl." Frank picked me up and gave me a bear hug. "Anyone got a problem needs to see me. What are they paying you to do, sit here in front of the television?"

"Very funny. I'm learning to use the electronic record."

Jeff walked over. "Everything all right, Maggie?"

I broke out of Frank's arms and introduced the two. "Yes, Jeff. I'd like you to meet my fiancé, Frank Ramirez."

I stepped back so they could shake hands. The way they sized each other up made my skin crawl.

"Frank Ramirez, Dr. Jeff Peters. I was hoping you would meet."

"Hey, Chief, good to meet you." Frank took Jeff's hand firmly in his own.

"Same here," Jeff answered.

Jeff seemed much more solid than I'd noticed before. His biceps were muscular. I couldn't help but compare the two. They were both big. Strong. *They had better get along.*

Frank seemed friendlier than I'd seen him in a long time, and I was relieved.

"Maybe you two have already seen each other in the ER? That's Frank's home away from home." I tried to read their body cues and keep things light.

"You know how it is," Frank said. "We officers are always coming in with a bus either protecting the injured or the criminals. You ever see that old black-and-white show *What's My Line?* Sometimes I'm not sure which is mine, get it?" He tapped Jeff lightly on the shoulder. "It's that way sometimes. When I get the chance, I come up to visit my lady here."

This was the second time I'd been called a lady that night. Still, I couldn't help but feel a bit apprehensive. Frank usually didn't do that well around men he didn't know, and I wasn't sure what he meant with that stupid line about the injured or criminals. Sometimes he was a jerk on purpose.

"Sounds like a tough job." Jeff touched his shoulder and moved slightly to the side. It was obvious he wasn't into the chummy tap after all.

"Well, somebody's got to do it." Frank began cracking his knuckles, and the pressure in my head started to rise again. He turned to me. "Can I speak with you privately?"

"Sure." I turned to Grecia and said, "I'll be right back. If Dulce comes back before me, tell her I'm taking a quick break."

I followed Frank down the corridor, when he turned around and pulled me toward one of the staff bathrooms. As soon as we were inside, he clicked the lock closed and immediately started yanking down my scrubs.

"No, Frank, really, we can't do that here."

"It's like a tomb out there. Except for that stiff and that robot, it's just us. The patients are asleep."

He propped me up on the sink. I bit my lower lip as he rubbed against me. I couldn't help myself. I knew it was the wrong place, but I liked the attention. We were one. Frank needed me and I needed him. My mind drifted to the good times we'd had together. I couldn't forget those. I held on to his broad shoulders as he moved his hardness inside of me, practically holding my breath so I wouldn't make any noise, until we came together, just like we did on the good days.

When we finished, I pulled my scrubs back up and he took my face in his hands. He opened my lips and popped a pill inside my mouth.

"Here, this will keep you relaxed, like you are now."

I swallowed it like a greedy baby. He knew what I

needed, even when I didn't. "Were you planning to meet me after work?" I asked.

"I'm working a double," he said.

Just before he left the bathroom, he grabbed my upper arm and pressed his fingers into my flesh. "Remember, you belong to me, okay? So, any ideas you've got, well, you might as well just get rid of them now. Got it?"

I nodded, closed the door, and looked at my reflection in the mirror. My mascara was smeared under my eyes, and I washed my face before exiting the bathroom.

The rest of the evening went by slowly. I gave up on the electronic record. Dulce came back and minded her own business. I helped Mrs. Graham with Amy Landry. This time I didn't try talking to my patient. The old lady was right. It was no use. If she didn't care about herself, why should I? Somehow I got through the evening, as my anticipation about meeting Jeff mounted.

13
The picture of concern

Jeff and I stood near the elevator. "Are you sure you want to go out for coffee?" he asked. "Your boyfriend might not be too happy about it."

"Why, are you worried?" I shrugged.

"Should I be?" Jeff glanced over his shoulder.

"Frank's doing overtime tonight," I said. "He's working toward being a detective and wants to impress his captain. I'm sure it'll be fine."

Frank had slipped that pill under my tongue and put a couple in my pocket. I found them later in the shift when I was looking for my locker key and had quickly swallowed them. I was feeling playful. He was the one who decided to work, not me. This gave me a nice stretch of time for coffee without worrying that he would follow me. Maybe for once he'd have a real case, like a murder, to manage. It was time he acted like a real cop and not a security guard in the ER.

We walked over to a diner a block away from the hospital and sat across from each other in a booth.

"So, how long have you been working at the hospital?" Jeff asked.

"I think we covered that, didn't we? Tell me about you. I want to know all about you."

"Okay." Jeff seemed surprised, but there was no break in the action as he stirred the milk in his coffee. His hands were more tapered than Frank's—just like I'd imagined.

"Where'd you go to medical school?"

"Just finished school in Antigua," he said, squirming in his seat a little. I knew it was a sore point for some

146

docs: it was such a competitive field. Spots in the United States were hard to come by. I didn't know how they managed, never knowing where they were going to end up.

"I don't think I could reroute my life so easily," I said. "But the positive is that you're back on home turf now."

"Actually, my homeland is California. I'm from L.A."

"I wondered about that."

"You did? Really?"

I laughed. "Yes, I did. I had the feeling you might be the sand-and-sea type."

"More like the inner-city type, but I like how you picture me."

Jeff's eyes searched mine. I didn't know what he was looking for, but his gaze was intense.

"I like you, you know," I said.

"You like me and that big rock you're wearing that's attached to *Big Man*," he said softly.

I shrugged. "I do like you. I hope you believe me. It would be nicer for us if you did."

"How much nicer?" he asked.

"Oh, I don't know. Pretty nice."

Our eyes locked. Suddenly I felt as though I were on fire. I found myself searching under the table for his thigh and began stroking it.

"You work out," I said.

"You were right," he said. "You are pretty nice."

I massaged his thigh with upward strokes until I came to his crotch. "Oh!" I feigned surprise, and we both laughed.

Things were going fast, and my breasts tingled. I

hadn't felt this excited in a very long time. I had enjoyed being with Frank earlier that evening, but with Jeff I felt like I was about to burst. I wanted to be with him. Frank would never have to know.

"Let's ditch the coffee," I urged. "Got someplace we could head out to?"

Jeff groaned. "Sorry. Roommates."

"Let's go over to my place." I stroked him harder. "We've got the night."

"I don't think that's a good idea."

"I wouldn't do anything to jeopardize you or our work. I live close to the hospital but not that close. It'll be okay."

The apprehension in his eyes told the story. I was worried too, but Frank was on duty and sometimes his nights cascaded into days. "Come on, it'll be all right. Let's go."

I took my hand abruptly off his leg, scribbled my address on a napkin, and stood up. "Give yourself a couple of minutes and follow me," I instructed. "The doorman is very *sometimesy*. If he's there, don't look at him."

"Are you sure?" he asked.

"Yeah, I'm sure. No need for fluff and stuff. Remember, I'm engaged." That said it all. There would be no romantic dinners. No flowers. I had to grab at whatever happiness I could.

⌛

The lobby was empty and James was nowhere to be seen. Jeff came in right behind me and we practically fell into the apartment. He pushed me against the door and pressed close, kissing my neck and rubbing his body

148

against me. I was on air. He picked me up over his shoulder, and I couldn't stop giggling as I pointed out the way to the bedroom.

We didn't waste a moment as he laid me down on my comforter and began removing my clothes. This time I wouldn't have to pretend that he was touching me. The hardness of his body was welcome. He was lying in my bed in the flesh and I needed him in me. I followed his moves and quickly began pulling his shirt off, and our skins embraced. He helped me undo his belt, and his pants came off easily. I was electrified with desire. My body was naturally open for him and I guided him into me. This was heaven. This wasn't Frank and his mechanical moves—pretending I was a metal bull that he rode. This was real and hard and sweet. I cried out when we came together.

Afterward, Jeff looked down at me and touched his fingers to my eyes, the tip of my nose, and then my lips. I was hungry for him and we started making love again, this time more tenderly. I couldn't help the tears that spilled from my eyes.

"Are you okay?" he asked, kissing my wet cheeks as we lay with our legs entwined.

"Yes, I'm better than okay," I said. I felt like I'd hit the lottery.

"You have to be careful."

"Careful?"

"You know what I mean."

I nodded. "I know, I know. I always have to be careful. I live *careful*."

"You're a little bit crazy, I think," he said. "Having me here."

"Actually, that makes two of us. Crazy, I mean."

This time I climbed onto Jeff and rode him like he was a bull—a live one. I was not going to stop. Still, I couldn't block out the vision of Frank or hearing my mother tell me that I couldn't *have my cake and eat it too*. She was dead wrong, and I was going to prove it. We made love until we were both exhausted, and then we fell asleep wrapped around each other.

I woke up lying in bed totally nude and alone. My nipples were tender and slightly reddened. I had that delicious feeling between my legs. I stretched and felt a vague soreness in my lower back. There was a crumpled sheet on the floor. I had the memory of us falling onto the rug. I jumped up and looked at my reflection in the floor-length mirror. Sure enough, there was a slight friction burn on my lower back. I raced into the shower, but the water made the irritation worse. I tried not to panic. I rummaged frantically through the medicine cabinet for some ointment. I couldn't let Frank see it. I would have to find a way to avoid arousing his suspicion. He wouldn't be back until late, and I had the rest of the day to figure it out.

The phone rang and I hurried out of the bathroom. "Hello?"

"It's me. What are you doing?" Frank asked.

"Dripping. I was in the shower. I ran out to get the phone because I know how you hate when I don't answer."

"Well, have you ever heard of towels?"

"Frank, what is it?" I asked. "I know you didn't call me to talk towels, or did you?"

I heard a sharp intake of breath. "You're a smartass, aren't you? The reason I called is to tell you that I won't be there tonight. I have some things to do."

"What things? You asked me to see your grandmother today and you won't even be here to find out what happened?"

"No. I can't. It's business. You know how my life is; it sucks. I don't have control over everything, as much as you'd like to believe I do."

"I'm sorry. You're right," I said. Those words were the magic balm that soothed almost everything. My prayers had been answered. At least for now, I didn't have to worry about him snaking all over my body. A wave of dizziness came over me and I was reminded of the knot in the back of my head. I also needed something, anything, to relax and take that pain away. My nerves were like a twisted and open electrical circuit.

"Yeah, well, do like I said, okay? Let her know that we're thinking of her."

"Sure, Frank, will do." I hung up, relieved that he wouldn't be in my space for a little while. That was good enough for now. I went back into the bathroom. I needed to find the ointment for that burn.

14
Put this near your bed

I had promised Frank that I'd go visit his ancient grandmother at the nursing home, but I was wired. This nurse thing was sometimes the bane of my existence. The old woman had Alzheimer's and had never laid eyes on me before. Going there would be a chore, but it was early and I still had plenty of time. He did say he wasn't coming around and I could go later in the day—this was no emergency. I straightened up my bed, lay back down, and picked up the journal. I was attracted to Ellen's story and eager to learn more about her.

September 15, 1903

Leather cases lined with velvet and pearls
Horses gleam from a thousand strokes
White gloves strewn at the bottom
of a sweeping staircase.
It is all so grand!

September 18, 1903

When traveling abroad
A lady must remember to keep her corset snug
But not taut so that she cannot breathe
Hold still
I will pull the laces a bit tighter for you!
Wait. Are those tears in your eyes?
Or are they in mine?

Bundled off to Europe. Miss Isabel and my wages both gone in an instant. That penny-pinching miser! Mrs. Allerton would be heartbroken to know that he sent her little sunflower away without a second thought. I must find somewhere else to work. It is not easy to get work as a first maid. Mrs. Allerton confided she hired me because she couldn't believe that I could hold a needle. When she saw my skilled stitches, she was dumbstruck. I remember her laughter. I don't think I will remember Miss Isabel's laugh, because it wasn't often that I heard it. I do believe that she loved Mr. Daniels. Mr. Allerton's preference to have Mr. Jones as his son-in-law only proves that money is thicker than blood.

October 3, 1903

There are some things that should never be written on paper.

November 15, 1903

The evening is icy. The streets are frosted. I must take care not to lose my footing on the slippery cobblestones. They resemble a glass floor at the Winter Palace. The many lights make for a festive atmosphere, but the night is maudlin. Still, on this cold night there are couples strolling on the boardwalk. They are all warmly dressed in furs and mufflers. One woman's hands are hidden in what must be an ermine muff. The Half Moon Hotel is well-lit. Travelers come from far and wide for fun and food. They frolic without heavy hearts. Does one have to

153

leave one's home for these things? I will find out the answer for myself. There is no one for me to depend on here.

My trunk is packed. I shut the lid after I placed the last of my belongings into it. My hope is that liberty will come with change. Miss Woodhull has promised this. A secret burns in my heart. I have told no one, not even Cook or Birdie, who toil by my side each day. I must hurry and leave tonight, before Karl returns. There will be no other opportunities, for I believe that if I do not leave at once, it will be my demise. If I do not move swiftly, either I or an outside force will hold me captive and I may never be heard from again. The boys have promised to bring my trunk to Ruby's. They begged me to tell them the truth of what happened. I will not allow them to be jailed for murder. Not this time or any other. If anyone goes off to jail, it will be me. It is my right to pay for any deeds I do, just as Miss Victoria Woodhull paid dearly for hers. I can hear Ruby in my mind as clearly as if she were speaking into my ear. She tells me not to be silly and that the time for decision has arrived, just as she had told me it would. She'd warned me not to let someone other than me make decisions in my life, but somehow I did. I allowed Karl to make my most important decision. The truth is, I didn't let him make it, but he took it nevertheless. Miss Ruby said I could stay with her. I am in deep gratitude for this wise gypsy woman.

I closed the journal and tried not to think about Ellen and Karl and all the things that the entries signified. I decided to erase Ellen from my mind for now. I couldn't deal with her darkness and my own this morning. I certainly didn't want to think about Jeff. It was the pills, the smoking; none of it had to do with me. The person who made love to Jeff wasn't me. I rubbed at my lower back and prayed it would heal before Frank could see it.

I brewed a pot of strong coffee. That would keep me awake. Even though I had to go up to East Harlem, I was going to enjoy my day off. I sat with my feet up on the velvety ottoman and filed my fingernails while I drank my coffee. As a nurse, I couldn't in good conscience have long ones, but I did the best I could to make them look nice with clear polish. I probably should have made plans for the day and not have acquiesced to Frank's harebrained request. Frank had a knack for making me do things that I was uncomfortable with.

Frank had told me very little about his grandmother. She had lived in El Barrio since she emigrated from Puerto Rico. He said her name was Marta. I wondered how old she was. Maybe I was being selfish, but I wanted my day to myself. I was feeling a little better. My head didn't ache as badly as it had for the last couple of days. I decided to leave Ellen's journal at home; I didn't want to look at it for now. Instead I would download something a bit more upbeat on my Kindle for the long train ride. I'd finish my nails and then do my eyebrows. Take care of me first. If not, I'd be sorry when it was time to return to work, knowing I hadn't done a thing for *me*. It was something I was working on. Self-care, what a concept. Sometimes it seemed that the last person I thought about was me.

But I couldn't help thinking about the captivating journal entries. I related so much to what Ellen had written so many years ago. The similarities between us were astonishing. We had both lived through unpleasant situations with our mother's boyfriends as young girls. I had hoped to forget about my childhood, and writing my memories down didn't seem appealing at all.

When my mother moved to Puerto Rico, I thought it was my chance for liberation, but instead I got stuck with Frank. Before that, it was Omar I couldn't shake off. I doubted that Ellen would get away from Karl. And her mother; her mother was just like mine. I didn't want to pick the journal up again, but every time I was close to it, I felt compelled. It read like a bestseller. It was astounding that no one else had picked it up over the years. It must have lain trapped in that box for a very long time. I wondered who found it and how it had ended up at the flea market. It seemed like it had been placed there especially for me. I shook my head and a spasm of pain went through me. I had to keep my focus and not just sit here thinking about the journal. I had a lot to do. I put the nail file down and got ready for the trip to see Frank's grandmother.

⌛

The nursing home was on Park Avenue, close to 101st Street. If I used my time well, I could go to a museum or to La Casa Azul Bookstore. I'd heard that the bookstore was a hub for Latino writers and artists. I could check it out. Afterward, I'd find a good place to buy a *café con leche*. It had been too long since I had savored one. I could easily get depressed about how I had stopped doing the little things for myself that I loved to

156

do. Sometimes I got sick of Coney Island. There was no culture in Coney—not like in New York City. I'd have to do a bit of walking, but the weather was nice. I was surprised at how excited I was becoming about going.

The train ride was long and I did my best to deal with the subway transfers and stairs—there were so many steps. I climbed out of the subway and held on to the banister. I was dizzy and a wave of nausea passed through me. I couldn't figure out why they came in surges and then disappeared for long intervals.

The street signs read *Lexington Avenue* and *E. 103rd Street*. I hadn't grown up in East Harlem, but I'd paid close attention to the stories my aunts and uncles told. It seemed like some of my family members had disappeared inside those buildings and never come out again. My *tías* told stories about epic house parties, *pachangas* and *boleros* that were danced so tight that the fabric flowers on the women's dresses were flattened to look like pieces of wet paper. They spoke about *Fulana* and *Fulano*, and an era that was over for my family. When my mother moved to Puerto Rico, I hadn't kept up my relationships. I had depended on her for that.

At the top of the subway stairs, I turned to the right and spotted a huge hill that seemed as if it was perpendicular to the street. I walked the other way to head uptown. Tantalizing aromas of sizzling dishes wafted in the air and I spied several restaurants. A few men hung out in front of bodegas, surveying the street, and I felt like an outsider. This was my neighborhood too, but without my family I no longer had a true connection with it. I was on a field trip all by myself. If I was going to do El Barrio, the least I could do was go up to 110th Street.

I felt alone as I explored the neighborhood. Frank only wanted to go from Point A to Point B. There was never any exploration with him. 'Get in the car.' 'Hurry up.' 'Who are you looking for?' That was the extent of his vocabulary. I don't think he ever took a train. 'That's for *pendejos*,' he said. Standing on the street corner, I spotted the bookstore—it was across from the church and right next to a funeral home. All three were sacred places.

La Casa Azul Bookstore was lined with books, but it was also filled with color and texture. I didn't know which area to go to first. At the front of the store there were tables full of jewelry and silk scarves. Toward the back, in the Children's section, there was a sweet little sitting area. I started to browse through the novels. I would work my way to the back.

"Hi! Welcome!" a couple of workers greeted me. They wore T-shirts that read *Got libros?* Books. I only had two and had gotten those at the flea market. I was such a loser, but I was in the right place. I had to change things up where I could.

The two salespeople had wide smiles on their faces. Their friendliness was like a punch to the gut. Who were these people? They seemed to genuinely like each other and me. If they knew about what I'd been doing the last twenty-four hours, they would turn away from me. I was glad they couldn't hear my thoughts.

I impulsively picked up a couple of novels without even looking at the titles and paid for them. On the way out, I saw a display of cookbooks and stopped to browse through them. The pictures showed gorgeous, elaborately prepared meals. The cooks, standing behind their dishes, looked so happy. The message seemed to be that any problem could be overcome with food. I should probably find new recipes and lose myself in the kitchen, but I barely had time to work and be either Frank's trophy or his punching bag.

I got out of there and began walking on Lexington Avenue, toward 110th. I'd savor my day before heading over to visit Frank's grandmother. I stopped in front of a Mexican restaurant at the corner and pretended to read the menu. After my excitement in the store, I wanted to be centered and grounded before venturing any further.

I heard a male voice behind me. "Aw, man, look, here they come. I don't want to see this shit."

"Come on, let's go," another voice answered. "It don't mean nothing."

I turned to see a couple of young guys walk past me. I followed them with my eyes; part of me was compelled to go after them, but I kept my distance. I didn't want them to notice me. This wasn't my neighborhood.

Coming toward us was a parade of people. It was a weekday afternoon, but a huge wedding party was walking down the middle of the street. *But this was no wedding.* The streets were filled with women wearing white bridal gowns. There were men walking alongside them. Whoever wasn't wearing a dress trimmed with lace and seed pearls was wearing a T-shirt with a picture of a young bride emblazoned on it. *Gladys Ricart.* They were carrying posters and banners that read 'A license to marry, not a license to kill' and '*El amor no duele.*' Another read 'Men who matter never batter.' Members of the crowd carried signs that read 'Remember all domestic violence victims' and 'New York Latinas Against Domestic Violence.'

My stomach began to twist and turn, and I needed to

get to a bathroom. I scanned the street in search of one. There was a café at the corner, but my feet seemed rooted to the sidewalk. The sounds of the people and the looks on the women's faces were all sending me a message, but I wasn't sure what it meant. *Why was I here watching this?* I took a deep breath and held on to a parking meter to steady myself. Maybe if I just waited it out, the churning in my stomach would pass. All it took was watching these women walking, dressed in white, and I was about to be sick right in the middle of the street. I grabbed the meter more tightly.

My grandfather stood in front of me and touched my arm. His fingers were electrified and I jumped slightly with the shock. No, it couldn't be. *Abuelo* had died a long time ago. This old man was wearing dark glasses and a straw fedora. I'd never seen him before. I felt the sweat pour down my face and arms. My breath was short and I flushed with heat. If I didn't get to a bathroom, or at least sit down, I would faint. I needed to get away from these people.

"*¿Estás bien, mija?*" His voice was gentle.

"*Sí*," I answered in Spanish. I hadn't said anything in Spanish for years, except to translate or to speak to a patient. "*No sé . . .*"

"I speak English," he said. "Sit down. You don't look so good." The cane he held came to life, and almost of its own accord began to tap on the concrete sidewalk. "*Ven conmigo*—you'll be all right." I knew that I would follow him wherever he went. I closed my eyes for a moment and he became my grandfather again.

As the old man walked me around the corner, I saw that the cane was a white stick that he used to navigate his course; he was blind. After opening the door to one of the street businesses, I saw that I was inside a *botánica*. I'd been in one before for a spiritual reading and sometimes thought of having another, but always chickened out at the last minute. The stranger pointed to a folding chair next to the counter. I sat down and took a couple of deep breaths. Suddenly, a woman was holding a Styrofoam cup filled with water to my lips. I drank and my skin cooled almost instantly and my stomach began to settle. I started to get up.

"No, stay here for a little while, until you really feel better," he said. The old man sat in another folding chair at my side. "You are still green."

"Green?" I asked, uncertain of how he could possibly know that. "I'm okay, really. I need to go to the hospital."

"You are sick?" he took his sunglasses off and his blue-ringed opaque eyes looked right through me.

I felt a chill. I knew that he saw more through that one look than any of those doctors who had examined me.

"No, I made a mistake, I meant a nursing home," I answered. Somehow I felt that I owed him an explanation. "My boyfriend's grandmother."

El viejo nodded and tilted his head slightly, as though listening. "Be careful. I don't mean right now. Tomorrow . . . tonight. You know what I'm talking about, don't you?"

Frank. "Yes."

"You're not safe in the night," he said urgently. "But you are not safe during the day either."

I lowered my eyes. I wondered if my experiences lingered in my aura like that *espiritista* once told me. *Taking spiritual baths isn't enough*, she had said. *You*

161

need to leave the evil thing and prevent it from looking for you anymore. It was easy to say that from behind a counter in a *botánica*. It didn't matter how many herbs, white flowers, and *Agua de Florida* I bathed in, Frank was here to stay.

"Take this. It will be your lucky charm." The old man took a tiny statue of St. Michael, the archangel, from the counter and placed it in my hand. "Put this near your bed."

I closed my hand around it. The sword and wings on the statue poked into my palm. "Thank you. What do I owe you?"

He waved his hand and took a business card off the counter. "Anything you need, call."

I stood up and felt like I was on solid ground again. My stomach had stopped doing somersaults. I took the card and the statue and put them in my bag. The card could go in my wallet later. I had to get out of there and spend some time with Frank's grandmother before I went home again. He'd be upset if he thought I had treated her like a hit and run.

"Thank you," I said, and started to walk out but turned around on an impulse. "*Bendición*," I added. I hadn't asked for a blessing in a very long time.

He gave a quick nod. "*Dios te bendiga.*"

I followed the demonstrators on Lexington Avenue until they turned on 106th Street and marched into a church. St. Cecilia's. I was tempted to follow them in but instead headed to the nursing home. My phone started vibrating. Frank, of course. I ignored him and continued my walk from Point A to Point B.

15
Doña Ana no 'ta 'qui

The slightly sweetish, decaying odor of the nursing home hit me as soon as I walked into the lobby. A cloying disinfectant hung in the air, intended to mask the other smells. They warned visitors to stay in the waiting room. *Don't venture in too deeply.* Frank said it was too painful for him to see his grandmother getting increasingly demented, but it was probably the smell that made him avoid this place.

The clerk at the nurses' station turned to me when I cleared my throat to get her attention.

"I'm here to see Mrs. Ramirez."

I took it for granted that her last name was *Ramirez*. I hadn't thought to ask him her name when I agreed to visit her.

"You're here to see *La Señora Marta?* That's sweet. She hasn't had a visitor in a while. Are you her granddaughter?"

The woman was smiling, just like the people at the bookstore. I didn't do that when visitors came to the desk at the hospital. I wasn't so nice.

"No, I'm her grandson's girlfriend," I said. What did that make me? Nothing.

"Just want to warn you in advance that she may not recognize you."

The clerk's nameplate said 'J. de Burgos.' I wondered whether she was named for *Julia.* My concentration was wavering. I was such an idiot for not waiting to find out if I had permanent brain damage.

"Actually, she's never met me before," I said.

"I shouldn't say this. HIPAA, you know." She

whispered loudly and craned her neck over the counter, making sure there was no one within earshot. "I don't want to breach her confidentiality, but no one really comes to see her, and you should know, she has Alzheimer's."

"I appreciate anything you're able to tell me. I'm a nurse."

"Then you know what I'm talking about. I'm glad. You know, for some family members, it can be heart-wrenching."

"I understand," I said. "Thank you for being so open."

"Last door to your right," she said. "Her last name is on the door. *Camacho*."

"No, I said *Ramirez*."

"Yes, but we dropped off the *Ramirez*. You know, double last names. It'll say *Camacho*."

I nodded and began my walk down the long corridor. It was funny how she knew that her full name was *Marta Camacho Ramirez*. There was probably no turnaround here in terms of the patients. Not like on a surgical unit, where every day someone was moving on or off the floor.

There it was. *Camacho*. How could I be sure it was his grandmother? I went back out to the nurses' station.

"Are you sure that *Camacho* is *Ramirez?*"

This time, the clerk glared at me. "Of course I'm sure. I've been here for fifteen years. At this desk. Don't you think I know our patients?" she sputtered. "Fifteen years, Miss!" Her face turned red and her eyes closed into slits.

"Sorry," I said, and turned away to head for the room.

Near the picture window, a tiny, withered woman sat dwarfed in a floral high-backed winged chair. Her eyes were shut tight in her caramel-colored face, which was lined with a million traveled roads. Straight black hair mixed with white strands was pulled back into a small knot at the back of her head. Marta Camacho Ramirez was wearing a print housedress and a crocheted sweater. Her hands were gnarled and they lay atop the pilled knitted afghan across her knees.

I tried to get her attention. "*Señora Ramirez, yo soy la novia de Frank.* I'm your grandson's girlfriend."

"Franklin?" she responded. Blinking, the woman smiled, showing her gums. She was completely toothless.

"Do you speak English?" I repeated myself. "I'm your grandson Frank's girlfriend."

"*Sí,* English," she cackled. "*¿Adela?*"

"No, not Adela. *Maggie,*" I said. "My name is Maggie." I moved closer to her, but I was repelled by the smell of urine that permeated her clothing.

"*¿Adela?*" She probed under her blanket and pulled out a stuffed rabbit. "*Coge, Adela, pa'ti.*"

Not wanting to hurt her feelings, I pulled my sleeve over my hand and covered my fingers before taking it from her. I put it on top of the bureau next to her bed.

Marta hadn't opened her eyes, other than a few blinks. She was probably blind. Meeting two blind elderly people in one afternoon was significant. Messages were usually not that obvious, but I still didn't understand what I needed to see.

I quietly surveyed the room. A stuffed owl stared back at me from the top of the bureau. It sat next to a crystal whale and a few fluffy little ponies. An old-fashioned kewpie doll seemed to wink at me. Somebody had to be supplying them to her. But the clerk said that no one visited her.

I bent close to her. "Marta, Frank loves you."

"Franklin? No. No Franklin."

"*Sí, Frank, su nieto,* your grandson," I whispered loudly into her ear.

Marta seemed to get agitated and then started humming a tune. It sounded familiar. I'd heard it before. As a very young child, my grandmother used to sing the tune to me while I played a dancing game. "*Doña Ana, no 'ta qui, está en su . . .*" She stopped and put her finger to her lips. "*Shh, Adela, escóndete allí.*" Marta Camacho Ramirez's statement was eerie. Why was she telling Adela to hide?

I wanted to get out of the room. It was stifling hot and the stink of urine was unbearable. No wonder they loaded on the disinfectant at the entrance lobby.

Suddenly, she spoke. "Get my book." I was surprised to hear her speak English.

"Book? What book?" I looked around for a book. There was nothing on any of the shelves but porcelain statues and glass figurines, along with the stuffed animals.

"*Mi libro,*" Marta said, and struggled to stand up.

"No, sit down, Marta," I said. "I'll be back. I promise." I tucked the afghan against her knees, but Marta continued to move about restlessly as I left the room. When I reached the nurses' station, the clerk was still there, picking up orders.

"Miss?" I called softly.

"Yes?" The clerk's bright smile was back. "Do you need something, hon? How did your visit with Miss

Marta go?"

"I just wanted to apologize for before," I started. "I didn't mean to doubt you."

"No problem," Ms. de Burgos answered. "And your visit; how did it go, dear?"

"Okay, I guess," I answered. "Do you know if she has a book she likes to read?"

"A book? Well, she can't actually read now, can she?"

"I didn't even think of that," I admitted. "But she asked me to get a book."

"Oh, that tattered poetry book that she has. She must have had it for years. It's falling apart. I'll ask Millie, I mean, Miss Johnson, her nurse, where it is."

"Thank you," I said. "Again, I'm sorry for any trouble I gave you earlier."

Ms. de Burgos's face broke into a huge smile. "I don't know what you're talking about. Come back soon. I'm sure she'd love for you to visit her again, dear."

On my way back home, the image of the stuffed animals and porcelain figurines started to gnaw at me. They were proof that the family, or at least Frank's mother, had been there often enough. I'd been taught by my mother that Latinos never put their family members into nursing homes. Alzheimer's was a tragic disease, and I should probably give Frank's family a break. But what really stayed with me was Marta asking for *Adela*. I'd have to ask Frank who she was; I'd never heard him mention that name before.

⌛

I rummaged through the medicine cabinet. I needed to turn my brain off. My headache was gone for now, but my nerves were jangled. I found a bottle of Vicodin. I had some left from a root canal that I'd had a few months earlier. A couple of pills would smooth my edges down. Sometimes my nurse knowledge came on too strong, but these were my pills, so I wasn't really self-medicating. I sat at the edge of the tub and swallowed them down. I turned the tap on and cupped my palm underneath. I drank a little of the water that trickled down and then wiped my forehead and cheeks. I could count on the pills to work; they always did. A while later, I went into my bedroom and crawled under the covers. I could still smell Jeff.

The old journal was on the nightstand, where I had left it earlier that day. The pills were already beginning to work because my stomach was empty. Relaxation set in and I relished the quiet as I began to read the entries that Ellen had written so long ago. Some of her notations ended abruptly. Maybe she had to hide her notebook. I didn't write in one because Frank dug through my personal things whenever he wanted. That was a good reason not to live with him, but now we were engaged. Things were bound to change for the better.

Some of the entries were unpleasant. When she wrote about that awful man her mother was married to, it reminded me of my mother's husband, Rafy. I didn't tell her about the way he looked at me or the things he said when she wasn't around. I did that already with Maximo, and that turned out to be a debacle. I wouldn't go down my old *Mommie Dearest* road. Instead, I opened the journal.

I am learning to read the cards too. Ruby says I'm a natural. First off, I should not call her Miss Ruby, she says, as she is not a lady but, rather, a flesh-and-blood woman. Secondly, I must pay attention to my feelings and remember that the moon and the water will never lie to me. Dusk and dawn are the in-between hours and that's when I should listen. She calls me her crescent moon child. She said if we were back in the old country, she would paint an indigo crescent over my third eye and set me out into the woods at night to sit under the dark sky. Ruby says the night belongs to women. She won't send me to the woods after all because we are not near the woods, and if we were, I'd be seen as a bit daft. Ruby went into one of her trances and said that other women might recognize me for who I am and that their hearts would stir with the commitments they have taken with me during our past lives. I had no idea what that meant, and when I asked her, she suddenly laughed and said not to worry about her rantings. Maybe I should draw the shape of a crescent moon on my breast, because while I don't understand much of what she's talking about, I feel it stir in my heart. I believe that I am connected with other women, like Victoria Woodhull, but that we may not remember what it is we committed to in our past lives. It was something together; that much I remember. Soon I will start gazing into that lovely violet sphere she has on her table and learn more of what there is to learn. Of what, I have no idea. But I'm sure it's something important.

The more I learn, the more I learn to keep secret. Some of the customers ask for me, as I am paid a lower fee than Ruby. She doesn't mind when they ask for me by name. We don't say my name is Ellen. That is too plain. My new name is Rosa—if only on the sign. Ruby thinks it's quite fetching. Ruby and Rosa. We tell fortunes. The feelings that I had when doing the laundry at the Allertons' were part of my women's gifts. Just by holding hands or a piece of jewelry I know what is coming toward the customer. Ruby says that I shouldn't let my head grow too big. She also said there is a dark man who is about to walk into my life. She said heed the word 'dark.'

June 25, 1904

Tonight I walked along the boardwalk and watched as couples strolled arm in arm. I looked about, hoping that the man whom Ruby spoke of would show himself to me. Is it the carnival hawker who calls out to the passersby, gaining their attention to sell tickets for the shows? I'm not sure I'd be interested in a man who wears a red-and-white-striped jacket with a straw hat decorated with a matching red ribbon. But, then again, I dress my head with a scarf and wear long beaded earrings when I tell fortunes. We wear costumes when we work, just as the officer does who rides his horse on the boardwalk and warns the children about roughhousing. Maybe my 'dark' man is the policeman. Or could it be one of the store owners? This I doubt, if only because most of them are too old, at least thirty years of age, with families of their own. I wonder about Mary and Edith. I try not to think about Momma, who didn't ask a thing when she saw me pack the trunk. She merely turned her head away. More aptly, she turned her heart away.

I am committing some of the teachings from Ruby to memory. None of what she teaches can be written down on paper. The knowledge should not be shared with anyone who may not use it for good. I don't truly understand that. Why would somebody use their knowledge for evil? Unless it were used against Karl, of course.

I think I saw him today. Tall and dark. Wearing a hat and holding a walking stick. More like brandishing it. I couldn't determine his age, but his eye caught mine as he walked along toward the pier. The blinding lights of Luna Park were behind him and I couldn't be sure of his expression. Some children circled 'round him, begging for a few pennies, but he pushed his way through. I'm not sure why I felt a shiver go through my body. It wasn't the nice kind.

I took another stroll to relieve me of all those who rap on the door asking for card readings. The women ask about romance and the men ask about money—how to get it, who has it, what they should do with it. So many questions roil around in my head. I am saving money. Ruby says I should because I will need it in my future and that I should never be dependent on anyone for money. I wonder what has become of Mr. Allerton and Miss Isabel. Their lives were entwined with money. It foretold her future. I must keep what happened to her in mind when I'm tempted to buy a sweet or new stockings, when the ones I have are perfectly fine. Ruby said that I should never be dependent on a man for money, and then she changed it to anyone.

July 20, 1904

*If I pen my thoughts on paper
Are they no longer my secrets?*

July 23, 1904

I was right. He spoke to me today. He tipped his hat and said, "Good morning!" My, he has lovely white teeth! They gleamed nicely when he smiled and wished me a lovely day. I think he's a traveler and here at the shore for the holiday. I will sit out on the walk and wait for him to pass each day. Ruby said that my skin will burn like toast. Her smile was cold and her tone took a turn; I don't think she meant burnt from the sun. She wouldn't say more when I tried to press her. It seems there are some things she believes I should learn on my own. The sphere will only share some things. I wish that I could see my future in it. I see everyone else's but my own. Ruby said that it is because I am still too young and have no experience. I disagree with her.

July 27, 1904

He sat next to me on the rocks and asked me my name. I was about to tell him that it was Rosa, but when he looked down at me, I heard myself say "Ellen." I became flustered, since I'd just taken off my boots and stockings. He was not at all perturbed and did the same. He sifted through the sand and picked up one of the prettiest shells I've ever seen and placed it in my hand. Pink and pearlescent was the way he described it. I accepted it but will return it to the sea, where it belongs, on the morrow. I will not tell him but will do it in secret. The sand was radiant white. The sea foam ebbed and flowed in a lazy rhythm. His name is Thomas, but he said I should call him Tom. I will not forget that. He asked me what I was writing and he seemed to stiffen a bit when I explained the idea of sharing one's most inner thoughts on paper. He got over it quickly, though, and teased and asked me if he could look at it. He stopped when he saw my face. I probably wore a look of horror. I am relieved that I already knew that I should keep my innermost secrets within me. One never knows where one's journal will end up! We listened to the sounds of the waves and the gulls, and when I returned to the shop, I found there was a long line of people waiting for me. It is the high point of the season and I barely had time to swallow my tea. It scalded my tongue. The biscuits helped to cool it down a bit. Ruby asked why I don't drink something cool in this scorching weather. She doesn't understand that old habits are hard to break. I must still fancy that I am living in a manor. Maybe one day I will be.

Maybe Ellen had hoped that someone would read her letters one day. *Someone like me*. The curtains moved as the breeze found its way into my bedroom and a chill coursed up my spine. I loosened the comforter from around my body and tried to get up to close the window but couldn't seem to move. The pills were affecting me in a way I didn't like; I was powerless to protect myself even against the cool night air. The aroma of the salty sea stole into the room like a silent vapor.

As I dozed, I began to feel the presence of someone in my room. I couldn't see an image or a figure but felt it close to my body. It moved slowly. Cautiously. Nearer and nearer. I couldn't do anything to stop the presence from advancing toward me. It sidled up very close, until it seemed to slither inside me. Someone was within me, enjoying my body and surroundings. I tried to move again and found that I still couldn't. I heard laughter. It was the same tinkling sound that I thought were bells when I came upon the trunk at the flea market. I knew then that Ellen had entered my body. I was sure it was her. I had come to know her intimately as I read through her journal entries, and now we were one and the same.

Time slowed, and I gathered my senses together as this new being I had become. I managed to stand up. My robe had become heavy. I stood in front of the full-length mirror. My reflection revealed that my robe had transformed into a skirt of taffeta, a party dress the color of gold, with the hem meeting the tops of the matching pumps on my feet. The dress's tiny floral decorations gathered it into a design of the most handsome sheath. Even my thinking was changing. I could see myself plainly, but I could also see Ellen. The glow of her countenance matched the shimmering hue of the gown. The thin cross I wore around my neck had turned into a stunning choker of white water pearls, with a large faceted garnet set at the front. My hair, Ellen's, was highlighted in golden strands and swept up into a pompadour, which must have been popular in her day.

My bedroom vanished behind me and I was swept into a dance hall. An orchestra played lively music, and ladies wearing glamorous jewel-toned dresses hid behind open lace fans. The men wore tuxedos and white gloves. They were all masked. The servers were impeccably dressed too. One came close to me, carrying a tray full of champagne glasses, and I was tempted to reach out and pick one up.

"I'm glad you could make it," a male voice said.

I jumped. Standing next to me was a tall gentleman who wore the uniform of the rest of the men in the room and a half mask across his face.

I touched my face and realized that I was now wearing one too. Beads and feathers adorned the right side. I wondered whether he would hear me when I answered. That tinkling sounded again, and I realized it was me. I sounded happy. When did I, Maggie Fuentes, ever laugh like this?

"I wouldn't miss this, Tom!" *How did I know that this was Tom?*

The gentleman placed his gloved hand on my arm and maneuvered me over to the expansive bay window. I, too, was wearing gloves that reached above my elbows.

He whispered into my ear and his breath was feverish as his lips caressed my cheek. "I know that I shouldn't be doing this here. I couldn't wait to see you, Ellen. You are divine. I see that you received the pearls. You haven't disappointed me."

"You haven't disappointed me either, Tom. The pearls are superb and match my dress magnificently. You always know exactly what I would pick out for myself."

"Would you have picked those out, my fine one?"

A pang of discontent in his response cut across my heart, but I didn't know whether it was me or Ellen who was sad. I was reminded that without him I would never have been able to afford these fine pieces of jewelry. That I would soon be walking the alleyway behind the boardwalk if he, on a whim, decided that I was no longer of value to him. I shook my head. Those weren't my thoughts; they were Ellen's.

"Let's dance," he said, and pulled me back onto the gleaming dance floor. The quartet was playing gay music and we moved quickly across the room.

"This is glorious, isn't it?" I wanted to take advantage of this splendid experience and immerse myself in the music. The other women's gowns were stunning. The fabrics were heavenly, and I had to hold myself back in order not to reach out and touch them. It was surreal, but the feeling of Tom's body holding me close to him was very real. *How is this happening?* As my thinking became sharper, the swirling ballroom receded. It seemed that the more I thought, the less I was able to stay in what had to be an illusion. Suddenly, I found myself back in my room, wearing my robe and lying in my bed.

That's enough for tonight. There was no way I could channel someone from a journal. No one would ever believe me. But, deep inside, I knew that was exactly what had happened. I tried moving, and this time I was able to get up and close the window. I practically leapt back under the comforter. The room was frigid and I needed to get some sleep.

Personal Love Monster

When he fills me up inside, I feel whole. Protected. Like he loves me. All I do is move around and around and it feels so good. Like something I can't get enough of. I want more and more. I think he loves me. I love him.

Maggie finished writing the sentence with a flourish. She placed the pen between the pages of the journal and closed it. She ran her hands dreamily over the textured cover. When she softened her vision, the greenish-brown color with shiny mermaid scales turned into waves.

"*Ayudame, Magaly,*" Abuela yelled from the kitchen in her broken English. "Come help."

Maggie snapped to attention and pushed the journal away from her on the top of the dressing table. A perfume bottle fell over and she set it upright.

Abuela was in the kitchen frying beef empanadas for her fourteenth birthday party at their church. Not sixteen. Definitely not eighteen. The way things were going between her and her mother, Maggie was sure that there wouldn't be a Sweet Sixteen party when the time came. *She hates me.*

"*Niña,*" her grandmother called. "*Ahora.*"

It was Magaly's job to wrap the empanadas and have them ready for the members of the congregation, who gorged greedily on the spicy meat and flaky shells. That was probably why they didn't mind giving her the birthday celebration. It came with food.

"I'll be right there!" Maggie opened the journal once

more for a brief glimpse of the poem she had written last Friday after spending time with Rafy.

Secrets
Nobody's business
You mind yours
I'll mind mine
He loves me
Not you

This time when she closed the journal, she hid it under the ruffled bed skirt. Her grandmother couldn't read English, but her mother could, and would dunk her head under scalding water if she found out she was fucking Rafy. It wasn't her fault that he pretended to be her mother's boyfriend.

The phone rang and Maggie leapt to grab the receiver before *Abuela* did.

Breathless. *Hello?*

Deep breathing.

You're so stupid. She giggled.

You know who this is?

Yes. Ted Bundy.

That's right. Your own personal love monster.

You're crazy.

Meet me upstairs.

I can't.

Just tell Granny you forgot your homework or something. Say that you're going to Jenny's.

I'll try.

There ain't no tryin'. Just doin'.

Maggie hung up the phone and went into the steamy kitchen. Sweat beads had gathered on *Abuela's* forehead and upper lip.

"Get me that pan," her grandmother demanded. "The one with the foil."

Maggie handed her the pan. "I'm sorry, but I forgot that I have to get an assignment from Jenny." The lies cascaded like a glittering waterfall.

"Jenny?"

"Yes. I was doing work for my teacher, Mrs. Castro. I couldn't get the assignment. Jenny said she'd give it to me."

"You stay to work for your teacher, but you're too lazy to help me?"

"It's not the same thing." Maggie smiled and hugged her grandmother. "It's for my grade."

"Your mother don't like you going out after school."

"It's only 4 o'clock. I'll be back way before she comes home."

Maggie gave her grandmother another quick hug and fled before she could hand her ten reasons not to talk to strangers. She ran into the hallway and slammed the main door shut, making sure that it was hard enough for the glass window insert to rattle. *Abuela* would hear that and think she left the building. Maggie counted to three and ducked as she passed the peephole of their apartment door. She ran lightly up the stairs to the third floor. Rafy waited behind his own door, holding it ajar.

Maggie was barely in when he began invading her mouth with his tongue.

"Stop!" She pulled her head back while pressing her

hand against his chest. "I can't breathe when you do that."

"Then what the fuck did you come up here for?" he growled, as he pressed against her.

"Because I love you."

"Now you sound like your mother." Rafy pinched her nipple right through her sweater.

"Ow, that hurts!" Maggie rubbed her breast.

"Here, let me do that." Rafy kneaded her breasts in the dark corridor, this time kissing her tenderly. "Stop complaining. I was kidding. You know I care about you."

"Sometimes I don't believe you."

He caressed her long, thick hair, whispering, "*I missed you, babe.*"

"It's only been a couple of days."

"Too long." His voice had become husky.

"I missed you too," Maggie admitted. "All I do is think of you."

This time she was ready for his deep kiss and accepted his tongue eagerly. If he took her breath and she died, it would be worth it. Rafy breathed life into her with his kisses. She could feel his hardness against her soft body. A perfect combination.

Rafy skillfully pressed her down to her knees with one hand, while unzipping his jeans with the other. *Oh, baby, give me what you got.*

Maggie willingly submitted on bended knees and accepted him into her mouth. Accepting all the love he gave.

After his last shuddering gasp, Rafy pulled her up. Maggie tried to put her lips to his, but he turned his face away.

"Come on, Rafy, kiss me. *Please*."

Instead, he laughed. "See that?" He pointed to the coat closet. "I'm gonna hide you in there. Whenever I want you, all I have to do is open the door and take you out."

This time he kissed her neck, catching her pale skin between his sharp teeth.

"Don't," Maggie whimpered.

Rafy interlaced his fingers in her hair and then pulled back harshly. "Remember, babe, if you tell your mother, I'll kill your grandmother."

Maggie's eyes widened.

He paused and then nuzzled her neck again, but this time gently. "Don't look at me like that, sweet stuff. I told you I love you."

Maggie nodded.

"I'm coming over for dinner. Not a word, okay?"

"You don't really love her, do you? My mother said that you two are getting married. In Las Vegas."

"Don't be jealous. I've got lots of love to give. There's enough of me to go around." He took her hand and pressed it against his crotch, which was beginning to bulge again. "This is for you, babe—just not right now."

Maggie remained quiet.

"And don't be sitting at the table looking at me with that *like-you-love-me* bullshit. It's getting late; you better go."

Maggie nodded. "My grandmother is waiting. I have to help her wrap the empanadas." She paused. "You wouldn't really do anything to her, would you?"

Rafy laughed again. "Save one for me, okay? I'll see you later."

Maggie left as quietly as she had arrived. *Abuela* was waiting.

16

Remember the beach

According to the clock, I had slept through the night, although I felt as if I had just closed my eyes. No more pills and no more all-nighters with Jeff before traipsing all over the City. But my head did feel clearer this morning. I hurried to change the sheets. Frank would be here in a few minutes. Neither of us had to get to work until four o'clock.

I raced against time showering and had just finished dressing when Frank came into the apartment. I scanned the room and prayed that Jeff hadn't left anything behind.

We sat in the living room. Frank unclipped his piece from his waist and placed it, still in its holder, on the glass coffee table. I should have been used to it but wasn't. I hated when he did that. Frank immediately started questioning me about his grandmother and all the details of the preceding afternoon.

"You know, I'm a little sick of how you're always asking me about every little detail of my life that goes on when you're not around," I said. "You're always grilling me."

"Again with the griping?" He curled his lip in annoyance. "All I did was ask you a question."

I was getting all mixed up and felt like banging my head against the wall, except I couldn't risk more injury.

"Read my lips," I said. "I saw your grandmother. Ask the nurse there if you don't believe me. I can't help it if she has Alzheimer's. I bet she doesn't even remember you."

"Really? It took you that long to go into the City and

spend, how long, a half hour with her?" Frank cracked his knuckles, knowing that the sound grated on my nerves.

"If you're so worried about her, I think *you* should go see her. I got sick to my stomach. I had to take my time."

My mind drifted back to the sea of white wedding gowns that floated by me on the street. I remembered the old man's warning. I made a mental note to hide the business card and the statue of St. Michael. I didn't want Frank to know about a lot of things, especially Jeff. I had to be careful. He would kill me if he found out what I was doing. Right now, I had become my biggest problem; it wasn't Frank.

I softened. "What I mean is that I know that you love your grandmother," I managed to say. "It must be hard for you to see her like that."

Frank burst into tears. "She doesn't even know me anymore. She gets upset when I go. The doctor calls it 'agitated' when she starts pushing me. She thinks I'm my father. *Abuela* always hated my father. That bastard was never around. It was because of him that my mother is the way she is."

This was the closest to him admitting something was wrong with her, but he still stuck up for her as though she were the Blessed Mother. The tension in the back of my neck started creeping upward. The doctor had showed me the different spots where I'd taken blows to my head. Some of them were old. Some of them were from before Frank. My mother, like Frank's, never seemed to know the limits of disciplining a child. Sometimes all Frank and I had was each other. Dulce once told me it wasn't right to love someone out of pity, unless it was yourself.

I still had a question I needed to ask.

"Frank, who is Adela?"

Like a shot, he changed the topic and started stroking my face and neck. "Forget about that. We have more important things to do. Remember what I came here for, babe."

Despite myself, I became aroused, but I didn't want to chance his seeing the friction burn on my lower back. I had to stop him, and quickly stood up with my hand outstretched toward him.

"Why don't we go to the beach?" I suggested. "The sun is out. It'll be nice to spend time there together. It's not going to last."

"What do you mean it's not going to last?" The urgency in his voice was thick. "We're engaged, aren't we?"

"I don't mean us. I mean the weather, silly." I really did feel sorry for him. He was like a big kid. Frank loved me. It wouldn't be right for me to be intimate with Jeff again.

Frank took my hand and got up, pulling me close to him. He kissed me on the neck and began moving closer to my breasts. "You smell really good. I could eat you up."

"That does sound good, babe, but the beach. Remember the beach."

"Let's go, then," he agreed. "Hurry up. We don't have all day."

I got our jackets and together we walked down the stairs.

I tried once more. "You don't know who Adela is?"

"No," he answered curtly.

It was probably better that I drop the whole topic for now. I'd come back to it when he wasn't so touchy.

"Are you coming back here after work?" I asked.

"No," he said. "I've got some things I need to do."

I was relieved, but part of me wished he would tell me more about what he was doing. If I was going to be his wife, he shouldn't keep secrets from me.

"Come on," he said. "Get your tight little ass in gear."

When we arrived at the beach, I thought of the last time we were there and how he acted when I told him that I wanted to end our relationship. He had become so angry. Today I sat next to him with the elegant, sparkling diamond on my finger. We held hands as we sat on the wooden planks of the bench. The sun was strong and comforting. I loved overlooking the water. A few people strolled behind us on the boardwalk and several were on the beach near the shoreline. Autumn in Coney Island was the best time of the year.

I snuck a peek at Frank. His eyes were closed and he looked relaxed. It made me feel calm to see him this way. I rested my head on his shoulder and took a deep breath, closing my eyes too. Sometimes I felt so secure when I was with him.

"Maggie, want some of these?"

I opened my eyes to see that he had his palm open under my nose. Different-colored pills. The white ones, I wanted the white ones. My mouth started to water, but I knew I should stay away from them.

"We don't really need these," I said.

"No, we don't." He agreed with me so easily. "We don't need them, but we like them, don't we?"

The twist. True. I nodded.

"Come on, take one or two. Lady's choice." He laughed softly, then kissed me full on the lips.

I took two and put them in my mouth. The slightly bitter taste would disappear in a minute and any bitterness I felt would also disappear. I could count on that.

A few minutes later, I was in a light sleep with the sun's warmth on my face. I felt fine and grateful for all the beauty that surrounded me. The gulls were shrieking, but the sounds were far away. When I sat alone on the boardwalk, I could never fully unwind the way I wanted. Sitting with Frank, I allowed myself to go under. I was there, but differently. My imagination soared, and it seemed that the boardwalk was suddenly busy and there were plenty of people walking back and forth.

People were strolling, wearing old-fashioned garb. The women wore long coats over their dresses, high-button boots, and large hats. A few had feathers sticking out of the ribbons above the brims. The men were dressed like dandies, carrying walking sticks and wearing bowlers. One of them came close to me, and I knew that if I reached out and touched his handlebar mustache, it would be silky to the touch. He winked at me and gestured for me to follow him.

Frank was snoring lightly. I got up to follow the gentleman. Just as when I opened the journal, it seemed I had no self-will.

"Missy," he said. "There's somebody here who wants to meet you."

I stood in the middle of Luna Park not knowing how I had gotten there so quickly. The crowd parted for us to walk through. I was a celebrity. Maybe it was Ellen who was waiting for me. Just yesterday, her energy had merged with mine. The nineteenth century-type clothing was right. Maybe I would find Ellen here, or find that, in fact, she was now me. I was confused but loved this feeling.

"Ellen?" I sounded her name aloud.

"Pardon me? Sam, the name is Sam," he said, while taking his hat off and bowing to me with a flourish. "At your service. Come along."

We walked farther, into the amusement area. There were colorful kiddie rides, music from a calliope, and children eating mounds of pink cotton candy on paper sticks. One little boy wore knickers under his serge sailor coat and hat. This was as vivid as the dream I'd had of the masquerade ball. There was a stand filled with sticky red candied apples. The salted air filled my nose. I was at a genuine carnival, and it was spellbinding.

Sam stopped suddenly and I bumped into him. He turned, and up close I could see every pore and crevice on his craggy face. His smile revealed brown stains on his teeth. There was a clay pipe peeping out of his jacket pocket.

"This is where I let you off," he said, winking at me for the second time.

In front of me stood the hulking figure of a gypsy fortune-teller encased in a large glass booth. Everything was so vibrant and colorful, almost larger than life. A golden bandana covered the male statue's head and a goatee covered his chin. A sardonic smile was plastered on his face, showing teeth that resembled Chiclets. The tunic he wore was of white silk and reminded me of something that Sinbad would wear. All that the mannequin needed was a sword. It had to be inside the booth where I couldn't see it. I knew that he had to have one by his side, and I stood up on my toes to peek over the shelf in front of the form.

Sam started to leave but not before reminding me to put a coin in the slot. "It's time to get your fortune read, Missy!" The next instant, he was gone.

I fished into my pocket and pulled out a quarter. I didn't usually have change on me but, inexplicably, there it was. I pushed my quarter into the slot. Nothing happened. I grabbed a second coin out of my pocket and did the same. This time I could hear the mechanical grinds begin to whir.

The large hands moved very slightly and made a pretense of shuffling the cards displayed in front of it. This wouldn't be a real psychic reading. It was a game. A gadget that couples on dates threw money at. Women hoped that a reading would somehow entice their beaux to marry them. Men desired a card that would foretell that a windfall of cash was on its way. I knew better but still believed that it would tell me something I needed to hear, a special message.

The figure's eyes met mine. They were glassy and a strange light color of blue, out of context to its swarthy skin tone. His eyes bore into mine and I couldn't turn away. It seemed that the smile was becoming larger. I wanted to leave. Frank would be angry that I'd left his side.

The machine started clanking and I heard a voice. It had to be a recorder of some type. It couldn't be the waxen figure's real voice.

"Your fortune is mine for the telling and yours for the healing." The voice was deep and heavily accented. "What is your question?"

"My question?"

"You've come to me for a reason. What is your question, Maggie?"

How did the mannequin know my name?

"You've put your coins into the slot and now you must give me your question, Maggie."

"I don't know!"

The sun began to drop over the horizon. The sea winds began to blow. The clouds gathered at an astonishing rate in the quickly darkening sky. The walkers had disappeared and I saw that I was alone with the fortune-teller. His goatee was bushy and thick, and I knew him from somewhere. I couldn't place him, but I knew him.

"Your question, Maggie! Maggie!"

Frank stood in front of me. His hands were on my shoulders and he was shaking me. I struggled to open my eyes.

"Where the hell did you go?" he asked. "I thought you passed out. You're such a pain in the ass."

"What? I was here," I said. "Where else would I be?"

I was sitting on the wooden bench on the boardwalk, just as I had been. There was no carnival or calliope or fortune-teller. There was no man by the name of Sam leering at me. Frank tightened his grip on my shoulder.

"Stop. Enough already," I said. "I'm awake. You're hurting me."

"What the hell? You can't take a couple of sticks? What have you been doing? I know you. I know that you can do more than two pills."

I rubbed my left shoulder, which still hurt from that day on the boardwalk. I'd been so focused on my head that I hadn't realized my shoulder had been injured too.

"Maybe we need to stop using," I said. "Take a break from each other, just for a while."

"What is this? Déjà vu? Is that what I have to look forward to when we come here? You telling me that we have to stop?" He grabbed my chin and squeezed. "I tell you when we're done. Got that?"

"Yes."

"And we both have to work."

It took me a moment to get my balance. I had awakened from a deep dream into a nightmare. My watch said two thirty. I couldn't account for the time loss.

Predictably, Frank was angry again. "What's wrong with you? Are you dizzy or something? Didn't you have breakfast?"

"You woke me from a dream."

"That's bullshit."

"No, it's not. I've been dreaming about Ellen. About her life."

"Who's Ellen?"

I hesitated. "She wrote the journal I bought at the flea market."

"A book? You're dreaming about Ellen who's in a book? Stupid."

"She's more than that."

"Just shut up," he said, and put his arm around my waist, moving me forward on the wooden-slatted surface as if I were a doll. "Let's go get some pizza. We've got to be in good shape for work."

I nodded.

Frank insisted we take the Escalade over to Totonno's. Like always, Point A to Point B. It had been way too long since we were there. This could be a date if

I wanted to make it one. I just had to adjust my attitude. The evening at Gargiulo's flashed before me. I wondered when those visions would finally fade.

When we arrived, the hostess escorted us to a table right away. We made ourselves comfortable. The last time we'd come, we had to wait on line outside for about a half hour. I took a picture of us together with my smartphone as we waited for our pie. I'd send that photo to my mother next time she started asking questions about what I was doing. The couple who sat next to us was intent on their pie. The crust was thin and the aroma of the sauce was tantalizing. I gazed at the newspaper articles about Totonno's that were plastered all over the walls.

"Maggie! What a surprise."

I shifted my eyes to see Dulce and Jeff standing in front of our table. My face flushed and my cheeks burned. Just a couple of days ago, Jeff and I were making love, and today he was with Dulce.

"Hey, didn't expect to meet up with you guys here."

"Why is that, Dulce?" Frank asked. "Why are you so surprised to see us?" He was immediately on the defensive.

"Hey, Brooklyn's happens to be a big place," I jumped in. "Totonno's is a not-so-big place. Want to sit with us?" Frank dug his fingers into my thigh under the table, making it clear that he didn't want them to sit with us.

"No, thanks, we don't want to intrude." Jeff shook his head. "But thanks for the invite. We're going to pick up a pie and walk over to the boardwalk. Dulce promised me that I would love Coney Island. Would you believe that I haven't really been out there yet? The hospital is the only place I've gotten to since starting my residency. She said it's about time I got to know the lay of the land and not just the hospital."

"Oh, nice," I said. "Just watch out for the seagulls; they love pizza."

The image of his body melded with mine was powerfully strong in my mind's eye. I wondered if he had also made love to Dulce. Maybe it should have made sense to me, but it didn't. I wasn't feeling humiliated any longer; my feelings were now turning to jealousy. Frank was right when he called me an idiot. Jealous over some Hick Town guy.

"We'll leave you two alone. See you at work, Maggie?" Dulce seemed uncomfortable and her eyes darted around the room, making no contact with mine. We hadn't really made peace the night that Frank had come onto the unit.

"Yes, sure, see you later," I said.

I watched them pay for and pick up their order. They turned back to wave at us before leaving the restaurant. My head started hurting again.

"What's with that guy?" Frank's expression was tight. "I see the way he looks at you."

"He wasn't looking at me."

"Go ahead. Play that game. It's not gonna get you anywhere. I'm not sure exactly what's going on, but you can be sure that I'm gonna find out if there's something to this. You know I've been upset about my grandmother. We're supposed to be out here relaxing, and instead I find out that I can't trust you for shit."

I kept my mouth shut.

"Eat." Frank shoved a slice toward me. "I brought you here to eat, so do it."

194

The pizza tasted like cardboard. We finished our slices in silence.

⧗

I was summoned by the journal again and opened it without a second glance at the clock.

📖

April 12, 1905

My, but I have neglected these pages! Movement has been so swift. I barely have time to breathe. My wardrobe is filled with pretty dresses, glorious gowns, and boots of the softest leather. Even Miss Isabel would envy me. Tom loves me and I care for him deeply. He said that acting as a gypsy fortune-teller is unbecoming to me and moved me into my own apartment. He explained quite candidly that although I am his lady, he is married, and had committed to his wife before knowing that I existed. Otherwise, I am certain that he would have married me under the eyes of God and the Law. I promised not to trouble him with such trifles. He is a loving and devoted man. His wife's (I abhor writing this word when the title does not belong to me, I daresay!) health is a concern and he does not want to frighten her or sicken her further with legalities. I am perfectly willing to remain here in my apartment with the beautiful white and gold furnishings. I was saddened to know that I couldn't bring my Mary to live with me. It is a bit lonely, but I do understand. I spend whatever time I can visiting with Ruby on the days that he is with his frail wife.

May 15, 1905

Although Tom made certain that I am no longer telling fortunes, I do feel as though I am still the gypsy. Her spirit stirs in my heart. I walked to the shore today and was pulled close to the waves. I took care not to wet my skirts, as dried salt on my garments would likely anger Tom. He has paid a fortune for my clothes and my care. I wear my hair in an upswept fashion now. No longer do I wear it long on my shoulders, other than when I am ready for bed. I am almost used to his touch on my skin. It often does not remind me of Karl. It pleases me to please Tom. He seems so gratified after he is spent from an afternoon in my bed. He says that one day I will be pleased too and that what we do is love in its purest form. I hope that on the day I find true pleasure in his body, I will believe those words. Ruby gave me a dark look when I told her that. She reminded me that to depend on anyone is to be in peril. I wonder if this is what Miss Woodhull meant about free love.

August 8, 1905

Tom sharply reminded me to keep my place today. I am well aware that I am not his wife. After that, we made up and had tea together. We read in the sitting room and the light from the setting sun cast a glow over him. I am so fortunate to have such a handsome companion at my side.

October 5, 1905

The night at the opera was incomparable to any other event that I've ever attended in my life. Sometimes my

Tom is unkind, but I am grateful for the wonders that he has shared with me. I must remind myself how hard the work of washing and cleaning for someone else is. I am independent now. Am I not? I would like to ask Miss Woodhull. She had been married to Mr. Woodhull and Mr. Blood. I wish I could ask her the true reasons she divorced those men.

November 21, 1905

Ruby tells me that I can walk away of my own volition. Tom is quite kind to me and it is only on the rare occasion that he slips and presses my lower back too hard or grabs my arm callously. My flesh is soft and bruises too easily. My love would never knowingly do something that would harm me. His love is too great. I am becoming more adept at pleasing him in our private quarters. He asked me if I have been entertaining someone else here in these rooms when he is away tending to business or his family. But then he somewhat apologized, calling his words a joke of sorts. I am baffled by his insecurity. I must show him that I love him.

December 3, 1905

As if in a dream
I stand by the window
Peering through sheer panels
That filter the night sky
The neighborhood children
Point at my shadow
I hear their refrain
Ghost!

197

Ruby turned over the Death card. Her laughter was harsh as she explained that this does not mean I will die. She said it means that a transformation from the old ways is at hand. I was frightened by the chill that brushed against my arms. What is it that is going to change? Will I be alone again? The distance I felt from Ruby was disturbing, especially when she reminded me not to be dependent on anything. I gathered my cloak as a lady would and left the storefront with a heavy heart. I feel the stirrings of disquiet. Ruby's features took on a sad expression and I gave her a quick hug before departing, and a promise to heed her words.

March 2, 1906

It is truly awful, this turn of events. Ruby is gone. The sign hangs from its hinges, but the storefront is empty. I am in great despair as to the reason she felt it unwise to share her plans with me.

March 5, 1906

The wind slices through me
I become slivers of ice
Afloat on the swelling sea
This green glass merely
a mirror of my dismal inner world
Reflecting a betrayal
I am at a loss
Alone

March 8, 1906

I cannot go home again. Tom thought it was amusing that Ruby had disappeared. He laughed as coarsely as she did on that last day of cards. I am baffled as to why he treats me in this way when he professes to love me.

April 23, 1906

I believe that I will cease to pour my energy into this journal. I am not a weakling.

May 18, 1906

The evening was again filled with the beauty captured by the moon, the lights of Luna Park, and the boardwalk. The smell of the ocean pulled me close to the sea and I ran down to the shore as the waves called out to me. I heard my name clearly in the wind. Tom argued that he didn't hear anything and pulled me back, admonishing me that I was becoming overly excited. I felt exactly that. Excited and feverish. The waters are my emotions. They tell my story as they move against the shore. If I were to lie on the sand, the wind and the waters would cover me as a blanket covers a child and I would be at peace. He told me that he will have me committed to a sanitarium the next time I attempt to run past the first waves. I am being called. I am being called. He does not understand this, and I have no words to explain it to him.

May 24, 1906

How is it that one moment I am in ecstasy and the next I

199

am floating in despair?

June 1, 1906

No forwarding address. Did she mean to hurt me in this way? Rosa disappeared as did Ruby. They no longer exist.

June 9, 1906

He struck me today and said that it was to remind me from where I come. He advised me to pay heed to him. He is short of patience. My face is reddened and raw. My skin stung when I applied balm to bring the swelling down.

June 11, 1906

Tom insisted that I accept his apology. I am not happy and am certain that something worse will happen soon. I have no one to converse with about these happenings. Miss Isabel would be horrified, but she is not to be counted upon, living abroad as she is. Momma is tending to her own welts. The children are children. Ruby is gone. It is she whom I mourn for the most—after myself.

August 12, 1906

If these words are read by another, I beg your pardon. That you may not suffer as I. Not by the physical duress upon my being, but by the slow demise of my soul.

📖

I had no words. Chills prickled my arms. I closed the book. It had become a novel. This time when I put the book away, I hid it under some blankets at the foot of the bed. Ellen's story had become my story.

The phone rang. Frank. I placed it under my pillow to muffle its sound. I needed some time away from him and I needed to get ready for work. I was on shift in less than half an hour.

"It feels like I haven't been here in a month, almost like I've been on vacation." I put my bag in one of the drawers in the nurses' station. I hoped this would keep me from going to the locker room to sneak more of the pills I had in my bag. I didn't want to lose my job.

Grecia sat in front of me at the station. "A day off and you feel like you've been on vacation? You need to book a real flight. We've been so busy here."

"You know what I mean," I retorted. Here for five seconds and Grecia was already on my nerves.

"We got her up today," Mrs. Graham's voice piped up. She stood next to the nurses' station while I stared at the telemetry monitors the technicians had placed there earlier in the day. We were now housing a small step-down unit. The administration had agreed to transfer patients to a few rooms near the nurses' station because of a breakout of MRSA in the unit downstairs. The changes added to the chaos on the unit.

"Who?"

"Five twelve. Miss Landry."

The day nurse had reported earlier that there was an attempt at removing Amy Landry from the ventilator, but she was still dependent on it for each breath that kept her alive. I didn't believe Mrs. Graham, and stood mute.

"Miss Fuentes? I'm talking to you." Mrs. Graham glared at me. "They disconnected her this morning. I'm doing two shifts. I was with her all day."

"You're telling me the exact opposite of what the outgoing shift reported just a little while ago." I couldn't conceal my accusatory tone. "Is she all right or not?"

There was madness surrounding me with the intensive care patients on the unit and a mistake might easily have been made. I couldn't blame anyone for that. I might have made the same error.

"Well, she sat up, but she's not really talking. The tubes—you know how that goes. Her throat is sore and she was pretty irritable."

"The tubes are out? She was sitting up?" The information was unbelievable. "Is she back in bed now? Why aren't you with her?"

Mrs. Graham flashed her Cheshire Cat smile. She turned her back to me and strode away on her rubber heels.

My fury quickly mounted and I had only started the shift a few minutes earlier. I had no idea what I would do to keep myself calm for the next eight hours. The small tin pill container that Frank had dropped in my bag flashed before me. I struggled against going for it. Instead, I got up to get a glass of water.

"On a break?" Dulce stood in front of me. "Didn't you just get here?"

"I don't need another police officer in my life. Frank is enough," I said, in what I hoped was a light tone. I needed to break the ice that was thickening between us. "I'm kidding."

"Why are we like this?" Dulce extended her hand to me. "We're best friends."

"You're right." I squeezed her hand briefly in response.

"Are you mad?" she asked. "Is it because I had lunch with Jeff?"

"No. What kind of question is that? Why would I be angry about that?"

"There's something not right here," she said.

I interrupted her. "Look, I have to check on my patient. Can you sit and watch this monitor while I go in? Marie will be back soon."

"Sure, I can do that, but I'm still not convinced everything's okay between us. We have to talk. There's something wrong here. You know what I mean."

"Honestly, I don't," I said, but I knew exactly what she was talking about. I wanted to get close to Dulce again, but part of me was resistant.

Before I went into Miss Landry's room, I got my bag out of the drawer and went into the nurses' lounge. That same craving had taken hold of me again. I dug in my bag for the tin holder. I opened it. Frank hadn't let me down.

By the time I reached Room 512, I felt like I was walking on air. It had to be a placebo effect. There was no other explanation for feeling so well so quickly. All my anxiety and thoughts about Dulce or anybody else were gone. *Pure tranquility.*

Miss Landry was lying on her back, still in traction. The ventilator was pumping oxygen into her lungs. I had no choice but to confront Mrs. Graham. She was such a liar, and I couldn't figure out what she had against me. I was glad that I had taken something to calm me down.

The nurse's aide was sitting in a chair near the window with her back to me. "Mrs. Graham, excuse me." I reached out and touched her shoulder, and she turned.

"Sorry, Miss, she's off tonight," a woman I'd never met before answered. "I'm on one-to-one here. I'm Joan Fitzgerald, from Pediatrics."

"You're floating from Peds?"

"You know how it is; that unit is always half empty."

"Sorry," I said. "I thought you were her."

The woman shrugged and blinked. Her expression was blank.

"Mrs. Graham was here the last few nights," I said. "I was mistaken. You both have red hair."

"Would you like to help me give Miss Landry skin care? I can do it by myself, but it would be easier with the two of us."

"Sure."

I put the siderail down while Ms. Fitzgerald went for fresh linen and a skin-care kit. I looked into Amy Landry's face and the bile backed up into my throat. A decaying smell came from her mouth and her lips were chapped and peeling. She was decomposing while still alive.

"Doesn't look like this one is going to make it." Ms. Fitzgerald had returned and must have seen my look of horror. "Do you know why she tried to kill herself? She might have actually succeeded. It doesn't look like she's long for this world."

"There's still hope," I said. "She's alive."

"But she smells so foul."

"It could be an infection around the tube. We can have a surgical resident come up and take a look at her. She might just need a tracheostomy tube, that's all. It's not good to have an endotracheal tube in a person's mouth for days on end."

"Whatever you say, Miss Fuentes."

The aide expertly provided skin care for Amy. The skin on her buttocks was reddened and darkish right at the sacral area. That wasn't a good sign. It reminded me of the scrape I had on my own rear from my night with Jeff.

We were done in only a few minutes. Amy looked peaceful, but the odor coming from her mouth made my stomach turn. The least I could do was call the resident to get a surgical consultation ordered. The residents never came close to the patients when they were on rounds. They usually stood at the foot of the bed, where they read the patient's vital signs sheet. I would be the one to clue them in; it was part of my job, and probably one of the things that I did best. I could always point out what others needed, while I missed my own needs by a long shot.

"Please do me a favor, Ms. Fitzgerald. While I'm doing this, would you go to the station and have the clerk page whoever is on call? They need to check on this tube right away."

The woman hesitated and stood at the other side of the bed.

"Is there something wrong?"

"No, ma'am. I'll be right back." She put the clean sheets she held in her arms down on the chair and left the room silently.

I finished putting lotion on Amy's feet. The bottoms were dry and cracked. *Had they been like that when she jumped? Had Amy been taking care of herself? What would have made her decide to throw herself out of the window?*

My voice competed against the sound of the ventilator. "Amy, it's me, Maggie, your nurse for tonight. I'm putting lotion on you, so that when you get better, your feet will be nice and soft. There's nothing worse than dry feet." She must have felt terribly alone when she'd tried to kill herself.

I laid the sheets out lengthwise on the bed and pushed them close to her body. When I moved her in the opposite direction, it would be a snap to pull them out from underneath her to make the linens wrinkle-free. As I tucked them under her, I felt her body resisting. It had to be my imagination. There was no way she could do that. She'd been unconscious for the last several days. The early signs of her stirring had stopped. The possibility of her improving was highly unlikely, but there.

"Amy," I instructed. "I'm putting some nice dry sheets under you. I'm going to put your hand on the railing. Try to hold on when I do this." I took her hand and closed her palm and fingers around the metal siderail of her bed. For a moment they stayed closed around the rail. Then her fingers relaxed again.

"Good job, Amy. I promise to help you get better. We're in this together."

The surgical resident walked in with Ms. Fitzgerald.

"Hi, Maggie. I was at the desk when I heard that the patient needed a trach. Ms. Fitzgerald was just about to page me. How's that for luck?" He winked at the aide, who blushed as red as her hair. "We'll get her on the OR schedule as soon as possible."

"I think she's awake, Doug," I said. "She held on to the rail for a minute when I turned her over. Maybe we should wait."

"No, you were right to call us. The smell in here is awful. I'm surprised no one mentioned it before. Infection. I want to culture that to see what antibiotic we should prescribe, but we'll start her on a broad-spectrum right away." He pulled a couple of culture packets out of his pocket and took a sample of the secretions from around the tube. "She's pretty young, isn't she?"

"About my age."

"A shame, isn't it?" The doctor was out of the room before I had a chance to answer.

"Did you ever feel like doing yourself in, Miss Fuentes?" the nurse's aide asked solemnly. She had none of Mrs. Graham's attitude.

"I don't think so," I said. There were many times I had flippantly said that I'd rather be dead than do a certain thing, or that life wasn't worth living after a fight with Frank or an argument with my mother. I didn't mean that I didn't want to live. It was just something that I said.

"My brother killed himself," Ms. Fitzgerald offered.

I was surprised at her admission. "That must have been terrible for you—and your family."

"He was high on drugs," she said. "LSD. We were young. It was a long time ago. He thought he could fly. He couldn't."

"I'm sorry to hear that," I answered, unsure of what else to say to her. I finished tidying up the sheets for Amy.

"You survive, you know. Once you figure out that you're not meant to die. You survive."

Her face had taken on a somber cast. She must have thought about suicide too. Again, I was tongue-tied.

Ms. Fitzgerald picked up the dirty linen and began to leave the room. She turned back. "I'm glad this lady made it."

I nodded. "Me too."

The idea that someone would decide that suicide was the best choice floored me. Some people didn't act on it for religious reasons, or for the sake of their children, or for the glimmer of hope that something would change. Ms. Fitzgerald's brother had killed himself by accident because of the drugs he was taking. People said that substance abuse was a slow form of suicide. Was that what I was doing whenever I let Frank blow that smoke into my lungs or took a pill? I didn't want to die. I just wanted release. But, then again, I wasn't a substance abuser.

"Maggie?" Dulce stood next to me back at the station.

"Yes?" I'd managed to avoid her for most of the evening. The pills had worn off and my superwoman buzz had turned into low-level irritation at every beep from the telemetry machines and the glaring fluorescent overhead light.

"Want to hang out a bit after work?" she asked. "Get a sandwich?"

"A sandwich?"

"How about some drinks?"

"Drinks?" I asked. "It's late. I just want to go home and turn in."

"*Late? Did you actually say late?* Are you kidding me?" Dulce laughed softly. "We always went out after work for drinks or whatever. Just to hang and relax. You've changed so much."

"Not really."

"Sure you have."

"Haven't we already had this conversation?"

"Really," she pressed. "When was the last time we went out to a club? Had fun?"

"I've been busy," I said. "I'm in a relationship now."

"I know that probably better than anyone. It's not

about that. You know what I'm talking about, don't you?"

"Yes. You don't have to spell it out. I'm not an idiot."

"I never meant any—"

"You don't have to say it," I said. "It's about Frank. I get it."

Grecia hovered near the chart rack. I had to take this conversation somewhere else. There was no reason to have the whole hospital prying into my business. It was a small place and it was hard to keep anything private here.

"Let's go into the nurses' lounge," Dulce suggested.

"No, I have a better idea."

I maneuvered Dulce back toward Amy Landry's room. "We can talk in here. No one will hear us."

"This is exactly what I'm talking about." Dulce was exasperated. "You would never have had a conversation like this in front of a patient before."

"I know we say that unconscious patients can still hear, but really, have you ever experienced anyone coming out of a coma and saying anything about what they heard? No, I doubt it. This is the stuff that people make up so that they can write bestsellers."

"I don't get it, Maggie. You don't want to be close. You're ready to fight for the smallest thing—"

"I don't need to listen to this. You. You. What about you? Could you stop criticizing everything I do for a change? I'm getting sick of it."

Dulce backed off. "You're right. We had this conversation already." She brushed past me and left the room.

I sank into the chair. Where was Ms. Fitzgerald? I'd

forgotten that Amy was still supposed to be on one-to-one observation. Dulce was right. There was something wrong with me. I looked up to see that Dulce was back in the room.

"I'm sorry," she said, "but you're getting a client tonight from the SICU."

"Me?"

"I know you're busy." Dulce seemed only a tad sympathetic. "We're all overwhelmed, but you have the empty bed."

"What is it?"

"Not *what* is it. See what I mean? *Who* is it? That's the question."

"Right, right. I mean, *who* is it?" I couldn't help the sarcastic tone.

"Sonya Harris."

"Harris? You mean the woman who survived the carjacking?"

Dulce nodded. "They're planning to take her off the ventilator soon. She's brain-dead. They need that bed in the unit for someone waiting in the ER."

"And I get her?"

"She needs care too, Maggie."

"The two of them? How is it that I get to have the pleasure of caring for both Harris and Landry?"

Dulce's voice was hard. "It had to be one of us and, like I said, you have the empty bed."

"All right," I said. "Just give me a few minutes."

When I was sure she was gone, I went back into the nurses' lounge and riffled through my bag. I dug deep and felt for its rounded edges. My pill tin. I rubbed my fingers on it before pulling it out. I took a deep breath and opened it. Empty. I searched further and only found pill residue in the lining of my bag. I dropped the tin back in and hurried into the corridor.

The elevator door opened and the team emerged, pushing a hospital bed with a thin female figure in it. Sonya Harris—it had to be. A nurse pressed and released an Ambu bag. That apparatus was the only linkage between the client and life. Multiple intravenous tubes snaked from a larger catheter in her neck and were attached to bags hanging on a pole connected to the bed. I had to hurry and find a monitor for her IV drips. They should have waited for me to tell them I was ready before bringing her up. They didn't really care about my patient load or me. I saw that there was no bag for urinary collection. I had to be ready to keep her skin clean and dry, because urine practically ate through skin. The more ominous meaning was that, since she wasn't expected to live, we weren't measuring her fluid output as we were for Amy. Ms. Harris's condition had changed rapidly. Just a few days ago, she was the patient expected to survive. The only similarity between the two women was their age; there had been different treatment plans and expectations for each. All of that had apparently changed.

I endured taking the lengthy report from the specially trained nurse. Her eyes barely met mine as she spouted off Ms. Harris's latest blood gases and other vital signs, like her blood pressure and pulse, which were surprisingly excellent considering she would probably die soon.

After sharing the technological information, the nurse lowered her voice and confided, "We heard that Ms. Harris was the victim of a carjacking. I have a friend who lives in her area. She told me that it's a cover-up.

The rumor is that her husband staged it. He supposedly beats the daylights out of her."

"No witnesses?"

"No," the nurse said. "I know that I'm gossiping, and I really shouldn't be, but I thought it was interesting."

I had no desire to speculate. I was burning out on this job. I should have been a bartender. Just serve drinks and let what people said go in one ear and out the other. I could tell them to 'take that to your therapist' if they got too chatty. I wanted to turn my ears off and not listen to another person's tale of woe. Here it seemed that even if the patient wasn't telling me something, someone else would find a way to share their problems. I was done. I'd had enough.

After report, Dulce and Ms. Fitzgerald helped me get the client into her room. 514. Right next door to Amy Landry. It was probably easier to have them located close together. It would cut down on my running around.

Later that evening, despite all the chaos on the unit, I was finally able to sit and write my notes. Amy Landry was scheduled for a tracheostomy in the morning and I'd already started the intravenous antibiotics. Most of the other clients were snoozing or knocked out on pain medication. Sonya Harris was snuggled in her sheets. There was really no hope for her survival. Basically, her life had been taken but her body didn't know that yet. Sonya's lungs continued to expand and contract while her heart beat strongly. It would take her organs a while to get the message from her brain that life was over. I hated that I was used to this kind of thing. After seeing so much death, I thought, I must have become immune.

My back was stiff and I had a crick in my neck from

turning and tugging my patients. I stretched my arms and realized that at least my headache was gone. I decided to take a walk down the corridor to flex my muscles. When I reached the end of the hallway, I stood at the large picture window that overlooked the parking lot.

Frank was at the door of a burgundy sedan helping someone into the car. I saw her face clearly under the parking lot floodlights. *Ann Marie Arroyo. Pablo's wife.* My stomach turned. I had to confront them. I ran back to the nurses' station.

"Dulce, I have to run out for a minute."

"No way. I'm about to help put a line into one of my patients. You can't leave. You have to man the front, Maggie."

"I have to go," I insisted. "It's Frank."

"Don't tell me, he's harassing you again?"

"Not exactly," I said. "Now—I have to go."

"Where? What are you talking about?"

"Go look yourself. Hurry! He's in the parking lot with Ann Marie. It must be her car they're getting into."

Dulce walked out of the nurses' station to the window and returned a few seconds later, shaking her head. "There's no one out there."

"You missed them." A sense of defeat engulfed me. "They must have driven off. You didn't see a burgundy car?"

"It's your imagination. It's just like the other day, when you swore you saw them in one of the rooms. You're not right. Something's not right."

Joining Dulce at the window, I scanned the lot for a sign that I had really seen that car with Frank and Ann Marie. Other than the parked cars and a pearl-gray SUV cab unloading a very pregnant lady, the lot was vacant.

It hadn't been more than a couple of minutes, but he could have taken off at his usual speed.

The only reason Ann Marie had come over with that thong was to throw me off the track of her affair with Frank. They probably amused themselves by figuring out ways to keep things confusing for me. I saw things a lot more clearly than they realized.

The only one with a key to my apartment was Frank. He was the one who'd taken the thong out of my drawer and hung it up on the door hook. Frank loved to tell me that I was gullible, and laughed in my face whenever he said it. But there was a big difference between saying things like that and actively doing what he was doing with Ann Marie. I had to find a way to stop him. But it wasn't going to be tonight. I was like a dress that was tearing apart at the seams. My fear was that nothing could sew me back together, and I had to gather every bit of energy to focus on Sonya Harris, Amy Landry, and the rest of the patients in my division, even if that meant basting myself together.

Amazingly, the rest of the shift went by quietly. I could take vital signs, turn my patients, and give medication without blinking. There wasn't anything out of order, as far as I could tell. The only thing I had to deal with was the insatiable craving that ran through all my muscles and bones. I needed something to take the edge off, and somehow, when I looked up at the clock for the five hundredth time, I saw that my shift was over.

I left the hospital after giving report to the incoming crew. Frank was nowhere in sight and I took a cab for the short trip home. I poured cereal with almond milk into a bowl and lapped it up like a cat. I took a quick shower and crawled into bed. The journal was on the comforter, and I opened it and began to read. Why did I think I had placed it under my blankets? Maybe I was more out of it than I thought. The journal would have to be my sleeping pill tonight.

November 1, 1906

My landlady, Mrs. Danzig, heard sounds, she said, and crept up to my door. Because of this brave woman, I was awarded a short reprieve. It seems that only yesterday he was kissing my cheek. The curls that he said he loved now cover my bruised brow. He has accused me of wearing lip coloring and that I style my hair as would a harlot. The words are harder to bear than the stinging of his palm across my cheek. I have done nothing to warrant this. Mrs. Danzig squeezed my hand in a gentle manner and advised me to leave as quickly as I could. She warned that his behaviors may become worse. To what? What could be worse?

November 3, 1906

I've listened to Mrs. Danzig. This morning I bought my ticket and stored it in my old trunk. It will remain hidden from his prying eyes until my boat sails. I hide the ticket as I hide my feelings and my wounds. He must never suspect my plan.

November 16, 1906

I am in a state of raw nerves. I dropped my purse and

gloves onto the dirty snow that fills the road. Tom reminded me that I am a clumsy and feeble woman and that a lady would never consider going out into such filth. I reminded him that I was never a lady, and that it was only with him that I mistakenly believed that I was. He is wrong and he is cruel. My life has become a pretense. If only I could write a note to Mary, but if she were to hear from me, she may come looking for me. Even as I write this, I am aware that my thoughts are false. No one is looking for me. Once I accept that fact, I will be better off.

November 17, 1906

I am tired and my mind jumps from thing to thing. I have written lists of things that I must take care of before the boat sets sail on the morrow. I hid the list under the pillows on the divan when Tom showed up unexpectedly, as though he sought to catch me in the act of betrayal. He is eternally accusing me of entertaining gentlemen here in my parlor when he is away. That is ludicrous. My desire to be touched is almost entirely gone. Ruby said her first love's passion for her came second to his queasy stomach and he chose to stay across the seas. She admittedly felt nothing for most of the men who asked for her hand on this side of the ocean. The story should be amusing, but it is not. Where is Ruby? Why did she pack up and leave in such a hurry? I miss her terribly.

November 18, 1906

Anything can be bought for a price. Tad Relkin has agreed to meet me with his coach to take me and my *trunk to the pier. I cannot wait to be away from this horrible place. There has never been anything good for me here and I must leave. Even still, I will miss it. I will miss the ocean more than anything else, but I am going toward another seacoast town. Cape May. It will all be the same in some ways; the wind, the stars, and the salty breeze. I hope I will be able to make a new life and not made to worry about lowering my hat or veil over my face. I wonder whether Tom will miss me, or even has the capacity to do so. Maybe he will go to the gymnasium and swing at the punching bag or another daft man who will allow it for glory. I want no more of it.*

My eyelids were heavy and I could feel myself entering the dreamworld. I didn't want to be in either my world or Ellen's. I hoped that the dream would be a place where I could finally get away from these sordid realities. I walked in willingly.

18
Make this your friend

The walls that surrounded me were made of a smooth glass-like substance. I stretched out my arms, and my fingers glided along the walls, which were cool to the touch. It occurred to me that the walls were made of huge columns of clear quartz crystal. I was in a cave, a crystal cave. The floors and ceiling were also made of crystal. I walked deeper and deeper into the vault-like structure and felt a vibration that sent a thrill through my body. My physical being sang.

Further into the cave, I noted some activity. There was a man on a pulley holding an electric saw. It was harnessed onto his torso and seemed to be extremely heavy, because the man's body arched backward. He held the saw to the crystal and the teeth began to shatter one of the columns. The shriek of the metal teeth against the shaft of the quartz was agonizing. I placed my hands firmly against my ears, but the sound cut through even as I tried to protect myself. Chunks of crystal came crashing down, but the man was oblivious to the destruction he was bent on wreaking, despite the piercing sound.

"Stop!" I screamed as loudly as I could. "Please, you have to stop!"

Another large piece of crystal came crashing down, and the sound of metal against crystal was magnified to immense proportions.

The shrillness increased in intensity until it finally cut through my sleep. I turned over to shut the alarm clock off, but I couldn't reach the clock; I had set it out too far from my bed. I stretched out my arm and managed to hit the button, but the sound wouldn't cease. If it wasn't my alarm, it had to be something else, but I couldn't figure out what.

I got up and hobbled to the front door. I cracked it open, but there was no one there. The lights in the hallway flickered and buzzed. The elevator door slid open and I ran toward it. When I reached it, I saw that the floor to the elevator was missing and the shaft loomed wide open, inviting me to enter the black void. I stepped back, terrified, and turned to my apartment. The entire wall was smooth. The door was gone. *This can't be real*, I thought. I needed to get back into my apartment. I ran my hands across the wall, which began crackling under my fingers. A thin crevice appeared and I probed my forefinger in, stretching the opening wider and wider. I peered in and saw that I'd come to a dark lagoon within the cave. I felt myself being pulled inside, as though a huge magnet were behind the wall, and I withdrew my hand. Suddenly, I found myself back in my bed.

I'd been in a dream within my dream. The screeching sound continued, though, as I managed to fully wake up. The noise was real enough.

I shook the cobwebs out of my head and thought for a minute; perhaps the smoke detector next to the kitchen was the source of the ear-splitting noise. The ringing seemed to cut through my brain. I pulled a step ladder out of the broom closet and put it under the alarm. I climbed up to turn the alarm off and saw that the red light was steadily on. If it were out of order, the light would be blinking. *Where was the sound coming from?* It was insistent and pressing. I covered my head with my hands, afraid that my ears would explode. The sound was excruciating and reverberated through my head. I got down off the ladder and dropped to my knees. I sat there rocking, holding my head.

The ringing suddenly stopped. I shuddered and went limp with relief. I gathered my strength and went back to bed, pulled the comforter up over me, closed my eyes, and wept. My sense of release was strong, and I lay there for what seemed like hours. I must have gone back into a dream state, because I could hear murmurs near me. Soft voices, which were comforting, and I felt soothed rather than alone. I wasn't in a hurry to move. The fear that the shrill noise would start up again also kept me still.

Hours later, I opened my eyes to see that my closet door was open. I must have forgotten to close it when I put my clothes away before collapsing into bed the previous evening. The closet was as cluttered as my head. I got up to shut the door but stopped when the image of a box that I'd forgotten I kept in there popped into my muddled thoughts.

There on the shelf, just where I had left it, was the box that Frank had handed to me when we first got together. It was a gift 'just for being me,' with the explanation that he loved me so much that he didn't want anything to happen to me. The box was cumbersome because it was so heavy. I'd hidden it on the shelf where I could barely see it and not easily reach it. I looked around for something to stand on so that I could retrieve it.

A box filled with items that I kept meaning to donate to the local church was shoved under the hanging teal-blue evening gown that I'd worn once, to the annual hospital fundraiser. The sequined fabric reminded me of the exciting life I wished for but didn't lead. I attended only one social event that counted in the last year or so. I loved to dance, but these days I never stepped into a club. I climbed onto the carton and reached out my arms toward the box. My hands instantly became gritty; I hadn't taken anything off this shelf for a long time and it needed a wipe-down. I pulled the box toward me and took it down, placing it on the floor next to the lower shelves, which were filled with boots. I brushed my hands clean on my thighs.

Sitting on the closet floor, I looked around from a different perspective. I had so many items of clothing and pairs of shoes. Everything was hung neatly, but the place had become a collector's camp. I had several of everything I really didn't need. I dressed for Frank, more than myself. Colorful party dresses, gowns, satin shoes, leather boots, parkas, raincoats, turtlenecks, and bikinis filled the closet—something for every occasion. Dressing for my own tastes and interests was lost a long time ago. I was nothing but a doll for a fiend who claimed he loved me.

The box was the perfect size for a handbag. In fact, there had been a handbag in it when Frank gave it to me. He laughed when he saw my shock as I opened the soft, heavy leather bag decorated with rounded metal spikes. I would never have picked that style of handbag. He'd laughed again when I refused to take the *real gift* out of the bag, telling me that the silvery design would remind me of what was in the bag—as though I could ever forget—and yet, I had.

I pulled the Glock 9mm out and went to sit on the bed with it in my hands. I turned it over a few times, admiring its smooth, hard surface. It was compact but heavier than it looked. If I rubbed it like a magic lamp, maybe a genie would appear in a puff of smoke and grant me a wish, maybe even two. This was the first time I'd really looked at it since Frank had given it to me. When he first gave it to me, I shoved it right back into the handbag. He called me "cute," as though that was all I could be. Today, I didn't feel that way at all.

I reached into the tissue paper and rummaged around in it for another, smaller, box. I opened it and it was still tightly filled with bullets. I pulled one out and rolled the sharp point between my fingers. I thought of the afternoons we had spent at the range, Frank proudly showing me how to target precisely and shoot. I loved feeling his hard body pressed against my back, and would lean into him purposely. He'd rub his hardness against me. Back then I thought of him as my very own protective casing, a second skin, cushioning me from danger. His dark brown eyes twinkled when he reminded me to keep my focus and promised to give me everything I wanted when we fell into bed that afternoon. I looked forward to going home after these sessions and opening myself to him completely. I was wild for him in the beginning.

Today, Frank's instructions came back easily. I thought of all the things he had told me: "Keep it hidden unless you really need it" and "Make sure that whoever you're gonna shoot doesn't get to it first." He added, "If you don't do these things, you're a goner. Make this your friend. Better yet, act like it's your baby."

One day, he abruptly announced that I had gotten all the lessons I needed. We were at the range and he told me that I was "good enough." I must have looked disappointed, because he laughed at me and pretended to

223

chuck me under the chin. "What the hell have I created here?" he asked, before turning serious and making me put the gun back in the box. He never mentioned it again, and I wondered whether he remembered that I had it. Why the memory of it was so strong when I woke up today was a mystery. One thing I was certain of was that I would no longer forget to take care of it.

I was so angry at how things had turned out. Maybe he was tricking me and was waiting for me to find it again. He probably wanted me to use the gun on myself. It would be easy to shoot my brains out and leave them splattered across the wall. Let Frank be the one to clean up the blood stains. I had my share of doing it. Let him explain to his beloved officials why his loving Maggie was nothing but a bloody shell blown to bits.

"That's what you want," I said out loud. "You want me dead, and I do too."

I was suffocating in the closet. Stifled by my hoard of clothes. The most irrational part was that I wasn't even seeing Frank that much these days, and yet his energy burrowed in me like toxic mold. I put the gun back into the handbag, replaced it in the box, closed the top, and pushed it under the bed. I was too tired to wrestle it back up on the shelf.

I took a moment to close my eyes, took some deep breaths, and tried to do a calming exercise by imagining myself back at the shore. My mind's eye took flight. I stood on the sand and my toes curled into its warmth, but the wind was strong and brusque, pushing me into the surprisingly cold water. The frigid waves slapped against my thighs. The soles of my feet were stung by shards of shells that were hidden in the murky water. I was pulled farther and farther into the ocean by the undertow. The sun hid behind dense, thickening clouds and everything around me turned iron gray: the sea, the sky, my life. I took a few deep gulps of air and broke the spell of my meditation. I had no control. Not even in what should have been a calming reverie. There wasn't anything in my apartment for me but misery. I threw some clothes on, picked up my coat, and walked out the door.

⧖

Walking along Surf Avenue, I passed the flea markets and various sideshow stands that had been boarded up for years. The neighborhood was getting a facelift, but there were still barren lots filled with shrubs and dumped garbage. Few stores were open. The breeze was sharp and salty. My hair was being whisked all over the place. I felt burdened, but at the same time, I felt free.

I thought about Ellen and whether she had walked on this very street. I pretended that the Carousel's painted horses were spinning around, the old-fashioned riders holding on tight while gazing up at the twinkling lights. That was turn-of-the-century Coney Island, in its heyday. This avenue was now a ruin. I'd grabbed for coins from the Carousel, but I had never experienced the splendor of Dreamland or the grandeur of the incandescent Luna Park in the early 1900s. I wondered about the droves of people who strolled along while popping pieces of saltwater taffy into their mouths or nibbling at sticky pink or blue cotton candy. I thought about all the different attractions and how many visitors had stopped on their way to the Steeplechase to sit with Ellen or Ruby to hear their fortunes told.

No soothsayer was going to change me. I was the only one who could make a difference. A chill went up my spine as I thought about the last entries I had read in Ellen's journal. Perhaps she had not gotten away.

I continued to walk down the street and spotted some girls laughing on a stoop in front of a dilapidated two-story frame house. Most of the houses on the block looked as though they'd blow over with one fierce wind, but at least this one was full of life. The girls were joined by a couple of lanky boys who teased them. They seemed to take the bait and gave it right back to the boys. I enjoyed listening to their banter. A few doors down, a woman pushed a stroller back and forth while she watched two little ones jump rope. The colorful clips in their hair bounced as they hopped rhythmically. Music blared from a car cruising by with the windows down. I heard lyrics that I knew too well; Exposé singing 'seasons change, feelings change.' I was used to hearing their music from Frank's playlist. What had been beautiful was now something sad and hurtful. My desire for Frank to change back into who I originally thought he was hit me hard. *I couldn't wait for that to happen, but I could change.*

As I turned toward home, the thought of going into some type of recovery program popped into my head. I didn't really have a problem with alcohol or drugs, but it would be great to get away for a while. I wished I could enter a twenty-eight-day rehab just to get my head on straight and to heal my body. My apartment building was in the distance, and as I neared it, I chuckled to myself. The walk had made a positive difference. I felt better. That was all I needed. Once I got home, I'd start all over again. I wanted to be my true self, not this person I was becoming, who I didn't really like or know at all. I could always start my day over, and today would be the day.

19
Percocet, Vicodin, and Morphine

Feelings never last forever. By the time I got to the hospital, I'd practically forgotten about my self-positive talk. I pushed open the door to the medication room and began to think about Frank. Since he lived with his mother, I was hardly ever at his place. She never told me that I wasn't welcome, but the vibe was strong and I made sure that I paid attention to it. While I was relieved that I hadn't heard from him, I was also somewhat annoyed. I hated when he ignored me. And I still didn't know for sure whether I had imagined him getting into the car with Ann Marie the previous evening.

As these thoughts were twisting around in my head, Dulce pushed her cart into the room.

"Hey, you." I forced a smile. "Can we talk? There's a lot going on." I came out from behind the medication cart.

Dulce nodded but didn't say anything, and I was glad for that. I took a deep breath and went for it. "Look, you've got to know that things aren't right. I woke up with a ringing in my ears. It went away, but I'm worried about it. It started in a dream but wouldn't let up. I don't know if the dream started it, or, you know, when things on the outside get caught up in your dreams . . ."

She stared at me for a minute, then got busy with the narcotics cabinet lock. It was obvious that she was in the middle of something. I annoyed her repeatedly without ever following her suggestions. It would probably be better to just leave things be.

"Never mind," I said.

"No, go ahead," she said. "I'm listening."

Talking to her had to be the right thing for me to do. Besides, I had no one else to confide in.

"I'm worried," I whispered. "I'm afraid I'm going to end up like Ellen."

"Who?"

"Ellen, the lady who wrote the journal. Things are kind of haywire. I don't know what's real anymore and what's not."

Dulce's eyes flashed wide open. "What journal?"

"Didn't I tell you about it? Frank knows. We went to a flea market and I picked up a journal. I felt like it had picked me. It was written by this woman who was being treated terribly, first by her mother's boyfriend and then her own boyfriend. I mean, she was his mistress. I know it sounds confusing. I'm afraid to read any more, because, what if she doesn't survive?"

"I get it," Dulce murmured. "If she doesn't live, then you're afraid that maybe you won't either."

"I guess," I admitted. "I hadn't thought about it that way before . . . maybe . . . I think so."

"I want to be straight with you, Maggie. Just because the character of a book dies doesn't mean you will too. Your dying by Frank's hands is a more realistic scenario than that magical thinking kind of stuff. You're in danger and you know it."

"You're right. I have to do something about him."

"You can't do anything *about* him. You can only change the way you operate. You know that."

"Yeah, yeah, you're right. That's what I meant."

Dulce's eyes narrowed and she clenched her jaw tightly. She knew to stop talking. We hadn't really resolved anything after all.

"I have to give out some pain medication," she said.

"Excuse me, okay?"

"Yeah, sure."

I watched as she hurried to sign the narcotics book and left the room. Hearing her say the words 'pain medication' triggered something in me and I felt that familiar longing. The narcotics cabinet was stocked with Percocet, Vicodin, morphine, and other pills. The problem was that each tablet had to be accounted for and I'd have to sign for each pill.

"Maggie!" Jeff strode into the medication room. "I was hoping to see you."

"Hey, is something up?" The pills temporarily receded to the back of my mind.

"You're driving me crazy," he said. "All I do is think about you."

"Really? If you hadn't walked in on me just now, how would I know that?"

"I know I haven't called you—" he began to explain.

"I don't want to step in between you and Dulce. We've been friends for a long time."

"There's nothing between us. Believe me."

I couldn't trust his sincerity.

"Okay," he said. "Dulce and I went out a couple of times. Just for fun, that's all."

"Just for fun? Like me?" I couldn't help but wonder how intimate he'd been with her.

He gave a low whistle. "No, it's not what you think. It's nothing like that. You're special to me."

I didn't want to ask anything more. Today wasn't a day for figuring out what was real and what wasn't.

"Can I see you tonight?" he persisted.

"After shift, you mean?" I watched myself as I began planning the evening in my head. "No, I can't. My boyfr—fiancé will be around tonight. I don't want to take any chances."

He paused for a minute. "We can always go to my place."

"I thought you had a roommate situation."

"I do, but it's a two-bedroom."

"I don't know."

"I do," Jeff said. "We're good for each other." He came close to me and smelled so fresh. I needed freshness.

I nodded. "Eleven forty-five in the parking lot."

"I'm in the residence across the street," he said. "Just ring 12C when you get off. I'll be there."

"What about your roommate? Will he be there?"

"No. *He* is a *she* and she's away for a week. Family issues."

"She?" I asked. In my head, girls lived with girls and boys with boys, unless there was a relationship. I was so old-fashioned.

"Seriously, she's just a roommate."

"I guess I don't get out much." My attempt at a laugh was weak. "See you then."

"Can you get out any earlier?" he asked.

"I doubt it, but I'll try."

"See you tonight."

I started to leave the room, but my phone began to vibrate. I pulled it out of my pocket. It was Frank.

"What's up?" Listening to his voice after chatting with Jeff made me uncomfortable. There was no way I wanted to see him.

"I have to work late tonight," I said. "There's a woman in isolation, pretty sick, and I need to do one-to-one. There's not enough staff."

"Are you kidding?"

"No. Why would I make that up?" I asked. "Why don't you come over tomorrow morning?"

"No way," he said. "I'm not picking up whatever bug you might get being stuck in that room."

"I knew I couldn't depend on you."

"Yeah, well, you know how I feel about infections and contagious things."

I knew very well that he wouldn't want to be with me. I'd have the whole night with Jeff and not have to worry that Frank was looking for me. He'd be far from the hospital and the residence.

"I'm sorry," I said. "I'll connect with you tomorrow. I love you."

"Me too," he said. "But please, make sure you wash your hands—a lot. Okay?"

"Yes, don't worry. Bye." I turned off the phone and put it back into my pocket. I fought to concentrate for the rest of my shift. I had Amy, Sonya, and twenty other patients who were depending on me.

⏳

At exactly eleven thirty, I hurried to leave. Dulce was finally giving me a break. I told her that I was feeling under the weather. I turned back to wave but couldn't catch Dulce's eye. It was quiet outside as I left the building. Evening shift hadn't ended and that made it the perfect time for me to get to Jeff's without being seen. I rang his buzzer and he rang me in immediately; he must have been sitting on his intercom system.

The steel elevator doors opened and I was relieved that no one was inside. I couldn't think of an explanation if a supervisor or fellow staff member saw me. They'd want to know whom I was visiting, and I couldn't very well say I was going up to have sex with Jeff. Crazy. Anyone who knew me at work also knew that I was in a relationship with Frank.

I'd barely arrived at his door when he pulled me inside and slammed it shut behind me. He grabbed at my scrubs and pulled them down. He was already hard as he quickly entered me. I was pressed against the door and he placed his hand over my mouth when I asked him to stop.

When he was finished, he gave a short, apologetic laugh and managed to look at me sheepishly. "Sorry. I didn't mean to catch you off guard."

I pulled my pants up. "I'm out of here."

"Wait a second. Are you upset or something?"

"I have to leave."

"Come on, Maggie, lighten up." Jeff pulled the tie out of my ponytail and ran his hands through my hair. "You're beautiful. Don't be angry. Maybe I came on a little strong, but that's nothing to be mad about. We carve out a little time and we want to take advantage of every minute."

My gut told me I needed to get out, but then what? We both knew why I'd come up to the apartment.

"Do you have anything to drink?" I asked.

Jeff gave me a squeeze. "That's more like it. Let's start again, as though you just walked in, okay?"

I took a deep breath and tried to relax. "Yeah, sure."

Jeff went into the kitchen and returned with a couple of bottles of Guinness. He handed one of them to me. I tried to swallow, but it was harsh. I managed to get only a mouthful down.

"You're not a stout drinker, I take it?"

"No," I said. "But thanks."

He took me by the hand and we entered his bedroom. It was dark and the bed was unmade as he laid me down on it. This time he touched me slowly. Jeff's hands were soft; a surgeon's hands. His skill lifted me to another vibration. He explored places that Frank had forgotten existed and his tongue reminded me how much I'd forgotten I existed. I entered a void that pulled me in, and I never wanted to leave.

I dozed off and woke up just as the sun was rising. Jeff turned to me and began kissing my shoulder and upper back.

"Time to get up," he said.

"No, I don't want to go."

Jeff laughed. "I have rounds. Gotta go." He patted me on the rear.

"I don't remember the last time I was so relaxed."

"Seriously, we've got to go," he said, and threw his legs over the side of the bed. "How about tonight? You can come back."

"No, I can't."

Picturing Frank and his usual state of paranoia made me shiver. If I tried this again tonight, he'd go to the hospital to make sure that I was really taking care of someone. Once he found out that I was lying, the whole situation would blow up.

"I'm jumping in the shower," Jeff said. "There's coffee on; feel free to get a cup. The kitchen is down the hall to the left."

Jeff was obviously in a rush and I didn't want to hold him up. I found my clothes, which were scattered on the floor next to me. After I gathered everything and dressed, I sat back down to put on my socks and noticed a small gilt box on the nightstand. Next to it was a pair of amethyst earrings and a gold bracelet encircled with garnets. I opened the nightstand drawer and saw that the inside was filled with women's expensive lingerie. I quickly got up and pulled the bureau drawer open. It was filled with men's underthings. I followed my intuition and opened the door to the walk-in closet. It was huge, almost the size of a second bedroom. One side held a line of men's suits and shirts. Lower shelves held men's shoes, sneakers, and some sports equipment. The other side of the closet was filled with women's things: business suits, dresses, and pants sets.

I listened for the shower but didn't hear anything. He must have jumped out as quickly as he went in. "Jeff," I called out.

There was no response, so I headed toward the kitchen.

"So, who's the lucky lady?" I asked.

He stood at the counter pouring rich brown coffee into two mugs. "Lucky lady?" Jeff seemed baffled.

"Those women's things." I kept my voice steady. "In the closet."

"Oh, those belong to my sister, Hope."

"Hope?"

"There's a lot you don't know about me." He put a mug in my hand and kissed me on the nose. "I hate to rush you, but we've got to leave. People are going to be getting on and off the elevator. I don't think you want anyone spotting you."

I took a swallow and practically scalded my tongue. I put the cup down on the counter. "You're right."

I grabbed my jacket and left without making plans to get together again. I didn't believe Jeff. He was seeing me and dating Dulce. It was possible he was in a deeper relationship. His sister leaving lingerie in his nightstand didn't seem plausible. Maybe he liked wearing women's things. He was right; I didn't know much about him at all, but I couldn't focus on those details right now. I had to concentrate on leaving the residence without being seen by anyone.

Luckily, the elevator door opened right away. I pulled my collar up and put on a cap that had been crushed at the bottom of my bag. It would probably be worse if someone saw me this way. It was obvious I was trying to disguise myself. I practically cried when the elevator reached the lobby floor. Finally slipping out, I breathed a sigh of relief. No one had seen me. I hurried to the corner to hail a cab.

⏳

When I fit the key into the lock of my apartment door, it swung wide open. Frank was sitting there with his service revolver in his lap.

He rubbed his eyes. "Is that you? Or am I seeing things?"

I took a deep breath. "Of course it's me. I told you that I was working."

"Working?" he asked, while running his hand over the gun.

"I'm tired," I said. "It's been a long night."

"I agree with you on that. It has been a long night." He looked thoughtful for a minute, then he said, "Come close, babe, so I can smell you."

"Come on," I said, "you've got to be kidding. I smell awful. I wore that isolation garb all night."

He wiggled the fingers of his left hand toward me,

while his right hand stroked the gun. "You heard me."

There was no way for me to walk past him. The fact that I hadn't showered would turn this into a disaster. I was so worried about not having people see me that I had forgotten about protecting myself where it counted. I stood there paralyzed in place.

"Don't make me come get you, okay?" Frank said.

Somehow I found myself standing close to him. I must have moved involuntarily, because one minute I was at the door and the next I was gazing at the sheen of his hair. Beads of perspiration were intricately woven on each strand like a spider's web in the early morning dew. I was the spider's prey.

Frank took my hand with his free one and brought it to his nose. He put my arm back down at my side and smiled at me. "Scared?"

I couldn't even answer.

Frank pulled me down to his level and I hit my knees with a thud. He began sniffing at my neck.

"You're right. You do stink." The air whipped with his lips so close to my ear. "Who were you with?"

"Nobody."

"Really?" He smacked my baseball cap off and grabbed my hair, weaving the strands in his fingers.

"Really. I swear." I put my hand on his. "Please stop, Frank, you're hurting me."

"The least you can do is tell me the truth," he said, tightening his grip. "Or, better yet, do me like you do 'nobody.' You're such a lying bitch; did you think you'd get away with your lies?"

"No, Frank, I'm sorry. Please." I'd been with him long enough to know what came next.

My eyes were stuck together. When I finally pried them open, the room had a familiar gauzy texture to it. My head was throbbing again. I couldn't open my mouth. My lips were swollen and the bottom one was split. I didn't have to look in the mirror to recognize the familiar metallic taste. My mouth was lined with caked blood. I moved my tongue around my teeth to make sure that none of them were missing or loose. Thank God, they were intact.

I slowly got up and sat on the side of the bed. Waves of nausea and dizziness passed over me. I'd just started to get my bearings, when Frank walked in from the kitchen.

"Have a good sleep?" He pointed to the bathroom door. "I think you might want to shower now, because I've confirmed it. You do stink. Time to get ready for work."

I shook my head, trying to get clearer. *How long had we been here? What had he done this time?*

"I can't go like this," I croaked.

"Oh, yes, you can," he said. "You're devoted to your work, remember? Now, git."

I held on to the furniture as I made my way to the bathroom. At least I could walk. I climbed into the shower and the hot water felt like pellets against my breasts. There were deep purple abrasions covering my upper torso and fingerprint markings all over my thighs. I took the bar of soap and made a thin lather to wash between my legs. I cringed, anticipating the burn.

I opened my mouth under the shower and let the water cleanse my lips and mouth. When the water turned clear from its initial muddy color, I turned off the faucets and toweled myself off as gently as I could. It was over and I had survived. He had threatened me with his gun, but he'd never use it on me. One thing I was certain of; Frank would only go so far. He cared about himself too much.

If you're lucky

The coffee pot was doing a slow burn. The bitter smell permeated the assistant dean's office. Mr. Gerald leaned back in his chair and flicked off the blinking amber light. He quickly pushed forward again.

"You sit there like that and no one can help you," he said. They'd been there for about ten minutes and second period was almost over.

"I'm telling you that I didn't do anything." Frankie's impassive expression allowed Mr. Gerald to fully appreciate the stark change from teen to young man. Frankie's facial structure showed high cheekbones and a settled brow. No anxiety there. That made it even more difficult to penetrate his resistance.

"I heard otherwise, Frankie."

"Don't call me that." The flare of his left nostril was the only indicator of any feeling in the boy—and his tone of voice.

Mr. Gerald laughed mildly. "Did I offend you? What would you like me to call you? Frank Jr.?"

Frankie's mouth turned white and he grabbed the shoulder straps of his backpack tightly.

"That bothered you too?"

"What do you want from me?" Frank's demeanor portrayed the depths of challenge.

"I knew your dad, son."

"I'm not your son, and I don't want to hear the history of my father."

"All right with me, but the day you change your mind, come look for me. But you're right that we're not

239

here to talk about history." Mr. Gerald paused. According to the clock, the bell would ring soon. Joey Reyes, the star quarterback, and his mother would take their places to discuss college choices during third period and then there was lunch duty for fourth. He had to set time limits with Frank Ramirez or every appointment would run late.

"Let's start over. How about I call you Frank. That better?"

Frank shrugged. "I asked you, what did you call me in here for? I've got to get to calculus." He started to rise.

"Sit."

Frank sat back down in his chair, closed his eyes, and waited.

"Let's talk about the girl," Mr. Gerald said.

"What girl?"

"Play dumb, Frank. Her father almost called the police. She's made some serious allegations against you."

"That's what you say."

"Let me give it to you straight. You're a young cock. It's going to take you a while before you start thinking with your head and not with what's between your legs."

Frank scoffed. "She wanted it."

"The only reason you're sitting in front of me and not at the precinct is that she begged her father to pull it back. She says she doesn't want to lose her senior year."

"What does that have to do with me?"

"The family is doing this for their daughter. Not for you. Get it?"

Frank remained silent.

Mr. Gerald's lips were tightly drawn. There had to be another way. He could report this incident to the authorities, but then he would probably be out of this job. Three more years to go and he could retire with a full pension.

"The family said it would be enough for you to change schools."

"No! I'm not changing schools. This is my senior year too." Frank's grip tightened.

The assistant dean tried again. "You've got until third period to make your decision. Your mother is ready to move on a transfer for you. To Lafayette."

"Are you kidding? Lafayette for that cunt? She begged me for it."

"Watch your mouth. And no, Frank, she didn't. Her aunt is a nurse. She didn't go to the ER, but she got a rape kit done. She can always change her mind. Her father is connected and is dying to call the ADA. He's pushing for them to report this and press charges. What do you say? Lafayette, or five to fifteen years upstate? They have your DNA."

Frank exhaled. "All right." *Motherfucker.*

"You know, it doesn't really matter much to me what you make of yourself. But what about you? What do you want to do with your life?"

"I'm going into the Marines."

"You're going to protect our country? With a record, you'll be standing behind some fast-food counter serving French fries with a Coke. And that's if you're lucky."

"No, I won't."

"I suggest you start making better choices. Or other people will be making them for you for the rest of your life. This is just the beginning."

"I get it," Frank said. *Just shut the fuck up*.

"I'll call your mother."

"Don't bother. I'll tell her."

"Will you, son?"

"What did I say? You got a hard-on for me, old man?"

"Hey!" Mike Gerald's complexion turned ashen. "Where'd you get that from? Something going on that you want to tell me about?"

"Hell fuckin' no. My life isn't your business. I said I'm going to transfer. That's not enough? You have to keep pushing me?"

"Cool down. You've got to make a change. That's all I'm saying."

"Yeah. Whatever."

"There's a good PAL program you might be interested in." Mr. Gerald riffled through some brochures, picked one out, and handed it to Frank. "Sports. After school. Saturdays."

"Keep me off the street, you mean?"

"Like I said, Frank, you've got to start making some decent choices. Or the police will be making them for you."

"The police have got that much power?" Frank quickly perused the brochure. "Is that what you're saying, Mr. Gerald?"

"They've got guns, son." The dean swallowed hard to hide his voice cracking. The image of Frank's father was still fresh in his mind after sixteen years. He never got a chance to raise his boy. "Stay away from danger is all I'm saying."

Police. Guns. Power. "Yeah, all right, I'll go to that Police Athletic bullshit. Sign me up."

"That's a good start, son. You'll see. Things will start turning around for you—in a good way."

20
Slow motion

Dulce and I met in front of the hospital. The street was lined with trees whose branches were filled with leaves of brilliant reds, golds, and oranges. A smattering of dried brown ones littered the curb. The day had that Indian summer feel, but autumn was well on its way. I wanted to be like the seasons, which changed without anyone's permission.

"I see you spent the night with Frank," Dulce said, shaking her head slightly.

"I hit myself with the door."

"Oh, that hurts." Dulce exhaled deeply. "You can't come in to work like this. Really, you need to look in a mirror. In fact, the only place you should be going is into the ER."

"Please, Dulce, I need your support, not your sarcastic tone."

"I've given you support. Maybe you missed it, though."

"I haven't. You don't know what it's like. He loves me. I love—"

"Stop," she said. "I can't. You're making me sick now. I can't hear any more, okay? You come to work and I make believe I don't know what's going on. Will that make you happy?"

"Yes, I mean, no," I said. "Look, I have to get inside. My division is pretty busy, or did you forget?"

"You haven't heard, have you?" Dulce looked over my shoulder. "I don't know how to say this, but—"

"What?" I couldn't believe she was going to drop the Frank topic that easily. This news had to be important.

"Sonya Harris."

"What about her?"

Dulce put her hand on my arm and stopped me at the revolving door.

She hesitated. "I hate to be the one to tell you."

"What?"

"She went into cardiac arrest last night."

"Cardiac arrest?" My own heart started to flutter. "How is she doing?"

"She didn't make it."

"What? When did it happen?"

"We found her at change of shift. We were on rounds."

I began to cry. "You didn't call a code, did you?"

Dulce shook her head. "Maggie, you know better than that. She was a 'no-code.' Ms. Harris was brain-dead."

The ground seemed to sway beneath me. "It's my fault."

"You need to sit down." Dulce steered me over to a concrete bench at the side of the entrance. "Are you all right? Do you want some water?"

I found myself gasping for breath. I was underwater. Drowning. Overwhelmed with everything.

"It's because of me that she died." I had betrayed one of my patients. If I had stayed, she'd still be breathing. "I left early last night. I should have been there with her."

"You said she was okay when you left. You wrote everything out in report. Get a grip, Maggie. She died. There was nothing you could have done."

"You don't understand. I didn't have to leave early

yesterday."

"I'm confused here," Dulce said. "I thought you said that you needed to leave because you weren't feeling well. It's burnout. You need to take time off. I've been telling you that for a while. You should listen to me before something bad really does happen."

The revolving glass door began its rotation and Jeff emerged. My stomach flipped. The *bad thing* was already happening. I hated myself.

Dulce suddenly smiled happily. "Jeff!" She practically sang his name. "I was hoping I'd see you."

"Dulce. Just who I was looking for," he answered without even a glance at me. "How about a quick burger before your shift starts."

She jumped up to hug him. He couldn't really love her. It seemed impossible after the way he had made love to me. But now wasn't the time for me to try to figure it out. Frank had just pulled up in his unmarked car. Pablo sat in the passenger seat, staring straight ahead.

"Hey, my love," Frank said, getting out of the cruiser and bowing with a flourish. "Fancy meeting you here."

Frank came around the car and put his arm on my shoulder, also smiling at Jeff and Dulce. "Missed my babe here. You know how it is. Love makes you do some crazy things. I'm starting my tour now but had to stop when I saw the three of you here."

Frank placed his hand on his hips and I could see his gun protruding from the waistband of his pants. He wasn't wearing a belt or holster. This was new. I didn't remember him ever wearing his gun like that before.

"Frank, man, what's up?" Jeff said. The smell of an explosion about to go off was in the afternoon air.

Anyone watching would think we were a group of good friends, but the undercurrent was sinister.

"We were just about to start shift. Dulce, come on." I touched her arm and hoped she would come in with me.

"Maggie's right," she said. "Sorry, Jeff, I hate to disappoint you, but we were about to go inside. How about later?"

I nodded. Grateful.

With an exaggerated tilt of his head, Frank let me go. "I'll let you go now, but tonight you're mine. Wait for me and I'll pick you up."

"Sure thing, babe." I looked at each one of my supposed friends, wondering how long I could keep up this façade.

⧗

The elevator doors slid open and I walked into chaos. I stopped one of the day-shift nurses. "What's going on?"

"Amy Landry." She barely stopped while whispering loudly at me over her shoulder. "We're in the middle of a code."

I threw my jacket and bag on the chair and ran in to help with the Ambu bag while the other nurse did chest compressions.

"Is she still a code?" Dulce asked.

"Of course," I sniped. "There are no DNR orders for her."

"Okay, okay, just asking." Dulce put her hands up as though calling a truce. "I'll put your things away in the locker room."

As soon as she picked up my jacket, the small glassine packet fell to the floor. Her eyes saw it the

247

minute mine did. We raised our eyes simultaneously and looked at each other. I gave my head a slight shake. This wasn't the time to deal with this. Amy was coding. The rest of the staff was busy either giving or taking orders and missed what had just happened.

"Please," I mouthed to Dulce. "Don't."

She nodded and slipped the packet into her bag. After picking up my belongings, she walked out of the room.

We worked on Amy for about a half hour. When it was over, her heart was beating again, but her blood gases weren't good. The attending on call muttered that we were using extraordinary means to keep someone alive who had decided quite a while ago that she'd rather be dead. I left the room as soon as I could. She had been stabilized and I didn't want to hear anyone's opinions about life and death.

⧗

Dulce and I sat across from each other in the nurses' lounge. She'd thrust my jacket and bag into my arms as soon as we met in the room. She hadn't put them in the locker and was just sitting there waiting for me. Then she opened her palm to show me the glassine envelope. Just as I expected, there was a small amount of dope in it.

"Do you want to tell me about this?"

"It's not mine."

She slapped her knee. "Maggie, what the hell is wrong with you? It fell out of your pocket. You saw it when I did. How can you deny it?"

"I'm not denying it," I said, "but I didn't put it in there."

"So now you're going to tell me that you've never

used this stuff? This little bag explains so much. This would account for what a different person you've become. But it's not you, right? It's Frank. Come on!"

"He put it there, Dulce."

I covered my face with my hands. I didn't want her to know that I smoked. If she thought that I had worked while high and reported me, I could lose my job and my license. My career would be gone with a snap of her fingers.

"Really? Frank planted drugs on you for what reason?" Dulce was tough. She would never understand what I'd been going through.

"He probably did it to get back at me. Frank was mad. He's been angry. He accused me of being with someone else."

"Why would he think that? He wouldn't tolerate that; that would make you dead. Both you and I know that."

"You know how paranoid he gets."

Dulce's eyes were penetrating. "I'm not buying it. You had that in your pocket for a reason. I don't have all the answers, but you do."

My phone started vibrating. I could feel it through the leather. I reached into my bag and took it out. "Can I take this? It's Frank."

Dulce shrugged and stood up, dropping the envelope on my lap. She closed the door quietly behind her.

I answered. "Yeah, what's up? You know that I'm at work."

Frank's sniffling was loud. It was obvious he was crying. I closed my eyes as I listened to him tell me that his grandmother was found dead earlier in the afternoon. Sonya Harris had died. A shiver went up my spine. We had almost lost Amy Landry this afternoon. I had heard and saw often enough that death came in threes. Did that mean we'd lose her tonight too?

"I'm so sorry, Frank." I tried to soothe him. "I'll meet you right after work."

Frank would see to the arrangements, no doubt. His mother would lean on his arm as though it were a cane. Their bond was incredibly strong. As I turned off my phone, I remembered the book that the clerk told me his grandmother had. I'd never see it now. I thought of the statue of St. Michael that was probably still in my bag. I'd never even taken it out. I hadn't wanted Frank to see it. He didn't believe in anything that had to do with spirits or saints. Maybe I didn't either.

I got through the rest of the shift in slow motion. Amy was still alive. I managed to avoid Dulce. I couldn't wait to get home.

21
You're finally here

I stood at the living room window. The ocean was dark, and so was the sky. The boardwalk was lit and I could make out the shoreline but without detail. Just like me, alive but with ill-defined edges. That black tar was in my bag and I knew how to use it. I didn't need Frank to light it for me.

I sat on the sofa and allowed the cushions to embrace me. I opened the glassine pouch and laid the foil on the coffee table. I prepared it the way I saw Frank do it more times than I had admitted to myself, lit it, and took a deep draw. Finally, I was at peace. Serene.

The bell rang and forever stood between me and the door. When I finally got there, Frank stood waiting for me. He leaned up against me and smelled my hair. I smiled up at him.

"Hey, why didn't you use your key?" I asked.

"I left it in my other jacket. I missed you so much," he crooned in my ear. He smiled at me, holding me securely in his arms.

"You're not mad at me, babe?" I was full of want for him.

"Nah, it's not like that," Frank soothed. "I'm not mad."

I rested heavily against him. We stood holding each other for several long moments.

"So, don't tell me," he said. "Let me guess. Chasing the dragon?" He laughed and shook his head. "The only problem is that you didn't wait for me."

"Oh my God, I'm so sorry. But, wait, did I ever show you this?" I couldn't stop smiling inside. Forget about chasing a dragon. I'd been chasing the feeling that I was feeling at that precise moment. I was elated to be with Frank. So much could come between us if I wasn't careful.

"What? What are you going to show me?" Frank pulled me closer to him, with his hands squeezing my ass just the way I liked it. The soreness I felt earlier had melted away. He knew me better than anybody. His hardness pressed into me. Why didn't I just give over to him and stop fighting it? I knew better. He loved me.

"My ring." I showed him my finger with the sparkling diamond. "My sweetheart gave this to me."

"Oh, really?" He caught me and threw me down on the couch, where we made love like molasses spilling into the ocean. It was lulling, rocky, and hard all at once. I fell asleep with him still inside me, so grateful for what I had.

When I finally woke up, I remembered his grandmother. I was a jerk. He'd told me that so many times and it had finally sunk in. Frank was right. No doubt about that.

"Oh, wow, I'm so sorry," I said. "I'm so stupid. Here I am, totally forgetting about your grandma. How can you forgive me for that?"

Frank smiled. "Babe, you gave me you. That's all I want—all I ever wanted."

His reassurance fed me like a baby and I was finally filled the way I longed to be. I drifted off to sleep again and my dream was as vivid as daylight. I got up and sat at the window. Frank snored lightly in bed. I turned to him for a moment and admired his magnificent body. I had to stop questioning myself. I turned again to look at the ocean and the boardwalk. Up high, the seagulls played whatever bird games seagulls played. A few people walked on the boardwalk and some on the sand. I found that I had joined the ones on the sand, and the little boy who had called out to me weeks ago appeared before me again.

There was a red and black ball on the white sand next to me. I picked it up and offered it to the beautiful urchin, who opened his arms to receive it. When it jumped into his arms, he smiled at me. His complexion was the color of toasted almonds and his teeth were tiny round pearls. The child moved closer to the shoreline and I called out to him so he wouldn't go too far into the water, but instead he purposely began walking into the waves. The water level was at his waist and I called to him again to come out. I tried to get closer to him, but my legs were heavy. I was paralyzed. He turned back to me once more and I could see tears rolling down his brown cheeks. He continued to walk into the ocean, until finally he disappeared under its surface. I heard myself moaning, trying to wake up.

Cold water splashed against my face, drenching me. I woke up to see Frank standing over me.

"I told you before that you can't smoke that stuff," he yelled. "Why do you make me buy it for you? You're gonna end up dead, only because you're stupid. If you die, don't blame me; you're the one who's killing yourself."

It took time for me to gather back into myself. It was harder than the last couple of times, when I could easily drift back. This time I felt as if I could just disappear between the spaces of life and death. I had no control over it, until he threw the water on me. I was as soaked as my pillow and I tried to get up, but Frank pushed me back down. The speakers were blasting Hector, singing *"Tú amor es un periódico de ayer." Your love is yesterday's news.* I wished he'd turn the music off. I didn't want my favorite music mixed up with this. I'd have nothing to rely on to keep me sane when I needed it.

"Please, Frank, could you just turn that down? My head is aching."

"You think that's your problem?" he asked. "It's more than that. You need to do something."

"What? Did I forget something? Did I leave something on the stove?"

"No, that's not what I'm talking about," he said. "You need to do something about yourself." The way his lip curled up told me I wasn't in good shape, as if I didn't know that already.

Frank continued. "You might think about a program—"

I sat up, incredulous. "A program? You mean a drug program?"

"Yeah. Look at you. You're doing it by yourself now. You only did it before if I brought it home. You know, like a treat."

"You left it in my pocket."

"A gift, that's all. It didn't mean that you had to run home and light up by yourself."

"Now I'm confused. With you it's okay, but by myself it's not?"

He shrugged. "I'm just saying. You're the nurse, right?"

"What's that got to do with it?" I was heated. "And you're a cop, so what? Does that make it any different?"

"Just check yourself. That's all I'll say."

254

"What? Check myself into a rehab?" I shook my head, furious. "You have a lot of nerve. I thought we were good here again."

"I'm telling you this because I want you to know that I'm not hanging around a strung-out dope fiend."

"So now I'm a fiend? A junkie?" I wanted to leave, but it was my apartment. *He was the one who should leave.* Something in my brain clicked. It would be best for me to take the sweet route and humor him. "Okay, you're right. It's me. I have to do something."

"Finally you said something sensible." Frank pulled on his briefs and began scrutinizing his arms in the mirror. "I have to go. My mother is waiting for me. What am I gonna tell her? Oh, Maggie isn't feeling well? My grandmother just died and all you can do is keep the attention on yourself."

"No, you're right. I'm sorry." Instead of feeling angry now, I was remorseful. He was so right in every way.

He picked up the pillow and threw it at me. "What you need to do right now is to get the fuck up; you have to go to work. Get your fat ass up and get going."

"Frank, wait, I'll need something." I couldn't face the job feeling like I did. I would need something to get me through the shift. I could feel myself getting sick.

"Whatever you need, you need to get it yourself."

Frank ignored me and finished dressing. He turned to look at me before he left. Instead of crying like the little boy in my dream, he laughed. I wasn't sure what he saw, but I couldn't blame him. I was a mess.

I watched him leave and peeled myself off the couch. The tears rolled down my cheeks and my stomach cramped. I was sick. Maybe there was another packet in my bag. I searched frantically, and instead of another glassine pouch, I found the small statue of St. Michael. He couldn't help me. No one could.

I imagined myself at work and called in sick. There was no way I could spend the evening giving out medication and following up on the nurse's aides, making sure they did the treatments properly. An evening of turning Amy Landry seemed next to impossible. I had to get out of this apartment, though. The thought of Frank laughing at me showed me that I needed to stop the pills and the dope. I probably had the beginnings of a virus. This couldn't be the dope. It was all coincidental. I wasn't an addict. I needed something or somebody to tell me what to do. I sat down to think about it, turning the statue over in my hand.

The old man at the *botánica* could help me out. He said he would. My stomach was sick that day too, but for a different reason. I got dressed and out of the house as fast as I could. Maybe he would do a reading for me.

⧗

The train moved like a prehistoric mammoth, but I was finally standing in front of the shop. A cool breeze pierced my body and I pulled my coat close. As I turned the doorknob to walk in, my coat belt got caught in the doorjamb and prevented me from going in any farther. I cut my thumb as I tried to disengage the fabric. The pain was sharp and small dark beads of blood appeared. Two women were leaving just as I tried to enter. They gave me the once-over as they stepped to the side and held the door open for me. I went inside.

I passed shelves filled with candles and liquids that promised money, love, romance, and even 'the world.'

The cartoonish pictures on the bottles were detailed images of desire, the devil, greed, what to go for and what to stay away from. There were carton boxes obstructing the aisles. The place seemed almost unusable in its disarray; vivid, yet surreal. Colorful, intricately decorated *soperas* and *tinajas* glimmered on the shelves. Some of the boxes held lush green plants, and the smell of the herbs was intoxicating. To the side of the counter stood a life-size statue of a saint, wearing a gold crown and a cape with dollar bills pinned on to it. A big decanter of cloudy water was set at her side. Her plaintive expression captured me for a moment and I stood before her moist eyes, which locked with mine. Could she be crying? I heard her say, "You're finally here." Except, of course, her mouth wasn't moving. The coral-colored, painted-on smile was stiff. She was a big plaster statue, not real. Everything seemed alive and dynamic. Every one of my senses was assailed. I was losing it.

I moved toward the counter, where a woman was separating portions of plants into newspaper that were being made into packets. It was hard to breathe with all the paper, carton, and frankincense wafting through the store. She barely looked up from her task but nodded at me.

"There was a man here before. Maybe you remember. He helped me." I opened my palm and showed her the statue.

The woman's lips twitched into a tight, mocking smile and she pointed her chin at the display case. There were at least ten of the same tiny statues lined up on the shelf. There were several rows of labeled statues next to the St. Michaels. I counted about twenty Mother Marys, twenty Santa Barbaras, and twenty Santa Clara statues.

There must have been a run on St. Michael statues. Did he get sick of the number of people who prayed to him?

Behind me, someone cleared their throat. I heard a raspy voice say, "Either he's going to kill you or *tú te vas a matar a ti misma.*"

I whirled around to see the old man standing behind me. He was wearing the same hat and dark glasses as before. The cane he held in his hand tapped against the floor.

"You need help that I cannot give you." The old man extended his free hand over my head. "*Que Dios te bendiga.*"

"Aren't you supposed to help people?" I asked. "What are you saying? Don't you do readings?"

"I'm saying that you need to get away. You need to stay away from that man. Both of them. You're full of questions, but before you can ask them, you must do something first. You have to choose life, not death."

"What? What is it that I have to do?"

He remained silent.

I already knew that I had to stop seeing Jeff. And I'd have to find a way to break it off with Frank. But that wasn't going to be so easy.

"Is that it?" I asked.

"Take care of yourself. Forget about everybody else." He turned and ambled out of the store, adding, "If you don't want to die."

The woman behind the counter didn't even look my way. St. Michael stared at me, along with the Blessed Mother. I walked out and passed the old man, who stood right outside the *botánica*. An iron cauldron filled with things I couldn't make out stood in the corner by the old man's ankles. The smell of incense permeated the air, even outside the store. He was silent, and I wasn't sure if he didn't know that I had walked right by him or if he was finished with everything he wanted to say. I knew that I had to keep moving. There was no reading for me other than what he had already shared.

I made my way back to the train station but stopped at the entrance to La Casa Azul Bookstore. Colorful tiles lining the entrance walls invited passersby to enter. The doors were open and a group of children sitting inside were rapt with attention as a reader held up a picture book. The book-filled shelves were almost vibrating. They reminded me of the old journal that I had in my apartment. I'd forgotten that I'd also bought books from this store the day I went to visit Frank's grandmother. Books were filled with stories of history, lives, and meaning. I wondered if it was still possible for me to get the little book that the nurse had told me about that afternoon, and I made the quick decision to head over to the nursing home.

⌛

It was nearing dusk. The air was chilled and fluorescent lights shone through the nursing home windows. I opened the heavy doors and entered. There were a few elderly people sitting on couches in the lounge. I walked up to the security guard, who protected his domain from behind the main desk.

"I'm here to see Mrs. Ramirez's nurse," I said.

The guard knit his unruly eyebrows and stroked his handlebar mustache. "Are you a relative of Mrs. Ramirez?"

"I'm her grandson's fiancée," I said. "I was here the other day."

259

"When was the last time you spoke with him?" The guard seemed perplexed.

"I'm not sure. Maybe a few hours ago." My timing was off.

"Hold on a minute." The chair squeaked as he swiveled, turning his back to me to make a phone call. After hanging up, he said, "Someone will be with you in a few minutes. Have a seat." I looked around but couldn't bear to sit in the only available seat, next to a grim-looking couple, so I stood where I was and waited.

A woman wearing a white laboratory smock over her cranberry-colored knit suit emerged from one of the offices farther along the corridor. She spoke to the guard for a minute and then approached me.

"I'm Mrs. Stoddard, the nursing supervisor. How can I help you?" Her wide-set blue eyes were large and her paper-thin skin was lined with fine wrinkles. Her hair was helmet-like and cut close to her head, and her age was impossible to determine.

"I came in the other day to see my boyfriend's grandmother," I said. "I spoke with her nurse that day. Did you know Mrs. Camacho, I mean, Ramirez?"

"I just told you that I'm the supervisor."

"I'm a nurse too," I said, and lowered my voice. "I understand about confidentiality and that you can't share information about my boyfriend's grandmother, but he said she passed."

The woman breathed deeply and nodded. "Yes, in her sleep. There was no discomfort, as far as we could tell. She didn't have to go to the hospital or suffer any of that process."

The nurse suddenly seemed more distressed now that she had shared the information with me. There was something going on—I was sure of it. I just hoped that I wasn't being more paranoid than intuitive.

"There's something wrong, though, isn't there?"

"There is, actually." Mrs. Stoddard wrung her hands as she spoke. "You're the first family member to come in. We've called them several times, but after the first call, they haven't answered any of the others."

"You mean her body is still here?"

"No, I don't mean her body," she said. "The funeral home took care of that." Up close, I saw that her skin was etched with dry patches and her lips were chapped underneath her rose-colored lipstick. The mascara she'd applied to her eyelashes had dried in thick globs.

"Then what's the problem?" I asked.

"Actually, it's her things—no one's made arrangements to come and pick them up. We can't keep them very long. It's a storage problem. I mean, at least if someone was to answer our calls, we could take measures, but they haven't—"

I understood that. The reason Frank sent me to see her was that neither he nor his mother could. I wasn't really connected to the elderly woman in any way. I didn't want Frank to know that I had returned tonight. In fact, the less he knew about where I went the better.

"Do you have a suggestion?" she asked.

"Can you give them to Goodwill? Or maybe some of the other nursing home clients could use them?" I stopped. "The truth is, I'm not authorized to tell you what to do with her things."

"We'll hold on to them for a couple of weeks. As I said, we don't really have adequate storage. She had a collection of, well, dolls."

I nodded. "Yes, I saw them when I was here a few

261

weeks ago."

"You were here?"

"Yes, I mentioned that already. I came to visit her. First and last time, I guess."

"And you are?" Apparently, she was as flaky as her skin. "I don't remember you giving me your name."

"You're right, I'm sorry. I'm Maggie Fuentes. I spent a little time with her. She didn't really say much, if you know what I mean."

"Her dementia was quite advanced." Moving back slightly, she peered at me through her lashes. "Could you wait here a moment? I'll be right back."

"Yes, of course."

I waited in the lobby with the elderly lounging in their wheelchairs and a couple who sat leaning forward on their walkers. Everyone was pretty much silent. It was a lonely place, even more depressing than the hospital. At least there was hope there. I had wanted to work with old people when I was in nursing school. My teachers had encouraged me to get hospital experience instead, and I never left. Something inside me was kicked up, though, around these people with white hair. They had wisdom that I almost never encountered in my home life. Some of them had been nice to me when I was a student nurse. The desire to have one of them tell me a story flared up inside of me. I could be like one of the children in the bookstore. Maybe my eyes would shine like theirs did.

I caught my reflection in a framed pastel on the wall. My eyes and nose were red and tearing. I hadn't noticed that my nose was running while I was talking to that nurse. I didn't need to take the train from Coney Island to East Harlem to hear that I was going to die by either

Frank's or my own hands. I could have stayed home and told myself that.

"Miss Fuentes?" The woman stood next to me. "It is a coincidence that you came out here today. I'd totally forgotten about this package. Mrs. Ramirez instructed us to give it to you."

"She did?"

"I know it seems unlikely, but on rare occasions she was oriented. This is an item she came in with years ago. It is one of the few things that she kept. Except for those dolls and knickknacks, everything either disappeared or just seemed to disintegrate," she said apologetically. "This is a nursing home. I'm sure you understand, dear."

"Yes, of course. Thank you." She was handing me exactly what I had come for. The notebook was fragile and felt as if it might fall apart in my hands. It was filled with notes and small pieces of paper. The handwriting was tiny and spidery. *Another journal!* Suddenly I was the keeper of journals, and both of the writers were dead.

"I'm glad you were able to meet her before she died," Mrs. Stoddard said. "So many of these poor folks are brought here and then forgotten. See, dear? You remembered your grandmother and she left you a gift." The woman smiled brightly at me.

I backed away from her. This lady had begun weaving her own tale. The true story about how no one came to see the old woman would turn into how her granddaughter had come in just before she died. Isn't life mystical like that? Well, no, it wasn't. I turned and fled the facility before I could hear her say another thing. I heard low chattering and wasn't sure whether it was in my head or not. I'd held it together long enough. I had to get back home.

22
Tres de Mayo

The train pulled in as I hurried through the turnstile. Because I was all the way uptown, I got a vacant seat. It was rush hour and the train soon filled with people who wouldn't move a half inch to let anyone else through. The rumbling on the tracks and the noise in my head were unrelenting. I stuck my ear pods in to help drown out the rattling that sounded like people talking. I couldn't understand anything that I heard. Noise. Lots of noise. No one paid attention to me.

People were listening to their headphones and playing games on handheld devices, and the guy next to me was watching a soft porn movie on a mini-television he had propped up on his lap. He was over six feet tall. His shortness of breath either had to do with his belly roll or the movie. I was certain he wasn't afraid that he'd be robbed or that anyone would tell him to turn that flick off. I kept my iPhone in my bag. I couldn't take a chance and have someone grab it from me. I leaned back and closed my eyes, rocking along with the rhythm of the train.

The ride seemed to take hours, but I couldn't bring myself to take the book out of my bag. The prattling in my head seemed to have started when I received the book, as though people were in a hidden room that couldn't be seen, but their voices came through the walls. I hadn't taken any pills or anything else. There had to be a plausible explanation for it, or maybe it was just a coincidence. I needed rest. I'd been going non-stop lately. The last thing I should have done was travel today.

After a couple of transfers, the train was finally on

the elevated tracks and the Cyclone came into view, along with the Parachute. The landmarks not only indicated I was almost home but reminded me that Ellen had walked on this same stretch of land too, over a century ago. Although I wasn't feeling well, I appreciated the fact that we shared this. I wondered if she had taken the subway too. If I squinted my eyes, I could imagine that I saw her reflection in the train window. When I walked out of the station, I took a deep breath. The salty breeze welcomed me, and I almost instantly felt better. I was home.

James, the doorman, sat behind the lobby desk. I nodded to him, but he didn't even look up. He seemed waxy, just like the mannequin in the booth I'd seen that afternoon on the boardwalk. For a moment, I thought that maybe he was a figment of my imagination. There were a few elderly people sitting in their wheelchairs in the lobby, just like at the nursing home. This was odd; it was the first time I noticed how many old folks lived in the building. I had to get out of there. I was afraid that I would turn into one of them. Sitting, waiting, lifeless. I shivered and forced myself to go past them. I practically crawled up to my apartment and had barely gotten my coat off when I collapsed on the bed.

The room swam around me. I was nauseated and my bowels began constricting. I kept my eyes closed because the room swirled around me when they were open. *All I need is sleep.* I wanted to call someone to tell them I wasn't feeling well, but I didn't know who to call. I didn't want to call Frank, and Dulce was probably sick of me. Jeff had turned out to be a jerk. I got under my comforter and slept.

I opened my eyes several hours later. The chattering in my head had stopped. I looked at the clock. It was eleven p.m. I'd slept most of the evening away. I got out of bed and stretched. I'd almost forgotten how. My body still ached. I needed a hot shower.

The water practically scalded my shoulders and upper back. Abrasions and bruises dotted my body, but they didn't hurt when the needle-like spray hit me. What I needed was a cleansing, and this was it. The water was healing.

After drying myself with the fluffiest towel I could find, I put on a pair of sweats and the oldest and softest shirt in my drawer. I sat in front of the dressing table. The mirror was darkened in some areas. It was a relic I'd found in an antique store on Stillwell Avenue when I first started decorating the apartment with Frank. He loved modern furniture, but some things I insisted on buying and keeping. I treasured this table and mirror.

My eyes were just as clouded as the mirror. My skin was pale and dry. I was too thin. I turned away from my reflection. My bag was lying on the floor next to my bed. I must have dropped it there when I came into the apartment. I picked it up and remembered the journal that was inside.

My gift from Marta. Even though she suffered from dementia, she must have meant for me to have it; otherwise, the nurse would never have stuck a Post-it with my name on it on the front cover. I opened the book and looked at the date of the first entry. *1954. Tres de Mayo.* Most of it was in Spanish and I hoped I would understand it.

📖

3/5/54

No hay luz ni calefacción en mi apartamento. Todavía hace frío. La temperatura me tiene encogida. Volver a mi país és más una pesadilla que un sueño. Que Dios me salve.

4/5/54

Fuí de compras. Dos mujeres se estaban riendo de mí porque no sé bién la idioma. Pan: Bread. Jugo: Juice. Leche: Milk. El Señor Ramirez me está enseñando unas palabritas.

📖

I snapped the book shut. I didn't want to read another hard-luck story.

I roamed the apartment in search of myself. There were parts of me in pictures that I'd framed and set on shelves. In some of the photos, my eyes were shiny. In one of them, I stood with Frank's arm around me, holding me as though he loved me and would never let me go. He had meant the part about never letting me go, but I'd mistaken that destructive possessiveness for love. In another picture, I sat next to him at a restaurant. I couldn't remember which restaurant it was or who had taken the picture. Whoever it was had caught me laughing, with my mouth wide open. *Had I ever been that carefree?*

I found other parts of me in clothing and accessories I'd left scattered about the living room. When I first moved in, I was very organized. I'd put everything away carefully, as though each piece were a treasure. My blue silk scarf, decorated with hand-embroidered petals, was now crumpled in a ball on a bookshelf. I picked it up and found that the ends were discolored and soiled as though dipped in something, but I had no memory of what. *When had that happened?*

I didn't remember the last time I'd cleaned my apartment. There were a few empty bottles of soda and cans of beer strewn throughout the room. Those belonged to Frank. I was never really a drinker. I tried to pick up a bottle near one of the windows, but the bottom was stuck to the ledge. I pulled hard. There were tiny ants milling around, and I smashed at them with my thumb. I bent over to look more closely and found that a colony had taken up residence in the corner of the window. I would have to call the super to bring in the exterminator. I was suddenly ashamed.

I sank down on the couch and began to sob in the dark room. The only visible lights were the ones outside. They cast a bluish light into the living room. I thought about the provocative writings I'd come across. If I continued journaling as I used to, I wasn't sure whether I could be as honest as either Ellen or Marta in my own journal musings. Like them, I probably wouldn't like what I wrote.

I got up and grabbed a pen and paper from the desk where I never sat. It was a prop to make visitors think I did, efficiently paying bills or writing letters to my relatives. It sounded good when I told people I loved to write the old-fashioned way, but there were years between today and the last letter I had composed. Like everyone else, I used the internet. Or I paid my bills at the kitchen table. While there was nothing wrong with that, the problem was that I tried to seem so unique. Nobody cared what I did, or came to my place to visit anyway. I was isolated.

I wrote:

You need to clean yourself up. Get help before it's too late.

I put the pen down. This wasn't what I wanted to write. I wouldn't write at all, and that would solve this dilemma. Writing was out of my realm.

My head started hurting again, with a vibration that I'd never experienced before. The chattering voices started up again and I couldn't decipher them. I couldn't tell whether they were male or female. It sounded like my mother telling me what to do, but she was in Puerto Rico, not in Coney Island.

I turned the radio on, full volume, which drowned out the voices. Lisa Lisa filled the room with "I may do something I might regret the next day." I couldn't get away from Frank even when he wasn't around. I changed the channel, and the sound of Rubén Blades filled the room. I lay on the rug for a while, covering my head with a pillow.

There was banging at the door. Instead of listening to my intuition, which told me to ignore it, I used all of my strength to get to the door. James's face filled the peephole. I opened the door.

"Yes?"

His face was expressionless.

"Can I help you?" I tried not to show my annoyance.

He flipped his hand toward the elevator. "A couple of people have called to complain about the music coming from your apartment. That's why I'm here, doll."

"Excuse me? *Doll?*"

"You heard me," he said. "Like I said, it's loud. So do your neighbors a favor and turn it down. You don't want them to contact Management, do you?"

"Five minutes, not even five, and you're up here? I don't believe it."

"Well, believe it, because I'm here." I might have been naked the way his eyes were taking in my body. "You know what time it is, right?"

I braced my foot against the door in case he tried to get in past me.

"Time for little chickadees like you to be asleep," James said.

I could feel the bile rise up, stinging my throat. "I get the message. Good night." I backed up and started to close the door.

James stopped it with one quick motion. "You're alone here a lot. Come home late at night. Here all day by yourself. I see all this, you know. I could protect you."

My mouth was dry. I didn't know how to respond. I tried closing the door again, but he had a strong hold on it.

"Maybe you could use my company."

"Uh, no, I don't think so. Thanks for stopping by, though. I'll turn the music down."

"You don't have to, you know," he said. "You could keep it up. Drowns out sound, you know. Sometimes when a woman is lonely, she needs a little company."

Again I tried to push the door closed, but it wouldn't

budge. He came close and his breath was hot in my face.

"Well, you think about it." James's face was about an inch from mine and the wetness from his lips arced across to mine. "You let me know. I'm gonna wait but not too long." He backed away, flashing his white teeth. As he neared the elevator, he called out, "Remember, I know where you live."

I had barely made it to the bathroom before I vomited whatever I had in my stomach. I had to get out of here. Move. Away from my home. Away from my job. Away from everything. Whatever it was I was doing wasn't working. I had to get away.

I sat on the toilet seat and put my head in my hands. Where could I go? How could I get rid of Frank, and Jeff, and James? Of myself? The only reason they acted like this toward me was because I let them.

I went back into my bedroom and tried to relax. The vibration and chatter seemed to have disappeared.

Marta's journal was on the bed where I'd left it. There had to be a reason that I, and not someone in her family, had been given that journal. I crawled into bed and began turning the pages with urgency. I didn't know where to begin. I placed the book against my forehead and concentrated hard on the book, opening to the lines that I felt compelled to read first.

I opened the book.

📖

6/3/62

Es la vida mía y de mis hijos o la de ese animal. Lo voy a matar. Te lo juro por Dios.

Again, I couldn't go any further. I closed the book and then my eyes.

☒

I woke up to sunshine. I looked out the window and saw that the people on the boardwalk were bundled up, wearing sweats, scarves, hats, and gloves. It was only early November, but the breezes at the ocean were always so much colder than everywhere else. I'd chill out a bit. Clean the apartment and go to work. The most important thing was to remember that there would be no drugs for me today. They were messing up my head. I had never experienced the vibration or the voices before. I wasn't psychotic. I wasn't schizophrenic. I probably needed to be seen by a doctor, but I knew that the first thing they'd ask was whether I was using drugs or alcohol, and I'd have to say *yes*. It never occurred to me that I drank too much, but the bottles I'd found all over my apartment when I made the half-assed attempt at cleaning belied that. Frank hadn't drunk all of them. I'd had my share. The way I went berserk looking for pills in my bag had given me a glimpse of how much I had come to depend on substances to calm me down.

I cleaned the apartment, scouring the bathroom and kitchen, and concentrated on getting rid of the ant farm that was about to take over the place. Afterward, I opened a can of soup. I hadn't gone shopping for food in a while and the refrigerator was almost empty. I seemed to remember that the last time I had eaten at home was the day Frank gave me the engagement ring. There was something wrong with that. I had to have eaten since then; otherwise, I wouldn't be standing.

The scalding soup burned the inside of my mouth and lips. I spread butter on the end of a dry loaf of bread and chewed that instead. It seemed to help. I thought about the sliver of glass I'd found on the kitchen floor when I swept. It had to be from the vase that Frank had broken. Since that suicidal woman, Amy Landry, came into my life, everything had gotten worse. *Maybe I should ask them to change my assignment.* I wasn't my sister's keeper. I was just a nurse.

I stopped at the door before leaving for work. I planned to clean that apartment until it was immaculate. I'd go to the bodega after work to buy a can of ant and roach spray. I wasn't going to be run out of my apartment by the ants, James, Frank, or anyone else.

23
Life isn't a bowl of Dim Sum

The unit buzzed with activity. Dulce passed me on her way out of the nurses' lounge just as I was going in. Visions of the glassine envelope falling to the floor rushed back to me. No more of that. Things were going to be different now. The old man said it: either I would change or I'd be dead.

"Hey," I said, putting my hand on Dulce's arm. "Can we talk tonight?"

I could feel an invisible wall surrounding her.

"It looks like we're going to be busy," she said.

"We can always find a couple of minutes. Like we used to."

"I'll see what I can do. I need to make up the assignment now. Excuse me." She tried to brush past. I started to move aside, when I remembered what I had planned to ask.

"If you're making up the assignment, can you do me a favor?"

"A favor?"

"Can you assign someone else to take care of Amy Landry tonight? I need some time away from her. After Sonya Harris, I don't think I can deal with Amy tonight."

"Well, that's a bit too bad; you see, it's just us tonight. We're going to have to split the floor. We have nurses' aides, but we don't have enough nurses on. Sorry." Dulce shook her head. "This isn't Dim Sum. We can't pick and choose what we like and let the rest get carried to someone else or sent back to the kitchen."

"I know that," I said. "If we can't, we can't. I get that. No need to get touchy."

"It's been hard working with you lately. I never know what you have up your sleeve. Or, to put it more bluntly, in your nose, Maggie."

I was stunned. "Is that how you see me? As an addict?"

"There is no other way to see you. This is what you've become. I never thought you, you of all people—you're one of my closest friends. Let me rephrase that. You are my closest friend, but you need to do something about your problem before the supervisors find out. You can lose your license."

"Are you planning to talk to them?"

"I refuse to have you on my conscience. You need to work this out yourself. It's about you and your patients. That's all I really have to say. Do you still want to meet this evening?"

"I don't know. Let's see how the evening goes." I went farther into the locker room and hung up my coat. I closed the locker and turned back. Dulce stood in the doorway.

"By the way, Frank is here tonight. He's guarding a prisoner. I don't want any funny business. Got it?"

I nodded. There was a time when I would have laughed at her and pointed out that she was the only person who ever said 'funny business' these days. Tonight wasn't that time. I'd find a way to get around Frank. I wasn't going to do everything he wanted me to do. What a big mistake I'd made having sex with him in the bathroom that night. I had to be out of my mind.

I left the locker room and passed the nurses' station, making a detour to the medication room. Frank was standing by the clean utility room. I'd have to pass by him all evening long. The prisoner was in the next room.

There were two reclining chairs in the corridor. There were usually two policemen guarding a room when the prisoner was a high risk. Whoever was sharing the task with Frank must be on a break or in the patient's room. I didn't know what the crime was, and I was glad that we were short-staffed after all. That meant I wouldn't have a minute to breathe, let alone entertain Frank. If he got any action tonight, it wouldn't be from me.

'Babe," Frank whispered, pulling me by the wrist. "Let's go take a break."

"Babe yourself," I answered. "Do you see this stack of medication I have to give out?"

"No. All I see is you," he said, along with that look I knew all too well. He tightened his grip on my wrist and looked around. The corridor was empty, except for us. With his other hand, he grasped my hair and twisted. The pain seared the back of my head. I felt myself lose consciousness as I stood in the corridor, and was about to collapse, but Frank held my arm tightly. He wouldn't let me go.

Frank's lips brushed against my ear. "I'm here with you and no way am I going to leave you. Maggie, I love you."

His voice competed with the others that filled my head. Once again, I heard someone call my name. It was Frank. Yet, there were other voices calling my name too. "Maggie. *Maggie*."

I made out Dulce's voice. ". . . wake up, Maggie. You have to wake up."

My head was heavy with pain. I couldn't open my eyes, but I could see the image of the little boy flashing the medallion at me. I tried to call to him, but something was jammed in my throat. I couldn't breathe. I was choking. I struggled to move my hands, but they wouldn't move. Just like the dream with the water. The boy was going back to the ocean, but this time he was laughing. He seemed so happy. I couldn't move my hands or my body. The tears rolled down my cheeks.

"It's me, Maggie; it's Dulce. Stop trying to move. You have restraints on your hands. Stay still. Rest."

Using all my strength, I was able to open my eyelids slightly, but all I could see was a gauzy white film.

"Your eyes are covered, honey." Dulce spoke into my ear. "We need to protect them from the light."

I struggled against whatever was pinning me down. It was impossible to communicate.

"You've been in an accident," she said. "You've got to stay still. You're injured."

I couldn't make sense of what she was saying. A shrieking noise came from close by. I could have sworn Frank had been whispering to me just a few minutes earlier. I couldn't keep my focus. The noise tormented me, but being held down was worse. I felt myself go under once again. I was drowning.

The little boy was back. He watched me from the boardwalk. I waved and he came slowly toward me, lugging a satchel. His tiny biceps bulged with its weight. The child wore a red skullcap, a red and gold vest, and ballooning black harem pants. The gold medallion on his chest flashed in the sun.

I moved my fingers around my neck to reach my medallion; it was important that we synchronize the flashes. I continued to search and found that my neck was bare; the medallion must have fallen off. I searched for it in my blouse and found that my top had turned into a soft white linen tunic.

"Miss, Miss, your book!" The child dug into his bag and retrieved a book. He attempted to hand it to me. I tried to reach out to accept it, but my arms were too heavy and I couldn't. He stood in front of me, but he was no longer a little boy. He had turned into a man.

"Here, take!" he urged, placing it in my hands.

I held it against my chest.

The man quickly transformed into a wizened old man. "You must write in it," he said. "It is your book. You must write your story."

I held it away from myself and opened it. The blank pages flashed bright white in the sun. A tassel hung from the binding with an ornate fountain pen. I closed it. On the cover, the medallion flashed like a beacon.

Then the old man-child vanished before my eyes.

Dr. Jeff Peters's voice was loud and clear. "You're back with us, Mags. Hang on. You're in the hospital."

The shrieking sound had stopped and now a steady hum and rhythmic beeps filled my ears.

Dulce's soothing voice sounded again. "Don't scare us like this, Maggie. You've got to fight!"

I tried moving my hand, and this time I was able to wiggle my fingers, but it was still impossible to lift my arms.

"You're intubated because you were in respiratory distress," Dr. Peters said. "That's why you can't talk, and why you feel like you're choking. When you start filling with secretions, we suction you."

That explained why my throat was on fire. *Why couldn't I open my eyes?*

Dulce must have heard my thoughts. "The back of your head was injured, honey. That's why your eyes are covered. But don't worry about that now. You're going to be okay."

Was I blind? What kind of injury? I felt Dulce's soft hand on mine and she gently squeezed it. I was barely able to return the squeeze, but I must have, because I heard her gasp and then softly weep. I was exhausted.

I fell asleep and began to dream again.

St. Michael stood in front of me in resplendent red robes. His long wavy hair flowed in his golden aura. The surrounding illumination was so bright that I had to shade my eyes with my hand. With my other hand, I reached out to touch his leather belt. The expression he wore was so gentle and serene that I was taken aback by the action he took. I didn't see, but rather heard, the movement so swift, the slice of the fiery sword he brandished. He cut the air around me and a glistening dark-blue snake slithered out of my belly. It had become part of me, entwined with my umbilical cord, simultaneously feeding and draining me. The snake slid away from me.

The archangel made several cuts to the air around me with the swish of his sword and called to the other archangels. "Uriel! Raphael! Gabriel!" They appeared, one by one, and each stood in his cardinal direction. When they did that, I recognized the elements that each angel represented. How I knew this, I couldn't say; I'd never paid attention to anything about the archangels before.

Michael stood at the southern gate, in his flaming glory, in the bright of day. The splendor of summer had become apparent. Uriel guarded the northern gate, which was surrounded by white snow that fell to the earth. The sky was dark cerulean blue and filled with magnificent twinkling stars. Raphael stood erect at the eastern gate.

279

The winds blew gently at the sunrise of a beautiful spring day, with new growth bursting forth from tender young saplings. Gabriel protected the western gate, guarding the healing waters. Sunset was offered by a magnificent orange sky. I was stunned by this vision of brilliance. I fell to my knees as the archangels lifted their swords and united above me in prayer. The radiant cone of energy was so magnificent that I couldn't keep my eyes fastened to the illuminated skies. I dropped my sight to the ground and saw the serpent had circled near me again. It stared straight into my eyes with its glittering slits. It hissed at me, and slipped away into the ground. I was no longer afraid. The four archangels disappeared one by one. I slept deeply.

I woke up to see Dulce sitting next to me. She lay with her head on the metal rail of my bed. The skin around her eyes was dark and her usually creamy café au lait complexion was puffy and dry.

"How long?" I mouthed.

"About two weeks," she said, stifling a yawn. "We weren't sure you'd make it. Give it a couple more days. The tube is out, but it'll take a while before your throat feels better. For now, don't talk."

I nodded and looked around me. I was in a hospital bed, surrounded by machinery. There was an intravenous drip going into a vein in my neck. A bandage pinched my skin. The bedrail prevented me from reaching out to Dulce. When I tried again, I saw that it wasn't the rail but my lack of strength that kept me bound to one spot. There was a pad of loose-leaf paper on the table. I pointed to it and Dulce handed me the pad with a pen. Both felt awkward in my hands. My mind was fuzzy and I still had the ache in the back of my head. The pen felt heavy as lead, and I dropped it on the bed. It would take time for me to write again.

"Where's Frank?" I asked.

"Oh, Maggie. I'm so sorry but his grandmother passed away. He had to take care of the arrangements for the funeral and burial."

Frank so rarely mentioned his grandmother that I sometimes hadn't believed that she was still alive. He'd said that she was in a nursing home, but I didn't remember where.

"Tell me what happened," I croaked.

"We've got plenty of time to talk," Dulce said, "but you need to regain some energy to do that. Rest now."

"Please," I begged.

"I'm going home to get some sleep. I'll be back in the morning. If the doctor thinks you're strong enough, we'll talk about the last couple of weeks. Trust me. Just get some rest tonight. Mrs. Graham, the nurse's aide, will sit by you. She may not be the friendliest flower in the bunch, but she's a good worker."

I suddenly had the image of flowers in a shattered vase. "Wait—my eyesight—blurry."

"The doc took the patches off and gave you drops that should help soon. We'll continue the drops, but the best thing you can do is rest your eyes and yourself. That's all you need to do."

I nodded again and fell fast asleep. The next thing I felt was a tugging at my bottom. I opened my eyes to see that I was still in bed.

"Hang on to the rail while I wash you up." Mrs. Graham stood over me with an armful of towels and a basin. She pushed me over on my side. My hips burned as she worked on me, but my skin felt tingly and alive when she rubbed it with lotion.

"They're going to send someone in to talk with you soon. You want to look presentable, don't you?" Mrs. Graham's brogue was thick. I'd never really noticed it before. "I'm going to try and get rid of some of those tangles. You might want to get a haircut—for the rest of your hair, that is."

This time when I reached up, I could touch my head, and gently traced around it. There was a bandage covering the entire back of my skull.

Mrs. Graham had turned around, so I couldn't see her expression. "Don't worry about your hair, Miss Fuentes. It'll grow back."

⏳

The next time I woke up, I found myself sitting in a high-back recliner. Some days had passed since I first realized I was in the hospital. The physical therapist worked with me every morning and I was getting stronger. My eyesight was getting clearer. The doctor promised that I'd be measured for a walker soon. Getting out of bed was hard. I never understood why my patients complained that it was so difficult. My eye roll told them I didn't believe it. I winced when I thought about my callousness.

My favorite time of the day was when the nurse's aide applied zinc oxide to my hips. It was an embarrassing relief to feel those efficient hands massage my skin back to life. An intern explained that to keep the back of my head off the pillow, they had placed a large roll of linen at my back. The roll kept me off my injury but had rubbed a friction burn into my hip.

I was talking again, with only slight hoarseness. The

only problem was that no one wanted to talk. Everyone suddenly became busy and left the room whenever I broached the subject of what had happened to me. No matter what I asked, I was assured that I'd be told at a more convenient time.

I depended on Dulce, who spent a lot of time with me. Even Jeff Peters visited and encouraged me to get better. He said that my patients missed me and wanted me back. I still felt too weak to think about work or, really, even Frank. Most of the last couple of weeks was a blank.

This morning, a male figure stood in the doorway, but I couldn't make out his features.

"Miss Fuentes, I'm Detective Holmes."

"Detective?" I asked. "Is something wrong?" *Frank.* "Did something happen to my boyfriend, Frank Ramirez? He's an officer—"

"No, ma'am," he interrupted, coming closer to me. The detective was over six feet tall and his shoulders stooped as if they carried the world. Someone had once told me that when a person walks around like that, it is because they are protecting their heart space.

"Oh, thank goodness," I said, exhaling a long sigh of relief.

"I find that quite interesting, Miss Fuentes. I came to ask you questions about the occurrence that landed you in here with a very serious injury, and the first thing you do is ask about Officer Ramirez."

"We're engaged," I responded. But the moment I said those words, I knew that it wasn't true. "I don't know why I said that. We're not. I'm sorry."

"No need to apologize," he said. "And if you're not engaged, I can't imagine why. From what your coworkers have told me, you are one heck of a nice person."

There was a twinkle in the detective's eye that captured me. His brown skin was a rich mahogany color. I instantly liked him. We smiled at each other.

"I was out a pretty long time," I said. "I'll do my best answering those questions."

"I'm sure you will," he answered. "First question is, how are you?"

"My head hurts and I've been sitting in this chair too long," I said. "Could you help me get back into bed?"

"Uh, no, ma'am," he chuckled. "I'm here to ask you questions."

"It will be easier for me to answer them if I am in bed."

"I guess your nurse friend and doctor weren't kidding when they told me how stubborn you are. Guess that's what's helping you mend so quickly."

"I've been told that I'm pretty hard-headed," I said. "But that's not really funny, is it, Detective—?"

"Holmes. Carl Holmes," he repeated. "Miss Fuentes, mind if we get to those questions before the nurse comes back?"

"Okay." I looked down at myself. I was wrapped in hospital gowns. It hadn't occurred to me until now that I didn't have my own pajamas and robe. Each day that passed I was becoming more aware of myself and my surroundings. It was quickly becoming a reality that I was a patient and didn't have much control over what was happening around me.

"We're trying to piece together what happened on the afternoon of the accident," he pursued. "Do you remember anything about that day?"

284

I shook my head slightly and touched my head involuntarily. The bandage was no longer there, but I could feel a ridge of staples that held the wound together.

"Not really."

"Take your time. Think back. Do you remember where you were going or who you were with that day?"

I thought hard but couldn't put anything together. "No."

"Let me ask you this, then. How do you usually spend your afternoons? I understand you were working the evening shift on the day of the accident."

Frank. "I must have been with Frank, my boyfriend."

It dawned on me that he hadn't even been here yet. Maybe he had been in the accident with me. Maybe Dulce had kept the truth to herself to protect me. If I was hurt this badly, it was very possible that Frank was too.

"Do you two live together?"

"No. He lives with his mother," I said. "Only because he's a police officer. His mother worries about him."

"Okay. I'd like to ask you one more time. Is there anything you remember from the afternoon of the accident?"

"I'm sorry, no," I answered. "I'm getting tired; do you think you can get the nurse—"

"Okay, no problem. I'll see if I bump into her on the way out." Detective Holmes stood up and extended his hand to me. He placed a business card in my hand. "If you remember anything about that day, just give me a call."

"My memory hasn't been the best, but I'll call you if I do remember anything."

I watched as he left. I should have been the one asking questions. I had plenty of them, and was sure that he had the answers.

24

Chasing the dragon

"Babe, wake up," Frank whispered. "I was so worried about you." I opened my eyes to see him sitting next to my bed, holding my hand.

"Where were you?" I asked. "Dulce told me your grandmother died. Is that true?"

"Yes," he said. He blinked back tears and brought my fingers to his lips and kissed them. "I wish I could have been here with you. I'm so glad you're all right after everything that happened."

"I'm still not sure what happened. Since I woke from the coma, all I do is sleep. Do you think it's the medication that's sedating me?"

"It has to be the accident," he said. "Nobody told you?"

"I know I was in an accident, but that's all I know." I pulled my hand out of his. Something didn't feel right.

"Pablo and I found you at the corner of Stillwell and Mermaid, under the El."

"Near my house?"

"Yeah. We were patrolling. It must have been a hit and run." Frank's voice trembled as he wiped away the tears that had pooled in his eyes. "I thought I had lost you."

Frank pulled the metal siderail down and climbed into bed with me. He put his head on my chest. It was heavy and my breath was short, but I didn't want him to move. We eventually fell asleep. When I opened my eyes again, it was twilight, and Mrs. Graham was tapping him on the shoulder.

"Excuse me, sir, you've got to get up," she

instructed, sounding like a drill sergeant. "I have some work to do here."

Frank immediately responded to her command and stood up. I felt a bit sorry for him.

"Mrs. Graham, this is Frank. He's my boyfriend. He's taking good care of me. You know, helping me do things."

She shook her head. "I know who Officer Ramirez is. I've been here the last two weeks, you know."

"You sound angry," I said. "What's wrong? I don't remember much."

"Well, the whole event was pretty traumatic," she went on. "That's why you don't remember everything."

"Oh, I didn't know you were the doctor," Frank said. "I thought you were a nurse's aide. Excuse me."

"Frank, please!" I said. "Come kiss me good bye; you were just about to leave anyway, weren't you?"

He half smiled and half smirked. "On my way, babe. You need me to bring you anything?"

"Yes. Bring me my pajamas and robe. The white one." I tilted my cheek as he bent to kiss me.

"No problem. I'll be back tomorrow. You can count on me."

Frank was just about to walk out the door when I remembered I didn't have underthings.

"Frank," I called out. "Underwear. I need underwear."

"No problem. *Mañana*."

⧗

I watched as the aide got the small basin, a toothbrush, and toothpaste from the nightstand. There was something so familiar about her moves. I knew I was being silly; we'd both done this a million times. Sometimes together.

Then I remembered.

"Mrs. Graham, that patient we were taking care of. I don't remember her name. How is she?"

"I don't know who you mean, Miss Fuentes."

"The young woman. Amy. Amy Lowery? Something like that."

"No, not that I recall." She gave me a cup filled with warm water, which I swished inside my mouth.

"Yes, I cared about her. Amy. Oh, I know. Amy Landry."

"Here. Dry." The aide handed me a thin white towel. "No, we haven't had a patient by that name here."

"Amy Landry. Of course. She was intubated. How could you forget?"

"I don't mean to rush you, but you know how it is. I have a few other clients who need evening care too."

Mrs. Graham was right; nursing care meant trying to do twenty things at once. I spit the water into the kidney-shaped basin and dried my mouth with the towel.

"Can you just turn that light out by the door tonight before you leave? I never realized how many lights are kept on here. Twenty-four seven. I'm taking an oath that when I start working again. I'm not leaving one unnecessary light on ever again."

"We need those lights," she said. "It's impossible to take care of our duties in the dark."

The aide was right, but she turned the light out and I turned over on my rear. Now that I could turn on my own, I gave my hips and butt equal time. As I settled in for the night, I promised myself that I would ask Dulce about Amy Landry. She'd remember. Sometimes Mrs.

Graham was a bit of a fruitcake.

"You're going to be discharged soon," Dulce announced. "Have Frank bring you a pair of sweats or something. Easy clothes, if you know what I mean."

"Oh my God, that's great news. Finally!"

"You know how it is in the hospital," she said. "We kick everyone out as soon as they open their eyes after surgery. Maybe not that soon, but close enough."

"Do you think I'm ready? I mean, realistically. I just got the stupid walker."

"Maggie, that stupid walker is your ticket out of here. Think of it as your wheels. Anyway, you'll get physical therapy while you're at home too."

"This is such an adjustment. The last thing I remember is—I don't even know what."

Dulce was concerned. "Nothing? Still?"

"The one thing I do remember is us taking care of a patient. I finally put it together. A woman. Her name was Amy Landry, I think."

"You were probably dreaming that," Dulce said. "You were hurt pretty badly, honey. But, no, we didn't have anyone by that name here. So it's not like you heard it when you were under."

"She was a suicide attempt."

"That, I would remember," she said. "No such patient here."

"Something's been bothering me and I want to ask you about it."

"Yes, sure." Dulce dumped out the vases filled with dying flowers. That was a sure sign that I was ready for discharge.

"I keep thinking that you're mad at me, that I did something to upset you."

"Mad at you? For what?" she sighed. "No one is talking to you about that day, are they? Like Frank?"

"Well, he told me that he was cruising with Pablo. He called me a *hit and run*."

"That's just like him. I'm sorry, Maggie, but he can be a jackass sometimes."

I shrugged. "He can be annoying, but he's the only one who's said anything about that day."

"To tell you the truth, no one is really sure. There weren't any witnesses. Seriously, I can't believe Frank and his partner just happened to see you sprawled there. Pretty lucky, if you ask me."

"It does seem crazy that Frank would be the one to find me."

Dulce looked as though she was considering something. Her gaze was off into the distance.

"Tell me, what is it?" I asked. "I know you're thinking something."

"There were a couple of carjackings at the intersection where they found you . . ."

I had a flash. "*Sonya something. Harvey?* She was a patient here too."

"No, the two women who were carjacked were sent to Kings County. They needed a real trauma hospital. Not that you weren't *real trauma*, but we thought you'd do better here at Seaside. Everybody loves you here. It would have been like sending a family member out, and we couldn't do that."

"Sonya and Amy never existed?"

Dulce shook her head. "You were probably dreaming. They had to give you a lot of drugs to keep you under. They were afraid you might start having seizures."

"Lots of drugs," I repeated. "I'm remembering some of those dreams. Chasing the dragon, I think."

"Chasing the dragon? You know what that means, don't you? It means using heroin. God, you were really out of it, weren't you? It was more like the dragon was chasing you."

"It's as though my head was wiped clean."

"Well, that's not really true. You are remembering bits and pieces. Give it some time. You'll get your memory back. I wouldn't worry about it. The most important thing is that they did find you." Dulce was pensive for a moment, then stood up. "I've got to get a move-on. I'm back on shift again."

"Wait, you mean you took time off because of me?"

"Yes, because of you. You're my best friend, and I'm so relieved that you survived."

"Me too."

"You were scheduled to come in that evening. We were supposed to work that shift together. You went to the beach with Frank and he dropped you off at home to get ready for work. You never made it. He went to work, and that's when they found you. You were probably ready to come in." She looked troubled.

"What is it?" I asked. "You're holding something back, aren't you?"

"No, I'm sure it doesn't mean anything. Let's drop this."

"Tell me, please. I have to know."

"When they found you in the street, you weren't in your uniform. You had your bathing suit on underneath a shift. The flower one that we both bought that day, remember? We promised each other not to wear them to the beach at the same time."

"I remember that dress. I went to the beach that day, but I was wearing my windbreaker over it because it was breezy. Frank and I had gone to the flea market."

"Okay, I'm really sorry, but I need to get to work. We'll talk later. I think it might help to retrace that day. If you're up to it, of course."

"I am. Thanks. You're a real friend, and always have been."

We hugged and she left my room. The door was open and I saw the number of the room: 512. This was so familiar, but in an eerie sort of way. I got up to stand at the picture window and had a flash of Frank getting into a burgundy SUV. That could be important, but I couldn't remember why.

⧗

"Babe, babe!" Frank woke me up out of a restful sleep. "I can't stay, but I brought you what you asked for. Hope it's what you meant. I'm back on shift this evening. Can't take off forever."

My eyes took a few moments to adjust as I accepted the package he was thrusting into my hands. "Thanks, I appreciate it, hon, but now they tell me I'll be discharged soon. I'm sorry, but can you go back to the apartment? Pick up the gray sweats I have in the chest."

"Sure, no problem," he said. "Anything for you."

I kissed him goodbye and watched him scurry out. I didn't remember him at my bedside, only Dulce and Dr. Peters. I reached over for the package of clothes and opened it. I looked forward to wearing my pajamas tonight. Mrs. Graham had washed whatever was left of my hair and I felt more like myself. I looked down at the contents of the package. Inside were my pajamas, white robe, and underwear. *My white thong.* I felt a pang of fear shoot through me. Something wasn't right. I bundled them all back together and shoved the pieces back into the bag.

Dulce came in and plopped on my bed. "I figured out that I can take my breaks with you here. That is, of course, until you start working again. Then we'll meet in the cafeteria like we used to. I miss that."

"Me too." I gazed out the window. It was dark out, except for the lights in the parking lot. "I have to figure things out."

"Try to be gentle with yourself about it. The psycho who did this to you got away. No evidence, no witnesses. That's so unlikely in this part of town. I mean, they got the two men who were doing carjackings and your name didn't come up at all. There's usually someone willing to come through with information. Unless it was a gang initiation gone sour or something. I'd better stop there." Dulce seemed embarrassed.

"You mean that they meant to kill me?"

"The injury to the back of your head was, is, real. You could have had permanent damage."

"I guess I was in the wrong place at the wrong time. That's what people usually say." I laughed lightly, trying to infuse some humor into this dark situation. But Dulce was so serious, and maybe I should be too. "Can I ask you those questions now?"

"Yes, shoot," she gasped, covering her face. "Sorry. Didn't mean that."

"Why? What are you saying?"

"Maggie, you were shot in the back of the head.

They never found the bullet. It only grazed you, but there was enough damage that you needed a surgical cleanup and sutures."

"My God, really? Why wasn't I told this? I thought I'd fallen on my head. For God's sake, why is everyone keeping the details from me? The detective is walking on eggshells, and so are you. Frank hasn't said a thing, other than he found me near my house. I'm alive, get it? No one has to shield me."

"You're right. That's it. There are no more details to share. I swear." Dulce raised her right hand.

"I have more to ask."

"I'm listening."

"Had you been trying to get me to go to the emergency room? You said that I looked like crap."

"You didn't seem yourself for a while but, no, you were brought into the hospital by ambulance."

"How come I didn't die? How come the bullet didn't blow my brains out?"

"The surgeon said that it was probably the position you were in when you were shot. There might have been a struggle."

"I want answers."

"You may never get the answers that you're looking for. You're a survivor, Maggie, but you've got to be patient. Literally."

"One more thing, and please tell me the truth," I begged. "Did Frank and I have a fight?"

"Not that I know of."

"Is he seeing someone else?"

"Frank?"

"Is that why he's never around? I know that his grandmother supposedly died—"

"Maggie, this is old stuff, you being insecure around him. His grandmother died, and you know he's been dealing with his mother, a never-ending drain. But, hey, it's none of my business."

"But it's mine." I took a deep breath. "Thanks for being my friend. I appreciate you."

We sat together silently for the remainder of Dulce's break, except when she shared an odd tidbit about her evening. I felt as if I hadn't been on the unit in months, but I was sure that I had been taking care of my patients yesterday. Dulce was right. I had to be patient with myself.

25
A witness

Frank opened the door and I slowly walked into my apartment. Everything was in its place. It was a bit stuffy, but I was glad to be back. I hadn't been there in a long time.

"Can you open the window, Frank?" I held on to the walls and went toward the easy chair to sit down. I hadn't gotten used to the walker and left it in the foyer. I'd gone to physical therapy every day in the hospital and I was doing everything I was told to do. I was gaining strength. It might take a while, but I was going to be stronger than before.

"It's cold out there," he said. "Do you want to freeze?"

"Of course not," I said. "But it's like a tomb in here. So stale. How can you stand it?"

"Yeah, all right."

Frank opened the window and the room immediately began to smell fresher.

"Thanks. You've been an angel."

"Yeah, sure."

I remembered the dream of St. Michael brandishing his sword around me. The dream had been so vivid. I had the image of the brilliant diamond Frank gave me.

"Oh, I just remembered that I dreamt we'd gotten engaged!" I held up my hand. "You put this huge rock on my finger."

"No. We didn't get engaged. Look, I can only stay for a little while. I gotta get back to work. I put some milk in the fridge and some bread. I got you strawberries. I know how much you like strawberries. There are cans of soup and tuna in the cabinet. I figured you can tell me what you need and I can pick it up and bring it to you in the morning."

"Thanks. I know I've been depending on you for a lot of things."

"No problem."

"Can I ask you something, Frank?"

"What?"

"I'm just not sure how you found me at the corner. How you happened to be there with Pablo."

"We cruise, Maggie, we cruise. You know that."

"You found me there while you were cruising?"

"Yeah, how else would we have found you? It was a coincidence, you know, working and living in the same neighborhood. I'm probably going to transfer. This was always thin ice, me being out here. My address might be in Gravesend, but I practically live here in Coney with you. Look, I gotta get out of here. I've got to get to work."

"They think a gang member might have tried to kill me. Part of an initiation thing. What do you think? You're a cop. Is that common around here?"

"Anything can happen," he said. "Is that what they told you?"

"Yes. Dulce did. Why, you don't think so?"

"I don't know why they tried to shield the truth from you, Maggie. You're a big girl. You tried to kill yourself."

"What? No, I couldn't have."

"You threw yourself out of the car. You just don't remember." He brought his face down to my level. "Read my lips. You tried to commit suicide."

"Frank!" My breath became short, my arms started

298

to tingle, and my heart beat hard. "Stop. Don't say that."

"Just calm down. You didn't succeed, did you?" He got up again. "I have to leave."

"No, you can't just throw that at me and turn around and walk out of here. Why? Just tell me why. What was going on that I would try to take my own life? I'm not crazy."

"You were under stress is what the psychiatrist said. You don't remember losing it on the boardwalk that day, do you? One minute we were okay and the next you started screaming. I tried to bring you back here and you totally lost it. We were at the intersection and the light turned green; you jumped out, but I had already started the car. You couldn't get your balance and you fell smack on the back of your head. I didn't think you were that bad off. But you jumped. Like a psycho. I'm sorry, but someone has to tell you the truth."

"I don't remember talking to a psychiatrist. How could they just let me leave if I tried to kill myself?" I began wringing my hands. Nothing was making sense. "No. Dulce told me that I was shot in the back of the head."

"That's bullshit. That never happened. Anybody show you a bullet? No, I didn't think so, because there was no bullet. Get it?"

"Why would I try to jump out of the car?"

"You were high." Frank's eyes were filled with disgust. "You were chasing the dragon. You have a problem, babe. You've got a big problem."

"That's not true," I protested. "I don't get high. Why would you tell anybody that? There's more to it that you're not saying."

"Whatever. Just get a grip. I'll give you a call later."

I watched his back as he left the apartment, slamming the door behind him.

⌛

Defeated. That's how I often felt around Frank. Had I really thought that things would be different between us because of the accident? Frank was rarely even nice to me. Dulce knew. That was obvious from the way she had spoken to me in the hospital. I had almost lost my eyesight. But I had been in the dark long before this.

I shivered and saw that he hadn't closed the window before leaving. I got up and stood there for a few minutes, watching people enjoy the brisk air and the surf. It was cold and they were bundled up. The last time I had stood at this window, it was a warm autumn day.

It seemed like he tried to insert bad thoughts in my mind all the time. Why would he say those things about me? There was no way that I would try to kill myself. Or get high. He hadn't treated me this way in the hospital. He didn't want anyone to know how he really acted toward me.

It took all my strength, but I managed to lower the window. I'd have to contact the Management office. That window always stuck. Like me.

Before taking a nap, I went into the kitchen and poured myself a glass of milk. Protein would help my body heal. As I got the glass out of the cabinet, I saw my crystal vase in the nook by the kitchen table. It was intact. I could have sworn that it had shattered into a million pieces. Perhaps this was yet another event that had happened in my dreams. I drank the milk and then went and curled up on my comforter. Sleep would help to restore me.

300

The quiet of my room was startling. I had become used to shrieking monitors, loud whispers, and weird sucking sounds. I got up and poured warm water into my tub. The nurses had told me to make sure someone was with me when I took my first bath, *just in case*. The only person who could do that would be Frank. But I needed privacy from everyone, including him. I refused to be an invalid.

After luxuriating in the tub, I managed to dress without too much difficulty and was drawn to the window again. I wanted to go outside. I lived only a few yards from the boardwalk. It was early November and, at the oceanside, that meant the harsh winds were already blowing, but I craved the sea air after being in sterile surroundings for so long. There were plenty of warm coats in my closet. I put on the navy-blue pea coat and then shoved my uneven hair under a knit cap. It took me a while, because I refused to push that ridiculous walker, but I got outside and plopped down on a bench.

I kept my eyes closed as the sea winds blew over me. This had always been a healing place.

"Oh my God, you're alive!"

My eyes flew open. I knew that voice and heavy Polish accent. "I know you," I said, "but from where?"

The elderly man tried to hurry away. The wheels of his walker scraped across the wooden slats of the boardwalk. I was slow but still faster than he was.

"Sir, wait, please." I reached out and touched the hem of his jacket. He was dressed in many layers.

The old man leaned heavily against the metal frame of his walker. "What? I can't help you." His expression was a combination of pity and fear, and I felt shame as I gazed into his faded blue eyes.

"Please, I need to ask you some questions," I begged. "Why did you say that? Where do I know you from? I do know you, don't I?"

"A mistake, lady. I thought I knew you. I was wrong. You look like my daughter."

"But why did you act like you'd seen a ghost when you saw me?"

"I'm an old man. I don't see so well. Please forget you saw me. I beg of you." He was clearly afraid.

"I'm not going to hurt you." I pointed to my own frail body. "Just look at me."

I'd seen him before; I was sure of it. Perhaps he was a patient on the unit. Or maybe it was right here at the beach.

"What did you mean when you said that I'm alive? You seemed surprised."

Tears welled up in his eyes. I wasn't sure if it was the stinging ocean air or if he was crying.

"I was here that day," he admitted. The old man's hand trembled as he lifted it from his walker and wiped his eyes. "I saw you and that creep. I thought he had killed you."

A rush of adrenaline surged through me. This man was a witness. The only person out that day who had seen anything.

"Please tell me what you know."

"The important thing is that you're all right," he said.

"No, I'm not all right." I pulled my cap off and showed him the suture line. "Look at me!"

He looked at my head and into my eyes, and nodded.

"Please, let's sit," he said. "I can't stand anymore

like I used to. Here, we sit on the benches." His cheeks were ruddy and spidery capillaries traversed his face. The whites of his eyes were the same—full of tiny red veins.

We hobbled together to one of the benches overlooking the wide expanse of white sand. The seagulls cawed overhead and a dog barked in the distance. I pulled my collar up, close to my ears. He did the same.

"I don't want no trouble," he said.

"No trouble," I said. "I promise."

"You can't promise that. You're just a little girl." He swept his hands in my direction and my eyes followed his gesture. He was right. I sat quietly and waited for him to talk. I knew that he would.

He cleared his throat and ran a hand over his mouth. "I was here that afternoon you were with that criminal. I tried to stop him, but I'm nothing but an old man. I was afraid that he would hit me. I made believe that I was minding my own business, like he told me to, but I didn't."

The afternoon that he described started to come back. I was there on the boardwalk with Frank. I remembered the old man standing near us. His eyes were the same as today—full of fear and resignation.

He continued talking. "I sat on one of the benches and waited until you walked down the steps to the car. He rammed you against the car and then pushed you in. He was so angry. His face was red and he was filled with hatred. After you were in, he slammed the door and got into the car. You were parked there for a couple of minutes. Then he drove off fast. The brakes were screeching. I didn't know what happened to you." His chest heaved as he sighed. "I thought he had killed you."

"Did you hear anything?"

"My hearing isn't too good." The old man pointed to his hearing aid. "The battery ran down, and my eyesight isn't any better. I didn't know the license plate number. It was a big black truck, you know, an SV, SUV."

The old man said Frank had pushed me. Frank said I had tried to kill myself, and Dulce told me that Frank and Pablo had found me lying on the street with a bullet wound in the back of my head but no bullet anywhere near me. All very different versions with one ending: me waking up from a coma in the hospital.

The old man cleared his throat again. "You lost your shoe."

"My shoe?"

"Your sandal," he said. "You were wearing sandals. That much, I'm sure I know."

I'd worn flip-flops for most of the summer on my days off from work. I hadn't thought about them in the hospital. When I was allowed to walk, I wore sneakers. The physical therapist said they would support my feet. She'd been concerned that I wouldn't be able to keep my balance with any other type of shoe. Frank had picked the sneakers up for me.

"I have it," my elderly companion said.

"You have what?"

"Your shoe," he said. "It's in my room. I saved it."

"Are you sure?" I asked. "You actually have my shoe?"

"I saved it, just in case."

"Can I have it?" I asked. "Would you return it to me?"

"It's yours, isn't it?" the old man muttered.

"Yes, I think so."

Evidence. My mind was swirling. That something bad had actually happened to me was starting to sink in.

"Can you bring it here tomorrow?" I asked.

"God willing, yes," he said with a small smile, and started to get up. "I will do my best to be here."

I stopped him when I realized I didn't even know his name. "I'm Maggie Fuentes. What's your name?"

"Stanislaw Zbigniew." He tilted his head. "You can call me Stan."

Zbigniew. *I knew that name.*

"Mr.—I mean, Stan. Two, let's meet at two."

"Like I said, Miss, God willing."

⧖

When I got back to the apartment, I heaved myself onto the couch. After lying in bed for so long with only a few trips down the hospital corridor, I was bushed. The gash might have been a graze, but it was nasty, according to Dulce. There was another bruised knot to the right side of my head, but my hair covered that one and wasn't as serious as the one to the back of my head. It looked as if I had been the victim of a hit and run, or, as Mrs. Graham put it, *pretty beat up*. I didn't doubt that Frank had done that. It hadn't been the first time, but he'd never pulled his gun on me before.

I rested for a few minutes and then decided to search for my flip-flop. I went to the bedroom and looked in my closet but couldn't find it. I did find my large tote with the picture of a cat on it. I forgot that I had that bag.

I opened my bag and found one flip-flop in it. There were also two books in there. One was a picture book about 1950s Coney Island and the other was a journal. An electrical jolt flowed through me. This was the book that had called to me at the flea market that afternoon. I opened it and saw the old-fashioned handwriting. Entries that had been written over a hundred years ago, in 1903. The afternoon was coming back.

I held the journal to my third eye and opened it, knowing that the place I should read would be revealed. I was astounded. Most of the journal entries were poems.

📖

September 4, 1903
     Anguish

My anguish has become my infant
I tend to her. I feed her. I nurture her.
She returns to me the only semblance
of feeling that I have
Then he cries and I hold his head fast to my breast
as though it were he
And not my anguish that is my babe.

September 10, 1903

Sometimes it is hard for me to remember what my tasks are, and I often stop in the middle. This angers Tom. Deep down inside I know that he is upset because his wife is ill. He wonders aloud why it isn't me who is ailing rather than his love, the mother of his children. When he says these hurtful things, I think of how much he must loathe me.

Tortured

I walk to the edge of the pier
The night darkness swallows me whole
Unseen
Invisible
The wind engulfs my screams
I tear clumps of hair from my scalp

October 7, 1903

Tonight I gather some of my possessions and go to the shore under the cover of the moon. It is late and only a few stragglers are still about. My hands conjure words that fall onto blank pages. Whose story is it that I tell? It is as though my body has become an instrument for Moonspeak. She is the only one who will protect me. I am secretly pleased when Tom calls me a lunatic. For, yes, I am. I go to her when she calls.

October 12, 1903

Luna calls

The moon casts her veil over me
She smiles
Clever, roguish, secretive
I cry
Throw myself down on my knees
The sand dunes surround me
I submit

Grandmother, what lessons have you for me?
Show me the ways of the crone
Wise beyond her years
Apparent in the snowy tops of her head,
the mountains, the wise owl that
hoots in the stillness of the night
Calling
Oh, Grandmother Moon
Cast your veil over me
Save this one
Who bends on knees
awaiting exoneration
for the crimes I have committed against myself

October 20, 1903

Today I sit by the pilings and enjoy the spray of the salt
as it cleanses me of all that has taken place. My words
tell all, but I say nothing.

November 5, 1903

Siren's song

Crying out in wonder
That the wind would find me so
Atop the wooded pilings
Crying out for mercy
Beg that the salt of the sea
will stop the burning at my lips
bruised from the slim-hearted one
who would commence to halt
the words of love that spill from my mouth

Watching, watching
The waves crash at my feet
Should I tumble?
Seek refuge in its fury
Allow its embrace to swallow me whole?
Return to my ocean mother's womb?
That my hair would tumble like
Seaweed
Lifeless on earth
As the sea glass shaped by
Centuries of turmoil
Forever bound to the music of the deep waters
Whose harps I play
Fingers entwined in thin cutting wire
Beneath the crests that shudder my name

December 1, 1903

Scorched

My arms reach out
Hailing the day star that hides in the night
Were it not for the bright sun
That parches my throat
Already raw from my screams
I would not know that
I am alive

June 2, 1904

Tonight he pulled me from the carriage. The horse gave
a snort the moment he dug his long, thick fingers into my
flesh. My skin has become an eggplant, purplish and

black in hue, yanked from its vine.

Passing

The stench of anger rides on his breath
Passes the lips used to caress my cheeks.
Mocked by cruelty
Rocked as a Moorish knight
Up high on his horse
My beast recognizes not my dilemma
I have fed it oats and carrots
Yet it remains unperturbed by my plight.
My shoes of velvet and skirts of taffeta
now thick with dust as I take flight.
I hope to be spared by his
disdain for my behaviors.
If only I were to learn how to avoid the
incendiary mannerisms that thwart
the growth of his love.

July 20, 1904

I do not truly want to die. I have barely tasted life. I have tasted the salt from the sea, but she pushes me out onto the dunes. At first thought, I believed even she did not care for me. But, no, that is a delusion. My mother, the ocean waters deep, pushes me away from her breasts that I may find my way to life. I will leave. Go to faraway shores. There I will hide from the one who is truly mad. I must find a place where I will be safe. I must pay heed to my feelings of urgency. I will leave before he returns

310

to my rooms.

My memory was coming back quickly, almost too quickly. Frank had pushed me into the Escalade after smashing me against it. He hurt me. I'd lost consciousness from the pain and woke up in the hospital. Frank. It had to have been him. I felt the bile rise in my throat. *He shot me.*

I wasn't safe. He'd come back. I needed to protect myself, but first I needed to let somebody know what was happening. That person could only be Dulce. I pressed the hospital's number into my phone. It was after four o'clock; she was probably preparing evening medications.

"Grecia, hi, it's me, Maggie," I said. "Is Dulce there? It's important that I speak with her. Yes, as soon as possible. Sure, I'll hold on." I waited.

Barricading the door would be impossible. The sofa was heavy and I'd never be able to push it that far. The delivery men had had a terrible time with it when I moved into the apartment. The image of those old-fashioned police locks flashed in my mind. They probably didn't even exist anymore.

The clerk came back on the phone. "Dulce said she'll call you back later, unless this is an emergency."

"It's urgent," I said.

Dulce came on the phone.

"Dulce, I found out what happened," I hurried to explain. "An old man has evidence. He was there the afternoon of the accident, except that it wasn't an accident. Frank did it on purpose. He was the one who shot me. The old man told me he found my flip-flop."

Her silence told me that she had no idea what I was talking about.

"Are you still there?" I asked.

After another pause, she spoke. "Maggie, did you get enough rest today? Take a breath. You're talking so fast that you're not making sense. Is Frank there? Let me talk to him."

"No! Just listen. Frank and Pablo found me. No clues to an accident. No shells or anything, even though it was obvious I was hit by a bullet. That was no coincidence."

"You're saying that it was Frank who did this to you?"

"Yes. Listen to me—"

"The detectives have no evidence, no reason to believe it was one of their own, Maggie."

"That doesn't matter. There's an old man who saw us on the boardwalk that day. I saw him today. He said he was afraid for me. He was shocked that I was still alive."

"You're sure?" she asked.

"Yes. I hid a lot from you, but he'd been escalating before that afternoon. Please believe me. It was Frank."

Through the phone, I heard her sharp intake of breath. I could tell she believed me, and was relieved.

"Maggie, you've got to get out of there. Get into a cab and go to my house. My niece is there. I'll call her and tell her to let you in."

"I have to be here tomorrow," I explained. "The old man, Mr. Zbigniew, said he'd meet me to give me the evidence."

"No, Maggie, don't be so stubborn," Dulce said.

"We'll both meet him tomorrow."

"Frank said he was going to work. He never comes back when he says that. I guarantee you he's going to be home with his mother, especially with his grandmother's burial. He spent way too much time with me already."

"Well, no, he didn't. Not really." I could hear the dots connecting in Dulce's brain. "He was barely here. He called a lot to ask if you'd regained consciousness. He only started visiting when you woke up. Oh, Maggie, you must be right. It had to have been him. That's the only way that this could have happened. But you think that Pablo helped him hide the evidence?"

"Yeah, I don't get that part of it. Pablo, of all people. I thought he cared about me." I shook my head. "But I'll be all right," I assured her. "I'll take a cab to your place tomorrow after I see the old man. I dreamt that I had taken care of him. That he was a patient we were prepping for surgery."

"Look, I have to get back to work. Those bells are ringing non-stop. I'll call you later, after medications. I'll check in on you, just in case."

"Thanks. That would be great. But don't worry so much. I can take care of myself."

⧗

I could take very good care of myself. Frank himself had prepared me as if I were going to be a Girl Scout. His voice resounded in my head: "Make this your friend. In fact, make this your baby." *The gun*. He'd given me one when we first started dating and had taken me to the range to teach me how to shoot it. I'd protested but he had insisted. Frank warned me about all those "sick psychos" out there and insisted I be ready to protect

313

myself. "You first, babe, above all" is exactly what he'd said.

Frank became easily aroused when he explained the connection between sex and violence, saying the two went together. He had pressed his stiffness against me and rubbed his forearms against my breasts as he showed me how to shoot at the cut-out figure. At the same time, he'd kiss me on my neck. Thinking about those days, I flinched. I thought he loved me, so I didn't say much, but I'd also get embarrassed that people might be watching. No one ever noticed or mentioned anything. They were all wearing ear and eye shields, and were focused on the forms in their vision. I learned how to shoot that gun. I made him proud. He called me his "sharp-shooting bitch," until I asked him to stop. "Don't ever get stale, babe," he'd say. "If you were ever in a dangerous situation, you'd be in trouble." He was right. It was his problem if he'd forgotten that I had learned my lesson.

⧖

I knelt and reached under the bed for the box. It was there. I never moved it. *Me first, babe.*

I climbed back up to my knees and sat on the bed, placing the box on my lap. I opened it. The gun was as shiny as I remembered. I opened the chamber. The cartridge was in it. He told me that it should always be ready. I held it in my hands, just as Frank had lovingly taught me, opened the safety catch, and cocked it. I put it down on the nightstand. It was ready for me to use if needed, but, mostly, I was ready.

I went into the kitchen, poured a can of lentil soup into a small saucepan, and lit a purple flame under it. I couldn't allow myself to get weak. I needed to keep up my strength. I poured and drank a tall glass of milk. After finishing most of the soup, I washed the bowl and pan, picked a banana off the bunch, and brought it with me to the bedroom in case I woke up hungry in the middle of the night.

Taking care of myself took precedence over Frank's needs for once. I hoped that I wouldn't have to use the gun on him and that I could get Mr. Zbigniew to tell the detectives what had happened that afternoon. Going to the precinct with one flip-flop wasn't going to be very persuasive.

⧗

Someone was tugging at my shoulders, trying to wake me up. I sat at the side of the bed. It was only a dream. I fell back into a fitful sleep and woke up with the sunlight streaming in through my window. Today I would meet the old man on the boardwalk and he would bring the flip-flop.

There was a sound outside my room. It wasn't a dream. Someone was inserting a key into my front door. My hands and legs trembled. Other than me, Frank was the only one who had the key. He was coming back, even though he had said he was going to work. He was probably coming back to finish the job.

"Frank, is that you?" I called.

Another familiar voice answered. "Miss Fuentes?"

I pulled myself out of bed, wrapped myself up in my robe, and walked slowly toward the foyer.

"James?"

"Hey, I'm sorry to disturb you. I didn't realize that you were back. When did you get in?"

The doorman stood in front of me. There was no

reason for him to be here in my apartment.

"I came back yesterday," I answered. "What are you doing here?"

"Officer Ramirez asked me to keep an eye on the place while you were in the hospital. He didn't tell me you were being released."

"Well, I'm here now."

"I'm real glad to see that you're back home, ma'am. I heard you were hurt pretty bad. Glad you're okay." The doorman shifted from foot to foot.

I took a deep breath.

"Yes, me too. I'm glad to be back." I smiled. "Do you think you could pick up some tomatoes and turkey breast at the deli for me? I have such a yen for a sandwich; you know, homemade."

"Sure, but it'll take me a few minutes. The elevator is out, by the way. The Castro family is moving out. Do you know them? They're on the third floor."

"No, I don't think so."

"They probably got spooked. They said they hadn't realized there was so much crime in the neighborhood. What with the carjackings, a burglary on 6, would you believe it, and then—oh, I'm sorry."

"It's all right. I get it. Don't worry about it. I will wait for the turkey and tomatoes, though, if you don't mind."

"Sure. I'll be back soon."

"Thanks, James. Wait a second and I'll give you some money."

"No problem."

I took a few dollars out of my purse and handed the money to him, wondering why he irked me.

"On second thought, can you have them make me

the sandwich? Turkey with tomatoes on a hard roll with a bit of mayo."

"Change your mind about the home cooking?"

"I want to conserve my strength. I'll be cooking real meals soon enough."

"I'll be right back."

I'd barely closed the door behind him when the doorbell rang. Since he was otherwise engaged, catering to me, he couldn't very well do his duties as a doorman.

"Yes?" I asked through the intercom system.

"Hey, Maggie, it's me, Ann Marie."

Pablo's wife.

"Come on up." I kept my finger pressed on the return buzzer. "Take the stairs; the elevator might be out of commission."

A few minutes later, she was at my door.

"The elevator isn't out of order." Ann Marie scrutinized me from head to toe and then gave me a big hug. "Gosh, Maggie, I was so worried about you. Living on Long Island is like living in Sweden. It's not that easy to get out here."

"Does that mean you weren't able to see me in the hospital? I don't remember a lot."

"No. Every time I made plans to come out here, something happened," she rambled. "I have the baby, you know, and I have such a hard time leaving him at daycare when I'm off. Did you know that I've started working part-time at the hospital center? The endoscopy unit, of all places. I hate to admit it, but we need the money. Pablo kept me updated. He said you were out of it—I'm sorry. I should have tried harder to come."

Ann Marie Arroyo looked fabulous. Her skin appeared fresh and dewy, and her makeup was skillfully applied. I had an entirely different picture of what she would look like as I waited for her to come upstairs.

My old friend made herself at home and immediately took charge in the kitchen. "Gosh, I've been away too long. Do you still keep the tea in there?" She rummaged through the cabinet as she continued to babble. "I'm here now, and that's what counts. It took me a while, but when Pablo told me you had been discharged yesterday, I knew that I had to see you."

The ease with which Ann Marie made herself at home reminded me how close we had been just a few years earlier. Her marriage to Pablo and move to Long Island had changed all that. At some point, we'd been good friends. We were the Three Musketeers: Ann Marie, Dulce, and me. We had met on Orientation Day at work, and depended on each other during that training period as new graduates.

"Coming to visit you is kind of loaded for me, you know, Maggie," she went on. "My life totally changed when we moved to Long Island. I didn't think we would make it—but, I should stop. I'm not here to talk about my problems; I'm here to visit you." She laughed and touched me gently on the chin. "I guess we should focus. Did they get the guy who did this to my little Maggie?"

"Apparently not," I said. "According to Frank, there weren't any clues."

"Frank? Are you serious? He's not the officer on your case. Didn't a detective come to see you, ask questions?" She busied herself making tea, with the flame under the kettle up high.

"Yes, but I was still out of it. I didn't really have anything to tell him."

"That's bizarre. Didn't he leave you a card? You

should contact him. This is serious. You could be dead."

I nodded. I should have thought to call the detective who had come to visit me at the hospital. But something Ann Marie said nagged at me.

"Are you and Pablo having problems?"

"Well, no, not now," she said, and turned off the boiling water. "We were. I got the feeling he was having an affair. Here in Brooklyn. I got so paranoid being all the way out on the Island. They work such long hours, you know."

"I'm sure that Pablo would never do anything like that. He's always loved you so much."

"*Loved* is the operative word," she responded. "I found evidence. It's ironic that you got shot in the head and they can't find any evidence, while he puts his dick into some floozy and I find her thong in the car. Under the seat. Would you believe it?"

I felt a wave of nausea pass through me.

"Sit down. You don't look too good," she said, and pulled out the kitchen chair for me. "We worked it out, though. We got a good dose of therapy and I had to get back to work. I can't sit on my duff and wait for him to make my life happen. The baby was a bit of a stressor. Wa-wa-wa!" She made a face. "Pablo Jr. You get it. It wouldn't be right if we separated."

"You seem so matter-of-fact about it," I observed. "How can you live with him knowing that he's been with someone else? I don't know if I could do that."

"Oh, honey, of course you could," she said. "I always talked about what I'd do and what I wouldn't do to anyone who listened, until I found the white thong under the seat. When something like that happens to you, and the car you find them in is your Beemer, you adjust.

319

When you stand in your kitchen with the double sinks and the granite counter that has little streaks of gold running through it that was specially ordered from Italy, you adjust."

"I get it." *A pinch under my arm or a discreet twist to my thigh at a bar a minute before a champagne toast to my sexy ass was acceptable. A punch to my stomach may have doubled me over, but looking up to see Frank's apologetic expression, along with a pair of sapphire earrings was acceptable.* Just like Ann Marie, I adjusted. No wonder we'd been friends for so long.

Ann Marie handed me a steaming cup of tea. "Here, drink up. I didn't come to complain. I'm about to head out. Traffic, you know. There's always some type of construction on that infernal expressway. Gosh, look what time it is. I'd better be going. The daycare charges extra if you're a minute late, God help me."

"Thanks for coming, Ann Marie. I really appreciate seeing you. I'm glad that you came when I could actually talk with you. That's not how it was in the hospital. I was intubated; did you know that?"

"Yes, sweetie, Pablo told me. Do yourself a favor and get in touch with that detective. Promise me, okay?"

At the door I hugged her and felt better than I had in a very long time. I watched as she walked down the hall toward the elevator. James passed her, with my sandwich in a bag. I couldn't miss the steady sidelong glance he gave her. Ann Marie had a gorgeous set of legs. He would have to be dead to miss them.

"Here you go," he said. "They gave you a side of macaroni salad. A promotion, I think."

"Oh—" I didn't know what to say. *Who promoted macaroni salad?*

"If you don't want it, I'll be glad to take it off your hands."

"Yeah, sure." I fished it out of the bag and gave the container to him. It wasn't until he left that I looked at the receipt. I had been charged for it. I was right; he was a sneak. *Another creep.* I gobbled down my sandwich and drained the cup of tea.

It was twelve thirty. The morning had flown by and it was important for me to keep focus. Ann Marie was right about me getting in touch with the detective again, but I didn't even remember his name. I looked everywhere for the card. It was either in my carry-all or my suitcase. I knew that I hadn't thrown it out. I pulled my clothes and toiletries out of the carry-all and spread them across the top of my bed. Keys, lipstick, tampons, a hairbrush, but no business card.

I had to hurry. Mr. Zbigniew would be waiting for me on the boardwalk at two. I had to get downstairs to meet him. The hands on the clock were advancing.

I had lost so much weight in the hospital that the only clothes that fit me were my sweats. My arms and legs were like toothpicks. The mirror that I loved to stand in front of was now just a symbol, showing me what 'love' had done to me. I took a moment to inspect my skin. My complexion, which once was vibrant, had turned sallow. I pulled up my pants and felt like I was moving in slow motion. Dulce had urged me to accept a home attendant when I was discharged from the hospital. I sat at the edge of my bed and began crying. I'd never get downstairs in time. Things would never be right again.

The phone rang. Another interruption. I answered. "Hello?"

"Hey, Maggie, it's me, Jeff."

The hospital intern. "Hi. Is everything okay?" My anxiety shot up a few notches. "Everything is fine. I just wanted to check on you." His voice sounded like buttered rum. Smooth. "I know you've been through a lot. I want you to know that I'm here for you. For anything, anything at all."

"Well, they sent me home with a walker. I'm not really using it." I paused.

"What I mean is that while you were in the hospital, I feel we got a lot closer. You know, like friends. Good friends."

I couldn't miss his meaning this time. His tone was confiding. The whole thing seemed bizarre. He was a co-worker. My colleague. I'd been a patient. He hadn't seemed interested at all. How could he? I'd been in a coma. I tried to dismiss the disturbing feeling I was experiencing.

The sound of the key turning in the lock of my front door got my attention.

"I'm sorry," I said. "Someone's at the door. I have to hang up."

Frank. I had to keep the charade going but felt myself getting weaker and weaker. He was right; there was no way that I would ever outsmart him, but I had to try. I never tried to kill myself and I would do my best for him not to hurt me anymore. By letting him win out, I would be allowing him to not only take my life but my legacy.

I was so nervous, I could barely stand up. I sat back and propped myself up against the headboard. I reached for the gun and cradled it between my two hands. I was ready.

The doorknob slowly turned and the door opened. Frank peeked in, and when he saw me on the bed, he walked in and closed the door behind him. The room was brightly lit with beams of sunshine. I shifted on the bed. My keys dug into the back of my thigh. I held the gun with my right hand for a moment while I pulled the keys out from under me with the other. I realized that I was too weak now to hold it only with one hand and grasped the gun firmly with both. I knew that whatever went down would have to happen quickly.

"Whoa, wait, what's going on here, Miss Maggie?" Frank gave a short laugh and pointed to the gun with his chin. "Are you planning to use that?"

"It was you, Frank, wasn't it?"

"What are you talking about?"

"You tried to kill me, didn't you?" I tried to keep the gun steady, but my hands began to tremble.

"It's got to be your injury," he said. "You're talking crap."

"Please, Frank, listen to me—"

"I'm calling an ambulance for you."

"I almost died because of you."

"Really?"

"Really, Frank. All I did was try to love you. You're incapable of knowing what that means. What it means to love or feel someone's love for you."

"So you're saying I'm a monster?" he asked, while advancing closer to my bed. "Is that what you're trying to say?"

"You don't get it. There's good in everybody. At least, that's what I thought."

"Do-gooder Maggie Fuentes." Frank's laugh was bitter. "Well, you got the wrong dude, I guess, didn't you?"

"Why did you hurt me?" I pleaded with him, trying to elicit a sincere answer.

My hands started to visibly shake and the tears began to roll down my face. They were salty on my lips and burned where the skin hadn't healed a hundred percent yet from the tube that had snaked down my throat. I grasped the gun more firmly between my two hands.

"What are you really asking me?"

"I already asked you, Frank. Did you shoot me? Did you really try to kill me?"

"I think that you have a hard-ass head and I think you were watching too many Lifetime movies while you were lying on your fat backside—that's what I think." He continued to advance toward me.

"Stop," I said. "I think you tried but didn't succeed." I knew I couldn't hold the gun much longer. My shoulders surged in pain from holding it.

"You're gonna use that piece on me? Really? I don't think so, because you are just a little bit too late."

Frank began to laugh and pulled his hand out from under his jacket. He pointed his gun at me and I pulled the trigger of mine. The last thing I heard was his laugh. I shot him just as he'd trained me to shoot those cardboard replicas of authentic men. He had trained me well.

26
Beginning to understand

Death often makes its appearance just at that juncture of life when one has come into an acceptance of their existence. Sometimes Death shows itself when we are convinced we will live life to the fullest and no longer merely exist. Sources that are more powerful than ourselves are exerted and we find that we are powerless to effect change that might have occurred only a moment before. The lessons, opportunities, and potentials that were given to me during this lifetime ended the day Frank and I spent that balmy afternoon at the beach.

As I sat on my bed, I realized some things. I realized that no matter how much I tried to change the ending of my story, I wouldn't be able to. I was told that attempting to redo the ending of one's life is just part of the process, part of the passage, of crossing over to the other side. A change would have had to happen before that afternoon on the boardwalk. Maybe months or years before that day would have truly made the difference. I wanted to make things right, but there are some things that we can't fix. Just because I wanted it to end another way didn't mean that it did.

My spirit stayed awhile in my sun-drenched bedroom. A couple of crystal pieces hung from the window and I admired the prisms of light that pirouetted grandly throughout the room. My bedroom was immaculate and everything was in its place. There was no shattered glass vase. There was no blood on my shiny satin sheets. The tote bag that I loved, with the cat wearing rhinestone sunglasses, was set to the side of the bed and the journal was in it, along with the picture book of Coney Island back in its heyday. My favorite white robe was laid out on the bed. I knew without even looking that there was no gun in the closet or in a box. I knew in my heart that this was no longer my place.

They say that death comes in threes and sometimes it doesn't. Frank's grandmother died. It was odd meeting her a short while after my crossing. She couldn't really talk because she was still affected by her dementia. It takes time to sort through those types of things, really heal illnesses and afflictions, on the other side. I could tell by the pain in her eyes that she partly blamed herself for what happened. Marta Camacho Ramirez kept her secrets to herself. She made it to this side, yet she has so many regrets. I see her every now and again, and she's shaking her head and pacing, as if to make sense of her existence. *What lessons has she learned? What lessons have I learned?* I'm no different than she, but maybe I am, and I can still change.

Adela is still a mystery to me. I've seen a sliver of a woman who sometimes stops to touch Marta's hand, but she moves quickly, in a hurry to be on her way. I'm here only a brief time, so I hope that eventually I'll know who she is and her connection to Marta or me before the crossing was made. I always thought that after I crossed over, all the mysteries would be instantly revealed. I was wrong.

I'm trying to sort out my own thoughts and feelings, like separating whites and darks for the laundry. I ask myself, *will this red shirt bleed into the whites?* My sense of humor is slowly coming back. For such a long time, I forgot that I had one. My misery is like a dress that I keep putting on that doesn't fit exactly right, but I keep putting it on anyway. I've got to stop that the next time around.

I really want to meet and talk with Mr. Zbigniew. As timeworn as he is, that guy isn't going anywhere soon. He has the gift of longevity and the wisdom that comes along with it, but for now he's just an old guy with a shoe. He can't save me or change things either. I will watch out for him if I can, because he really cared about me. Mr. Z. at least saved my flip-flop and placed it on a pile of clothes in his room. I don't blame him for not going to the police, either. The fear he harbors runs deep. Sometimes he has nightmares about that afternoon. It's too bad he can't enjoy the surf when he sits on the boardwalk, but thoughts of how he might have stopped Frank fill his head. Mr. Z.'s daughter is on this side, and she goes to sit next to her father on the bench all the time, yet he doesn't feel her presence. He's one of those people who have yet to realize that you can still communicate with your loved ones after they leave. He'll probably be annoyed at all the time lost when he finds out that he could have spoken to her during their years of separation.

Frank. What do I think about Frank? I believe that Frank has no soul. He sits in his patrol car with Pablo. They sit there like stones waiting for the next job, the next call, the next *anything*. They don't talk about the day that Frank called Pablo, distraught, crying, over what happened that afternoon in his car. Frank used to tell me "I love you, babe" so many times that he believes it. I don't believe his words, even as I watch him—especially at night. He wrestles with his inner demons. Sometimes he looks like he's suffering, when he perspires in his sleep, tossing and turning, but then he wakes up and looks as fresh as a flower in bloom. I can't fight that fight any longer. The trick is for me to remember that. I don't hold rancor toward Frank or Pablo. It's funny. When I finally figured out what really happened that afternoon, I should have been enraged. My feelings might have been on mute. I've been asked if I figured out my part in the whole thing. Yes, I have—it's the only way to keep moving forward.

Ann Marie is struggling to save her marriage with Pablo and has no idea why he is so distant. She's busy trying to keep up family appearances, and I believe that to do that, she can't go too deep. I see her trying so hard not to ask questions. She wipes her hands on the kitchen towel and then twists the cap off his beer when Pablo calls to her from the family room. Ann Marie hands him his cold one, and he stares at the TV and takes the beer without moving his eyes away from the screen. She's teaching Pablo Jr. how to pick up his toys before reading him his favorite story at the end of the day. There were a couple of times when I watched as she picked up a framed picture of the four of us. Ann Marie was working with me at Seaside Medical Center when that photo was snapped. We were all smiling, except for Frank; I mean, he was smiling, except for his eyes. She shakes her head every time she picks the frame up and then she places it back on the mantel of their wood-burning fireplace.

An incredibly sweet thing happened. My best friend, Dulce, and the intern, Jeff, fell in love. They were swept up by it. You know how that happens, when people who care about something or someone work closely together and they look up and see light in each other's eyes. I like to take credit for that one thing. I won't tell Dulce that she'll have a lively little boy and sweet girl. She hears me when I talk to her and she still cries just a bit. Not many people hear me. I think they may be too afraid to listen, but who am I to judge? I won't tell her about the children beforehand, because I want her to be surprised. I've learned that unexpected joys come to people who are good and care about others, and they recognize the blessings when they arrive. Those are the people who have a bit of courage and a dash of humility. I'm beginning to understand.

I didn't realize that I'd look up and see life so clearly. Simple things like leaves turning from greens to rich oranges to translucent golds, Dulce's funny Christmas sweater and long- haired shaggy dogs make me happy. When the fear of what might come next was gone, lots of room for me to experience new things appeared. Nurses wipe away cauls from the faces of newborn babies. They say that these babies have the gift of 'seeing,' of clarity of vision, clairvoyance. I think I know what they mean now. I feel as though I am one of those new beings who have yet to experience life. I had a background, some ideas, and concepts. Added to those, I now have hope, a gentle feeling, and tenderness toward myself. My arms are open and I embrace the new.

That day I visited my bedroom, I was called to go toward the stillness. I found myself lying in a small rowboat. I sat up and looked around me at a beautiful lake. The water was a dark azure, but I could see clear through to the reflections of many existences. There were trees surrounding the lake that were plentiful and filled with dark-green leaves. The sky was tranquil with mists that I wasn't altogether sure weren't clouds. I heard no birds, but an occasional ripple in the water showed me that there was life where I floated. The boat moved toward a wooden pier that appeared through the foggy patches. I made out a figure and there stood Ruby. She extended her hand to me and helped me climb onto the pier. Ruby's smile was just as I remembered: pensive and caring. She wore an indigo crescent moon on her forehead and touched her finger to my forehead. I knew that I wore one too. She welcomed me to this side and I knew that I was finally free. Again, because I knew in my heart that I'd felt this way before. I recognized this feeling of liberation. We laughed joyously together for a moment and then she hugged me close. I was home and had no fear. This is the middle place. It's a place to reflect on actions taken and manifestations of those decisions. The place I will stay until I am ready to move forward again, in a new direction.

I'm told that here at the middle place, I prepare to fully walk away from my past. The choices that I made will reverberate throughout my lifetimes. Whether I'm Maggie or Ellen or whatever form I come back in, if I keep making the choice of remaining silent because of my fear, I'll be forever voiceless. I am fervently trying to work on it this time, and that's why I've decided to tell my story to whoever will listen.

I would love to have my robe with me, but I don't. Maybe I'll put in an order for one the next time around. That's what I'll do. I'll ask for fluffy robes, good friends, a beautiful sandy-white beach that I can dig my feet into and let the ocean foam rush over my toes. The little boy walks with me. His name is Ahmed, and he has the soul of an ancient one. He cares for me and promises to walk by my side wherever I go. Ahmed and I play on the waters. We communicate silently by using the elements and light waves and, at other times, light particles. It's important for me to learn more about the light, because I spent a lifetime working the element of compassion in the dark. I didn't even know that compassion was an element. Ahmed teaches me a great deal with his kind ways. He says that I can thank you for listening to my story because it's very possible that you hear me. That it might make a difference for you, and that it makes a significant difference for me.

One more thing before I move on. Here's a poem I've written for you to help you understand, as I do now. Fare thee well.

Luna lives

Our pact with the Moon
Signed in blood
An exchange for the energy of her love
Contracted to wax and wane together
As done for millennia
Each time slightly different
Forlornly witnessing images of men jump
effortlessly on her face
In fear they would mar the terrain
No longer would she smile at us again
from the sky
Yet she reappears as promised
through the midnights of our lives
Our stains always refreshed
When we lay our hearts down on the Earth

—Until we meet again—
Maggie, 2019
Coney Island, Brooklyn

Author's Note

I sat in the theater recently for a revival production of *Hello, Dolly!* and had the overwhelming sensation that Ellen was with me. The feeling was more of a *knowing*. I shared with her the love of the dresses worn by the female participants of the ensemble, along with their high-button boots and colorful parasols. Ellen never really had the experience of innocence, singing and dancing her way to happiness. I don't believe Maggie did either. The relief of Maggie's burdens came in her attempts to remove herself from being present through whatever release she could find.

When I write, I am propelled by the protagonists to tell their stories. When Maggie began whispering in my ear, I was thrilled that she took me to the beach, the ocean, and especially to Coney Island. My family spent countless days there when I was a child. I, in turn, took my children there often to enjoy the water, the sand, and the sun. I am an initiated daughter of Yemayá, in the Orisha tradition. She is the Great Goddess of all, who rules over the waters. The water is my home. A couple of summers ago, during warm days, I was often found at Coney Island. My father had Alzheimer's disease and we sat on the boardwalk, whiling away the afternoons in deep serenity. I wrote about Mr. Zbigniew before I began those short forays with my father on the boardwalk. Realizing afterward that my father shuffled with a walker just like Mr. Z. was a clue to the authenticity of this story. I often receive small signs that I'm on the right track.

When Maggie began arguing with Frank, I could see where the plot was heading and was none too thrilled. I speak with many women who struggle with domestic violence in my work at a women's shelter in New York City. Trauma, self-esteem, self-blame, substance abuse, and desire for love are often the foundations for complicated and tumultuous relationships. Although I was initially hesitant, I moved forward and did what Maggie and Ellen asked me to do. They wanted their stories told. There's a reason; maybe it's for growth, theirs or yours. I know that I've learned a lot from them. I'm sharing a listing of contacts that are available for those involved in domestic violence situations. Maggie's trauma started early on; she witnessed such violence in her mother's life. You or someone you know may be assisted by the contact information I've added on the next page. All it takes is one step toward wholeness during this lifetime. Maybe your child can be helped by your action, even if you think it's too late for you. We don't think it's ever too late.

I thank Cindy Hochman, my editor, for her honesty, precision in her work, and suggestions in lifting this story. I'm grateful to Orlando Ferrand, who assisted me with the Spanish translations. I'm thankful for my spouse, Patricia Dornelles, for her photography and designing skills, her encouragement, and for listening to me work out the stories for months, sometimes years, before completion. I am especially indebted to Maggie and Ellen, who shared stories of their desire to be loved.

In light and love,

Theresa

Domestic Violence Contacts

IF YOU ARE IN IMMEDIATE DANGER, CALL 911

The National Domestic Violence Hotline
P.O. Box 161810
Austin, Texas 78716
1-800-799-SAFE
1-800-787-3224 (TTY)
www.thehotline.org/is-this-abuse/abuse-defined/

Domestic Violence and Abuse: Recognizing the Signs of an
Abusive Relationship and Getting Help
https://www.helpguide.org/articles/abuse/domestic-
violence-and-abuse.htm

New York State Office for the Prevention of Domestic
Violence
www.opdv.ny.gov/help/helpfor.html

Safe Horizons: moving victims of violence from crisis to
confidence
https://www.safehorizon.org/
1-800-621-HOPE

Frequently Asked Questions at the New York Police
Department
http://www1.nyc.gov/site/nypd/services/victim-
services/frequently-asked-questions.page

Award-winning Puerto Rican author Theresa Varela was born and raised in Brooklyn, New York. She is the recipient of International Latino Book Awards for *Covering the Sun with My Hand* in 2015 and *Nights of Indigo Blue: A Daisy Muñiz Mystery* in 2016. Dr. Varela holds a PhD in Nursing Research and Theory Development, and currently works with the mentally ill homeless population in New York City. She is a member of the National Association of Hispanic Nurses and a member of Las Comadres Para las Americas, and is on the Advisory Board of the Latina 50 Plus program. She is co-founder of La Pluma y La Tinta, a Writers' Workshop. Her blog, LatinaLibations on Writing and All Things of the Spirit, can be found at www.theresavarela.com